END of the ROAD

EDITED BY
Jonathan Oliver

An Anthology of
Original Short Stories

En

S

WA

This

The
a furth

Also edited by
Jonathan Oliver

The End of the Line
House of Fear
Magic

END of the ROAD

EDITED BY
JONATHAN OLIVER

INCLUDING STORIES BY
PHILIP REEVE
BENJANUN SRIDUANGKAEW
IAN WHATES
ZEN CHO
PAUL MELOY
LAVIE TIDHAR
JAY CASELBERG
ROCHITA LOENEN-RUIZ
HELEN MARSHALL
RIO YOUERS
ANIL MENON
SOPHIA MCDOUGALL
S.L. GREY
VANDANA SINGH
ADAM NEVILL

SOLARIS

First published 2013 by Solaris
an imprint of Rebellion Publishing Ltd,
Riverside House, Osney Mead,
Oxford, OX2 0ES, UK

www.solarisbooks.com

ISBN 978 1 78108 153 2

Cover by Nicolas Delort

10 9 8 7 6 5 4 3 2 1

A CIP catalogue record for this book is available from the
British Library.

Designed & typeset by Rebellion Publishing

Printed in Denmark

CONTENTS

INTRODUCTION

JONATHAN OLIVER

THE ROAD STORY is a genre explored widely in film, from the dark – *Mad Max, The Hitcher, Long Weekend* – through to the comic – *Any Which Way but Loose, Identity Theft*. In literature, the road story is a central part of fantasy, the journey itself often making up the better part of the tale – *The Lord of The Rings* and Steven Erikson's *Malazan Book of The Fallen* series being good examples. However, while there are fantastical elements to many of the stories to be found here, this is not a fantasy anthology per se. Like its sister anthology, *The End of The Line* (2010), *End of The Road* presents stories that are dark in tone, often venturing into outright horror. The key word I used when contacting contributors to submit to this collection was *weird*.

And we certainly start in a very weird world, with Philip Reeve's 'We Know Where We're Goin', in which our young protagonist embarks on a journey that cleverly subverts the expectations of the quest narrative. Destination (expected or otherwise) is a theme running throughout this anthology, but often it is the journey itself that is the key to the tales. And that needn't be a physical journey (though, naturally, the majority of these stories do feature one); the journey into the self is also explored in various ways. Benjanun Sriduangkaew's beautiful and moving 'Fade to Gold' explores identity and desire while depicting a creature from Thai myth. 'Through Wylmere Woods' by Sophia

7

McDougall likewise plays with identity and self-discovery in a rich tale that is a companion piece to 'MailerDaemon' from *Magic* (2012). I also love the way Sophia plays with the idea of what constitutes a road, with her depiction of the electronic highways of the World Wide Web. Lavie Tidhar's 'Locusts' mixes the cultural and spiritual journeys of its protagonists with a story from history that is told in an usual and immersive style.

Nightmarish hitchhikers have often featured in horror movies and I was somewhat surprised to have only one hitchhiker story submitted for this anthology. However, 'Without a Hitch' by Ian Whates is a cracking tale, and Ian cleverly subverts our expectations of the weird hitchhiker story. As this story demonstrates, strangers met on the road may not be what they at first seem. Paul Meloy's black-as-night horror story 'Driver Error' certainly stands as testament to this, as does Rochita Loenen-Ruiz's rather more exotic 'Dagiti Timayap Garda (of the Flying Guardians)', in which a Filipino soldier makes the mistake of thinking he knows the person he meets on the road. In Anil Menon's 'The Cure' we have four strangers on a very unusual pilgrimage; a tale that plays with the nature of story itself.

Every time we venture out onto the road, either in a vehicle or on foot, we take a risk – the nature of which is starkly revealed with grim regularity in news reports. The violence that potentially awaits us on the road is chillingly explored in S. L. Grey's stark tale 'Bingo', in which desire and a car wreck meet, echoing Ballard's *Crash*. Rio Youer's 'The Widow' meanwhile tries to find meaning in the wreckage only to find herself face-to-face with a phantom. Jay Caselberg gives us 'The Track' in which a journey into the Australian outback meets with a faceless horror. 'Always in Our Hearts' by Adam Nevill tells the story of a hit-and-run driver and the horrifying manner in which he pays the price for his actions.

We travel to arrive, and arrivals are key to several stories here. 'Balik Kampung (Going Back)' by Zen Cho tells the story of a ghost reluctantly lead to an understanding by her personal demon. 'I'm the Lady of Good Times, She Said' by Helen Marshall starts with an arrival and works its way backward to unravel a tale of a haunted man. In 'Peripateia' the scientist protagonist arrives at an understanding of the universe that changes everything, but also very little.

As travel features so much in this anthology, I wanted a bit more of a world genre feel than I've perhaps had with my previous anthologies. I made sure to source writers not just from the US and the UK, but also from other areas of the globe. In this I am indebted to Lavie Tidhar for his help in leading me to brilliant writers whose work I wasn't already familiar with.

It's been a joy to embark on every journey you will find here, so, for you, it's time to buckle up, sit back and prepare yourself for the ride.

Jonathan Oliver
August 2013, Oxford

WE KNOW WHERE WE'RE GOIN

PHILIP REEVE

Philip Reeve's story begins with a journey and a destination set very firmly in its protagonist's mind. But like many of the journeys in this collection, the unexpected starts to happen the moment the first step is taken. There are shades of Russel Hoban's Riddley Walker *here, in the fragmented language of the tale, but shining throughout is Reeve's own dry wit and a compelling story that will draw the reader along the Road and into the heart of the unknown.*

FROM THE CAMP at Frunt End I liked ter look back sumtimes the way we'd come, an see the Road stretchin away from me down into the low lands. Strate as a measurin stick it lay across the ruffness and muddle o them wild places. But instead o feet an inches it was marked with my 'memberins, and the graves an birthin places o my family.

I could 'member back to when I was just a bitty girl an we was pushin the Road thru kindly country, along a wide valley with woods an green hills on eyther side an a river windin down its middle like a silvry snake. There was plenty o time in them days fer me an the other kids ter lark an laze along them shady river banks while the growed-ups discuxed how best ter get the Road across, an the smiths an carpinters got busy buildin the bridges that was goin ter carry it.

11

But that was all so long back that I could scarcely see that green valley now from up at Frunt End; jus the far twistins o that river sumtimes, shinin faintly thru blue distance an white ruffs o mist. Past few years we'd bin climbin agin, up stony steeps where nort but black pines grew, towards high mountins that walled off the sky. The huntin parties had ter go long miles ter gather all the food we needid, an there was scarce enough forage fer the piggs nor grazin fer the cattle nor timber fer makin the gas to fuel our trucks an diggas. The goin was so bad the Road had ter be laid in zig-zags some places, tho each ziggin an zaggin section of it was still strate as a ruler, so Foreman Skrevening sed it did not deviate from Rightchus Strateness.

We was following a path that stretched up inter them mountins like a ghost Road. My Ma tole us mebbe it was the way some other Road had gone, built by other folks in the long-back. Sumtimes we found a cuttin they had made, an sumtimes on a river bank there'd be the crumblin stone piers where a bridge had stood. But even so it was slow hard goin on them steeps an screes, an often there would come a girt landslide an take away the work o weeks, an half a dozen o the workers with it.

The year I turned 14 we only made ten miles, an the year after that was wurse. Back in that river valley me an the other kids had dreamed such dreams o how things would be when the Road got all the way ter Where We're Goin, the fine houses an cloaths we'd have there an the food we'd eat. Nowdays all we hoped fer was ter reach the top o them mountins fore we died, an look down inter the lands that laid beyond. But mebbe that was somethin ter do with growin up, too. When you get older you learn ter make your dreams littler, cos the little ones don't die so easy.

So up an up we went, cuttin an levellin the roadbed, layin the first fill o gravel fer drainidge an then the hardcore on top. Rollin it flat, then meltin an porin over all the black ash-felt that was delivered by the supply convoys from Where We Started.

An then 1 day Foreman Skrevening went drivin his jeep up ahedd to see what would be needed fer the layin o the next stretch, an he came back lookin like his own ghost, so wan an woeful. Turned out the way was blocked by a girt heap o massy bolders that must have come tumblin down off the mountinside since the surveyors last checked the route.

I was 16 by then, an workin as a mechanic in the motor pool, so I was amung the first ter hear that doalful news. I listened ter Foreman Skrevening tell it ter Purser Judd while I helped Steg Carrack ter fix a leaky gas pipe on one o the diggas.

Can we go round? asks Judd.

Not without deviatin from the way o Rightchus Strateness says ol Skrevening. An not even then without goin twenty miles from the path that was planned. An how many years an lives would that take? We must blast our way thru with splodeys, that be the only choice we has.

Purser Judd shook his head at that. We ant got no splodeys, he said. We used up the last back in the spring, clearin that long cuttin 5 mile back. We won't have none now till the next convoy comes up, an that could be 6 months more.

Well then, says Skrevening, we'll have ter send someone back along the Road ter Where We Started an fetch some. Or else sit an look at that rockfall fer 6 months.

But who we goin ter send? asks Judd. We need all the workers on the Road. Can't spare noboddy.

An thats where I stuck my noase in. Scrambled out from under the digga an grinned up at them ter let them know I'd bin listenin ter it all. I was promised ter marry Purser Judd's boy Danil the followin year, an I knew after that my life would be nothin much but babies an women's work fer a long way, an tween you an me that was not a prospeckt I girtly relished. So here I saw a chance ter have 1 bit o time ter meself, 1 proper adventure fore I turned inter a mum. Added ter which, I'd bin thinking o them nice green places we'd took the Road thru back when I was bitty, an it seemed ter me it might be sweet ter look on them agin.

So I says, I'll go.

An naturally there was a certin amount o old-mannish worryin an head shakin on account o me bein a girl. But they all knew I was as strong as most o the lads, an as brite as any o them. An I'd bin working as grease monkey fer Steg Carrack fer years, helpin tend all the jeeps an steamrollers an diggas, so I'd be able ter sort out any breakdown that befell me on the way. So fore too long it was decided, an then it was just a matter o sayin my goodbies ter Ma an my sisters an brothers an Danil.

Danil was the worst o all o them. I think Ma understood why I wantid ter go, an mebbe wished she could have gone herself. My brothers an sisters was too bitty mostly ter proply unnerstand what dangers I'd be goin inter. But Danil knew all right. Dimpsey, he says, you plannin ter drive that rig all the way back ter Where We Started on your own, an you just an unwedded girl?

Maybe I wont hav to go the whoal way, I tells him. Your dad reckins there might be supply caches here an there along the way, in case o 'mergencies like this. An if not, well, I got the Road ter drive on, ant I? The best Road ever built, what'll take me strate ter Where We Started.

Them caches will be empty, Danil says. Ant you heard, the hills back-a-way are full o wild crooked men, an they'll have robbed them caches out by now. An what'll they make o you, Dimpsey?

Well, says I, I recken I can cope with crooked men, an I showed him my Da's ol gun what Ma had gived me, an the belt o bullets that went with it.

That still wernt enough ter make Danil happy. Yore duty's here with me, he says. But I din't think it was, not yet. When I got back an we was wed he'd get ter order me about however much he liked, but till then I reckined I was free, an the Road was callin me. I spent my whoal life helpin build it, I thought, it would be a proper pity not ter travel it, just once.

THE RIG WAS a big 6-wheeler. Not as big as the convoy trucks that brung the tar an ash-felt up, but big enuf that I felt like a queen sat up in the driver's cabin, with my hands on the wide steerin wheel an Steg Carrack lookin up at me with oil on his ugly face an worry in his eyes like it was his own child I was takin out o camp.

You treat her proply, Dimpsey, he tole me, an she'll carry you ter Where We Started all right. When your comin back all loaded up with splodeys, you go slow, an let some air out o the tyres mebbe. You jostle them splodeys too much an they're liable ter blow you ter bits an my rig with you.

An I laughed an tole him I'd be careful an started the big roarin engine so I couldnt hear what further wise advice he had ter offer, nor any o the things Danil shouted as I went rumblin out o camp an away down the Road, with my brothers an sisters running alongside fer a way an then fallin behind 1 by 1 till I was alone at last.

SO OFF I set, drivin back down the Road we'd made, back past old campsites an cuttins an infills I 'membered bein built the year before, an the year before that. The rig ran well down them long zig-zags, an soon Frunt End an the smoke o the camp an the ash-felt vats was outer-sight behind me, an I was passin thru country I'd clean forgot. I went past little fields and vegtabble plots that had helped feed us for a season and was now gone back all to weeds and wild agen. An I saw knobs o rock an white roarin rivers that had bin part o my life fer a week or a month or however long it had took ter get the Road across them, an all sorts o 'memberins woke in me now I saw them agen.

I parked up that night in an old campsite, near the place where a landslip had took ten workers lives. Their grave markers was standin by the Road, dark mountin slate with names scratched on, the usual Judds an Vaizeys an Skrevenings, an also some Tains, my own kin. I shared some o my supper with them, scatterin crumbs o black bread an sprinklin beer on the graves in the hope the ghosts wouldn't come botherin me while I slept. An they din't, so that was OK.

Next day an the day after I pressed on, an found meself pretty soon down at the bottom o those mountins it had taken the Road half my life ter climb. Ahead o me lay that green valley o my happy 'memberins, an beyond it the Road climbed up agen inter more hills, but lower an kindlier ones, I hoped.

At first the land on either side was clear, just stumps showing where we'd hacked the trees down for wood gas, but new trees was growing, and the further I went the taller they was. There had bin rain, but now the sun was out, an the wet ash-felt line o the Road was shinin in the light, stretchin away an away inter the farness, an I felt so proud just lookin at it, an thinkin o all the people who'd laboured so long an hard ter draw this Strate an Rightchus silvery line across the world.

That evenin I came ter the first o the supply caches that Purser Judd had tole me of. Sometimes a freight rig on its way ter Frunt End broak down along the Road, an if its cargo couldn't be shared out tween the others in its convoy it would leav them by the roadside, burrid, with a marker ter show where they was. The idea bein that if there was dire mergencies at Frunt End, or if some delay kep the next convoy from gettin ter us, we would not have too far ter go ter get provisions. The caches was burrid in locked boxes, an the markers was subtle an secrit: a blaze on a tree-stump that lined up with a wite mark on a stone high on the hillside, stuff like that. Purser Judd had tole me where ter look fer this one or I'd not have seen it. But still the crooked men, who lived wild in the hills an would not share in the girt an rightchus work o Roadbuildin, had found it fore I did. The ground had bin torn up, an bits o broken crates an boxes scattered here an there among the bushes. It did not look ter me as if any o those crates had had splodeys in them, but even so it was a 'minder ter me that I was far from help an in wild country.

I gunned up the rig an drove on, an that night I did not stop, just turned the headlites on an kep goin, watchin the smooth black back o the Road rush under my wheels an listnin ter the hiss an hum o my tyres on the ash-felt.

All thru that night I drove, till by the time dawn started comin up pink an peach color over them eastly hills I could scarce keep my eyes open an my head seemed ter grow heavier an heavier, till I longed ter put it down upon the steerin wheel in front o me an just sleep. An then I did sleep, just fer a second, an woke sudden at the rush an rattle as the rig veered right ter the side o the Road an started brushin thru the trees an bushes that stuck out their branches there.

Then I knew I must stop an rest, fer it would not do ter wreck the rig in that lonely place. So I put on the brakes an slowed an stopped, an then turned off the engine, an silence came rushin inter the cabin, startlin at first after the engine's roar, till I realised it weren't really silence at all, but made up o wind in trees an the call o birdeys an the nearby laughter o a river runnin.

Then I slept a bit, an when I woke I opened the door an stepped down out o the cab inter long wet grass. I knew that place; the 'memberins o it came crashin down on me as I went down ter where the river waited. We had camped fer a month or more just there, on that flat place where young trees was growin now. In them deep pools me an my friends had splashed an played an made our plans. It made my eyes grow teary, lookin at it, ter think how bitty an how happy I had bin in them times, before the Road started up inter the mountins.

So I tended to the rig a bit, raking the ash out of the burners an loadin in fresh wood chippins, and afterwards I washed meself in them kind cool waters, an they flowed over me full o sweet 'memberings. And when I was dry agen I went back ter where I'd left the rig, an that was when I saw the crooked men.

I was lucky. There was just 2 o them. Not a raidin party; just a pair who'd bin huntin or fishin mebbe, an heard my rig an come fer a look at it. They was circlin it now, an 1 stepped up an tried the door, but I had locked it; I wasn't stupid. An also, not bein stupid, I'd brung my Da's ol gun with me when I went ter the bathin place. As far as I could see there weren't no guns in the hands o the crooked men nor in their belts neither, so I figured I had the edge on them.

Get away from that rig, I tole them, or I'll shoot the pair o you.

Now tho we call them crooked men, you mustn't get the idea they're really crooked. They ant all crippled up, nor twisty faced like Steg Carrack. We calls them crooked just cos they don't help with the buildin o the Road, or understand how Glorious is its Rightchus Strateness. In actual fact they was not bad lookin fellas, these 2 who turned ter face me, all surprised ter find a girl walkin at them out o the sunlight an the tree shadows, pointin that big ol gun at them.

Run, says 1, but the other tells him, stay. An he came forward as if ter meet me, squintin his eyes a bit against the light. Nice eyes they was too; light brown an pretty as any girl's. An his hair fox ginger, falling over them. But this wasn't the time ter be admirin his prettiness, so I jabbed the gun at him an says, you just stay put if you don't want a hoal in you.

An he grins an says, why, I don't beleev you'd put a hoal in me, Dimpsey Tain.

Which came as a surprise ter me just as big as if he'd pulled a gun o his own. Cos how did this wild wood wanderer get ter know my name?

An then I looks some more at his eyes an his foxy hair, an it comes back ter me. One o them kids who used ter splash an lark with me down in them river pools had hair like that. An a grin like that too. An that same way o tippin his head ter 1 side an shadin his eyes gainst the sun with 1 hand. Carter Vaizey was his name. I'd thought he was lost far behind. Thought he'd gone back with a supply convoy ter Where We Started after a landslip killed his da.

Seemed not, tho.

You're Carter Vaizey ant you, I asked, an he said yes he was.

The other 1 I din't know: some friend he'd made in the hills, I supposed. Ant you ashamed o yourself, I asked, turnin your back on the Road, turnin ter the paths o crookedness?

The Road? he says, all jokin, just like I 'membered him in the before-times when we was bitty. Ant you ashamed o yourself fer wastin your life away on the buildin of it, Dimpsey Tain? You used ter be bright. Ant you stopped yet ter ask yourself what your glorious Road is fer, nor where tis goin?

I don't need ter stop an ask, I says. Everybody knows that! It's goin ter Where We're Goin.

That's what I used ter think, says he. An then I changed my mind, an I decided I'd sooner find my own path out than help build yours.

So you hide in the woods an rob honest folks' rigs, says I, spittin sideways ter show him I was not impressed. Well you picked the wrong rig ter rob this time, Carter Vaizey. Tis empty.

It's got *you* in it, he says, an his brown eyes was twinkling like the river. *You'd* be useful ter me Dimpsey, up in the wild camps, fer cuddlins an such.

I tole him he had a pretty high pinion o himself if he thought I or any other girl would turn from the ways o Rightchus Strateness fer the sake o cuddlin *him*. Sides which, I was promised now ter Danil Judd, what would be purser when his dad gave up.

Danil Judd? he says, an I felt meself blushin an wished I hadn't tole him that bit.

Anyways, he says, I don't reckon you're going ter use that ole murderin piece on me, Dimpsey. An he holds out his hands an starts coming towards me some more.

An at first I thought he might be right, cos all my 'memberins o those river days was stirrin still an I kep seein him as the laughin boy he'd bin an not this robber he'd become. An then suddenly I 'membered meself an my finger clutched tight on the gun's trigger an there was a bang that seemed ter make the whoal world glitch. Loud as a splodey goin off it was, an all the birds flung up black out o the trees like flyin splinters. Carter's friend took fright an ran. I saw him trip on a stump an fall flat on his face, then he was up agen an runnin. The echoes boomed, comin back at us off the hills. An Carter sat there in front o me, knocked on his bum, with a poppy-flower o blood all wet an shiny on the shoulder o the old felt coat he's wearin an a look on his face like he's gettin ready ter cry.

What dyou do that fer? he asks.

Tole you I would, says I, you shoulda lissened.

He put his hand ter the place I shot him, which was just under his sholder on the left side. Then he took it away an looked at all the shiny blood. While he was busy doin that I got another round inter the chamber, ready ter shoot him all over agen if he got up an come at me. But he just sat there an after a bit I decided he wasnt gona try nothin so I went round him ter the rig an unlocked it an got back in.

What are you doin? he yells at me. You can't just leave me here!

Don't see why not, I says.

I'll die, Dimpsey!

I spect yer friends will come an find you, says I, startin up the engine. An if they doant, I'll stop an bury yer carcass when I come back this way, fer ol time's sake.

He shouted summin more, but I was movin by then. The holler o the engine drownd his words an the blue smoke o the exhaust hid his face from me an I was on the Road agen.

I DROVE ON up that valley all thru that day an most o the next, but it din't feel so sweet somehow lookin out the pretty places I 'membered, not after runnin inter Carter like that. And after a time I wasn't sure if I really membered em or not anyway: I'd couldna bin scarce more 'n a babe-in-arms when the Road came thru there. The bridges it went over was lookin old an shabby now. The ash-felt o the Road itself had turned grey with the passin o the years, an cracks ran over it, an the woods an weeds was crowdin in thick an close on either side.

Then after a while more the Road got to climbin agen, up inter them eastward hills an then wet moorland where a zillion puddles shone in the sun. I 'membered tales the old uns tole o how hard it had bin crossin the high moss, where every hole you dug filled in agen an every spadeful o hardcore you put down was swallered up by the bog. They had done it in the end tho, an here was the proof o it: me bowling along in the rig, goin strate as an arrer cross them high wet places with the sun risin ahead o me an settin behind me.

I didnt see no more sign o crooked men after that. Didn't see no sign o nobody. One day I come across another cache, buried by an old campsite, an this 1 had not bin robbed out, but there weren't no splodeys in it, so I pushed on. The Road was gettin old under me; I reckened I was drivin by now on a stretch my grand-da had helped ter lay. Old an grey like elefant skin it was, an cracked where the Jack Frost had worked his fingers inter it, an potholed where the rain had got in thru them cracks. Now an then the rig ba-DUNKed thru 1 o them potholes, an now an then it went rumblin over a darker patch where some gang sent out with the convoys had made repairs, but even the repairs needed repairin.

After a wile it started ter make me sad, seein the Road all crackled an patchworked so. It 'minded me of things I'd heard the old uns tell, of how the ash-felt of nowadays weren't so good as ash-felt used to be in the long-back. I'd always thought that was just how old uns talk, making out everythin was better when they was kids, but rattlin over them cracks and pot holes started me to wonderin.

Sides, it was lonely up there, an Carter Vaizey's crooked lies was echoin in my brainpan still: where is the Road goin? What is it fer?

An then 1 day the Road started ter drop agen an I realised I was leavin the moors behind me, an I was glad ter see the last o em. Down thru woods I went, an as the night drew in I saw lights ahead o me, laid on the darkniss there like a girt bunch o dropped sequins. Sometimes the lights was hid from me by folds an wrinklins o the land, an then theyd shine out closer an briter than before.

I stopped fer a bit around midnight, but I dint sleep long, an set out agen soon as I woke. Come first light I was driving inter a girt camp, so big it made our camp at Frunt End look like a den children make, playin in the bushes. There was smoke hangin everywhere an the noise o work goin on sumwhere, an

all the big trucks an tankers parked up. I thought at first I must
o come ter Where We Started, tho I could not tell how I had got
there so quick.

I soon found my mistake tho. When I stopped the rig an
climbed out an asked a woman there if this was Where We
Started she just laughed at me an said Bless you, girl, course it
ant. Turned out it was called Depot, this place I'd come ter. It
was another girt campsite edging westwards like our own, an
it was where all the ash-felt an tar an spare parts an stuff was
gathered an made ready fer the convoys ter take it on ter Frunt
End.

Mardi was this woman's name, an she seemed friendly enough
once she'd stopped laughin. I showed her Foreman Skrevening's
letter asking fer more splodey an she went with me ter an office
where another Foreman looked at it an whacked it with a rubber
stamp an tole me I was a brave girl fer comin all that way an
how they would start loadin my rig that very day with splodey,
an some wood chips an provisionins fer the journey back.

Then Mardi says come ter my hut we'll find some grub fer
you an a place ter sleep. So I follows her across the tyre-tracked
mud, past parked-up rigs an jeeps an diggas, an it felt so like
Frunt End it made me homesick. Even the work-noise was the
same, comin from over yonder beyond the huts an motor pools
an all that smoke; the growlin o the diggas an the chink an
scrape o picks an shovels, an men singin. An that hot ash-felt
smell hangin over everythin, same as at home.

What is the work they do here? I asks Mardi, when we're in her
hut an she's fixing some stew fer me. Are they repairin the Road?

Mung other things, she says.

Seems ter me the Road won't never be finished, I said. By the
time it gets ter Where We're Goin the whoal lot'l need repairin.

Now that's not Strate talk, says Mardi. You're tired an don't
see things clear. Eat up now, an I'll make up a bunk fer you.

So I slept the rest o that day away, an when I woke it was
evenin. Mardi was out sumwhere an I was alone, so I went out
o the hut ter get some air.

The sun was going down behind them girt moors I'd driven over, an the line o the Road was stretchin out towards it, an all I could think on was how many generations o my kin had lived an died a-buildin o that Road, an how I hoped Where We're Goin would turn out ter be worth it when we got there.

The sound o the work was still goin on. It made me curious ter see what they was doin, cos with all them diggas growlin an pickaxes chipping away it sounded ter me like some pretty big repairs. So I went down tween the huts an tents an rows o vehicles an soon I came ter where they was workin.

An I didnt understand it at first. It made no sense ter me. All them men an women hacking an hewin at the fine flat ash-felt o the Road, what our grand-das an our grand-da's grand-das laid. Hackin an hewin at it they was, an liftin up girt chunks o the blacktop, an passin it back ter others who slung it inter big meltin vats, from which that hot ash-felt smell was comin. An shovellin up the hardcore underneath an passin that inter big waitin hoppers too.

They wasn't repairin the Road! They was takin it up!

I couldn't beleev it. I went runnin down between the work gangs, with the smoke stingin my eyes an the men callin out cheek ter me. What are you doin? I asked 1 who was busy heavin chunks o ash-felt inter the vats

Recylin says he. This stuff's needed fer the Roadbuildin. When we've recycled enough we'll pack it all inter the trucks an it'll be sent up ter Frunt End. Then we'll press on, recyclin the next stretch.

I WENT PAST him, down thru the smoke an the dust an the growlins o the diggas ter where the Road stopped. Back End, I suppose you'd call that place. Oh Carter Vaizey, I says ter meself, you was right an I was wrong. Cos where the work o the recyclin gangs had finished there was nothin left no more that you could call a Road. You could just see the scar o the roadbed, that was all, stretchin away eastward, back over the curve o the world towards Where We Started. Just a line thru the grass, an mebbe here an there there an old cuttin, or stone piers crumblin on a river bank where a bridge had stood.

    Just the ghost of a Road.

    Nuthin more.

FADE TO GOLD

BENJANUN SRIDUANGKAEW

Lavie Tidhar introduced me to Benjanun's fiction and I'm so glad he did. The story that follows is a journey into Thailand's past and its mythology. It is also an exploration of desire and the tragedy that conformity can bring. It's an extraordinarily rich and exotic story, beautifully told.

THEY SAY THE afterlife is a wheel and that is true, but I am between, and so for me the way is a line. It unspools interminably into a horizon that shows the soft gold of dawn, always just a little out of reach.

Before the war this was only packed earth and grass and dirt to me; before the war I trod this path from home to capital thinking of the sweetness of rare fruits. Now that my back is to Ayutthaya, the ground is sometimes baked salt where nothing grows and sometimes wet mud bubbling with the voices of the dead. Inside my arteries there is blood which throbs and pumps, and my belly growls at emptiness as might a bad-tempered dog. But it is difficult to be sure, after so much soldiering, that one is still alive. It is difficult to be certain this is not all a fever dream.

It can be difficult to remember who you are, having watched Queen Suriyothai die.

These are the common ailments of any soldier, though few will admit them.

*   *   *

A BURNT VILLAGE, a burnt temple. I see such often, these days, defaced by the Phma who melted off the gold and stole every metal coin. Sometimes in their savagery they kill the monks, even though theirs and ours wear much the same saffron. The Phma have faces no different than any mother's son, four limbs and a head each, but it strains belief that anything human could have slaughtered holy men. Do they not have luang-por like second fathers, who taught them to read and write? Are some of them not orphans taken in by a temple, to shelter beneath the steeple and the bodhi shade?

Slaughter is what might have happened here, or else flight, for I find neither a living voice nor a body thick with flies. Toward the end everyone fled for Ayutthaya until the walls strained at the seams, until every house and hovel splintered at the edges. It should have been comforting, so many people, but when there was so much desperation all I could feel was desperation in turn, a sour and unrelenting fear that turned everything I ate – and even the king's soldiers hadn't much to eat – into rotten meat on the tongue, with an aftertaste of cinders.

I take shelter where I find it, in spite of ghosts that must've seeped into the fissured walls and the desecrated murals. In spite of knowing that Phma soldiers have been here too, that the air bears the stink of their sweat, the reek of their filth. Being a soldier has taught me to forget delicacy.

It has also taught me to put on sleep light as dead petals, to be shaken off and scattered at a blink. So when the mud makes sucking noises I am already awake; when the woman comes into view I have a hand around the carved wood of a hilt.

She must have seen the blade glint, for there is a hiss of breath.

"I thought you might be a thief," she says.

"What could a thief rob from a place already thieved to every final clod of dirt?"

"There is always one last bit of painted glass, one last talisman." She closes the distance, her apparent fear set aside.

"One last child to murder."

"Have you lost one, then?" There's still room in my breast for softness, still room to be cut by another's hurt.

"It's a season for losing children." The luster of her lips and hair seems brighter than dawn's light warrants. "You can only be passing by. Which way calls you?"

"East, to Prachinburi."

"The same direction, then." She gathers her braid in one hand, twisting it. "Might we not share company?"

I have collected myself, spine straight, eyes clear. In the back of my mind phantom flies buzz. There is no escaping the noise. No battle-hardened veteran ever tells you it is the flies that haunt you most, over the cannon fire and your fellows' screams, over the throb and burn of your own veins. "You would trust a strange soldier?"

"When she is a woman, why not?"

My alarm must have been immediate, for she laughs.

"Even officers go bare-chested the moment they're free from uniform. You remain as neat behind yours as a captain newly promoted and pledged to His Majesty." Her head moves from side to side. "I'll not pry – too much. I want only safety, for if you've survived the Phma you must be as fit to the business of combat as any man."

I should ask how she has been unscathed so far. I should ask from whence she came, and where she was going other than in the same vague direction as I am. But in the army I've been solitary out of need, and there comes a point where a person must hear another human voice or break upon the cliff-face of loneliness. My secret is already laid bare to her, so where's the harm?

We set out at daybreak, keeping parallel to but avoiding the road, for not all soldiers recently unyoked from duty are vessels of honor, and I've heard news of Phma stragglers along this way, ready to avenge themselves upon any Tai.

She breaks open one of her bamboo tubes as we walk, and hands me half the sweet roasted rice. Her name is Ploy, a widow, and when she hears my name is Thidakesorn she smirks at the florid grandeur of it. "A princess's name," she says.

"My parents had expectations." Years living with an aunt who married upward, wife of a merchant grown wealthy on trade with the Jeen. So successful he's sailed to the Middle Kingdom twice, and his fortune tripled by a wife shrewd with numbers and investment. She would tutor me, it was hoped.

"Instead you took up the sword."

How do I say that I went to the capital to learn to be a lady and fell in love with the queen despite the hopeless stupidity of that; how do I say it was for this love that I fought and that when she fell it shattered me? How do I say that I resent the king's continued life, for she was the braver of the two, the finer being, and that he did not deserve a wife as incandescent as she? So I seal my lips and pronounce none of these wounds. Better they suppurate than my shame be cast into the day.

She may have the secret of my gender, but this is mine alone to nurse.

The day brightens and Ploy acquires a clarity of features. Before, I thought her soft and plain; now there is an angle to her eyes and mouth I've failed to notice in the dim light. Sharp from nose-tip to chin-tilt. It does not make her beautiful, if such a comment may be leveled from someone as blunt-featured as I, but she would snag the attention and hold it fast. A little like the queen. The dead queen, whom I must not think about, whom I must bury under the blackest soil of memory.

When I shut my eyes I see elephants draped in black and silver, trumpeting for death. I see the edge of a glaive passing through flesh and bone, opening a queen inside out.

Noon claims the sky with fingers bright and fever-hot. It is a month for rain, but I harbor a childish fancy that the season has upended for Queen Suriyothai's demise.

Between my waking delirium transmuting earth to a sanguine river and us stopping to drink from a pool, we hear the Phma.

Away from the shields bearing the king's crest, away from his banners and helms, it can be difficult to tell Phma deserters from our own men. Loinclothed and bare-chested like any Ayutthaya soldier, bearing much the same type of blade. There is a wild look to them that I can spot even as we take to hiding, and I wonder if the penalty for desertion is as harsh for them as for us. Harsher: victors can afford generosity that losers may not.

When they are gone Ploy murmurs, "I thought you'd challenge them, for are these not your sworn enemies and murderous animals?"

"There were five of them, and one of me."

Her sneer is vicious. "If I needed confirmation you were a woman before, I would've required none now."

"What did you lose to the Phma?"

"A family." Her mouth tightens; she says no more.

I study her more closely for signs of who she is or might have been. *Widow* says little, designates merely a specific sorrow. Strange that we will confess but one loss at a time – I am a widow, I am an orphan; how to say in one concise word *I've lost everything*?

Evening approaches, and Ploy looks to me, asking of game and hunt. I mean to scavenge and work for food on the way, and point out that the army taught me to ambush enemy warriors, not edible meat.

"You make an inadequate man." She passes me her satchel. "I'll be back."

I wait beneath a tabaek whose trunk is garbed in a purple sash. There's not much of worth on me, but I smooth out the cloth as best I can and pour out a handful of rice for offerings.

Ploy returns with frogs fat and glistening, her arms wet to the elbows, pha-sbai and pha-nung damp. "Tell me you can make a fire."

"That at least I was taught. You must've been very fast, or those frogs very old."

"And you do not know how to flatter anyone. How are you going to find a husband?"

"By changing out of this into silk and silver." I touch the edge of my helm. "By combing out my hair." In truth I aspire to spinsterhood, for how do I explain the battle scars once all that silk is stripped away? Not evidence that I was wayward as a child. Marks left by a blade resemble in no way marks left by a switch.

I sharpen twigs and skewer her catch. The meat is succulent, and she carries a jar of the best fish sauce I've had in months. I leave two crisped frog legs by the tabaek's roots, among bruised flowers, for the tree's spirit.

The next village is empty too. I begin to think perhaps all the villages in my path will be unpeopled save by wraiths, that this is beyond death after all and I'm rotting beneath a fallen war-elephant – but I must not think so, for when I do the trumpeting and the cannon fire gain strength between my ears, and if those are bearable, the buzzing is not.

Ploy is as disinclined as I to the sin of theft, and so we limit our looting to two rattan mats and some oil. We find a creaking riverside house and rest on its veranda back to back. I remain awake enough to know she slips away long before dawn. When the sun is up she comes back with two roosters. It was not a clean kill: blood everywhere, on her and them, their bellies ragged as if they've been chewed to death.

She sets them down. "A wild dog must've been at them."

This time we've banana leaves to wrap the meat, and proper seasoning – sugar, garlic, coriander root. Afterward we find a rain jar and a coconut-shell dipper. No jasmine water to scent ourselves with, but I've been long crusted in sweat and filth, and Ploy is glad to shed her gore-stained clothes.

She looks on, frowning, as I disrobe and breathe in relief to have the binding off at last. "How did you have those cuts tended without the entire army discovering you have breasts?"

"I had patronage." Her Majesty's handmaids understood so simply a woman's need to be in arms.

Ploy produces yet another wonder: a pot of tamarind paste and turmeric. She bids me turn my back and spreads that across the width of my shoulder-blades, down my spine, in a bright tart-smelling lather. My breath catches once and she asks if there's a wound as yet unhealed.

"It's nothing." There is no way of saying that I've never had another woman's hand on me so except that of kin; there's no way of saying that her touch pulls the strings of my nerves taut, a note so loud in my skull that for a moment all else is mute.

I make myself indifferent while she, nude, washes her clothing. But my eyes stray and my skin craves. Is it any wonder that the monks tell us earthly desire is a shackle, material lust a disease? Rest comes slow, and I am not even drowsing by the time Ploy steals away.

"I've no appetite," she says when I offer her chicken in the morning. Then she scrubs at her teeth with a khoi stick, rinsing her mouth over and over as though she's swallowed unutterable foulness.

We circle back toward the main road. For a relief we meet a family: two grandparents, their daughter and son-in-law, a buffalo-pulled cart laden with supplies and children. Ploy takes my arm before I can speak, introducing me as her husband. The breastplate and helm purchase respect and welcome; they share food with us and their spirits are high. Here is a family that went through war untouched by tragedy.

I keep my words few, my voice low. I've allowed myself to speak freely with Ploy, and if I never trilled or chirped as some women do, still my natural pitch would have given me away.

They would have missed it, and I might have too if not for the flies. That sound – I would know it anywhere. Gorge rising, I stride into the bushes; Ploy calls but she is muted, for black clouds close in about me, red eyes the size of longans, wings larger than open hands. When they disperse and my sight clears there are the corpses.

Phma, by the color of their bandannas. A painful death, by everything else. Their bellies torn out, entrails wetting the earth, dense with ants and flies as though they're both sweet and savory.

The son-in-law has followed to see what's afoot. "This wasn't done by knife or arrow," I say, turning to him. "Do you know of any blade that could make wounds so messy?"

One look at the carcasses and he recoils. "I'm no fighter."

Ploy is not far behind him, and when she bears witness to this massacre she merely says, "A tiger."

"This close to the road?"

"Who knows? It is justice."

"We could cremate them."

"A waste of oil." She tugs at my hand. "Leave them for the worms. Were you reborn one, you'd have been glad of the gift."

I should like to think I haven't been so heinous as to reincarnate so low, but then I was a soldier. We do not burn the bodies.

At a river's crossing we part company with the family, them turning south while we continue east. Ploy's gaze follows them as they go out of our sight. "I wasn't entirely truthful," she says. "I don't have a home left to return to."

"I know."

"You aren't going to ask why I disappear after dark?"

"You never ask why I became a soldier, or any of the hundred other questions you could've put to me."

She looks away, but her hand slides into mine. "Could there be a place for me in Prachinburi?"

"There'll be work." I hesitate, this close to pulling my fingers away from hers, but they knit and there is an easy fit to our hands. "My grandmother might want another woman in the household. Toddlers running underfoot."

Her gaze lifts, fastens to mine. "We could see each other every day then."

My pulse races. It is a terrible affliction, to have your heart lurch this way and that at nothing more than another's glance, another's breath. "If you like."

"What a shame it is you aren't a man." Ploy's smile is only one half edged; the other, perhaps, is turned inward to cut herself. "Then I could have married you, you'd have returned garnished with not just a rank but also a wife, and all this would have been so perfect."

THERE ARE A hundred breeds of madness, one of them called curiosity. Her naming of it has roused mine, and where before it lay dormant, now it is a frenzied thing, stirring in my skull, a thousand wing-beats in time with the cicadas and owls singing the moon up through pale clouds.

A hundred breeds of madness, and I haven't been sane for a long time.

I resist it. I look at her face in the light as we draw nearer to my home, and become desperate that her taunt was truth – that I was a man, that the possibility she offered in jest could grow to actuality. But in Prachinburi I may not remain behind this garb. I must step out of it and return to pha-sbai that bares my shoulders, pha-nung that must have some gleaming thread to it. I must catch a man's eye and hope he will find me worthy of dowry. And Ploy, being without kin to give her station and place, will remarry.

This is only pretense: my hand in hers, and sometimes lying face to face as evening cools and dark comes, it is all make-believe. She wishes I were a man so I might provide her security and a roof; beyond that there is nothing.

This terrible knowledge – that this is all we will ever have – it tears at me, it claws. Even the distraction of ghost elephants and ghost queens only I can see proves unequal to it. My monstrous desire eats; my curiosity waxes.

Five days from Prachinburi and I give in.

She makes no secret of leaving my side now. Always it takes the better part of the night, and her outing brings meat more often than not. Perhaps it embarrasses her to be good at the hunt; I convince myself this is her secret, and if so what injury can come out of my confirming it?

Ploy is not difficult to follow. In those first evenings she might have been, when she stole away on light and cautious feet. Now her tracks are clear, as though she's giving me a test of trust. My failing of it pricks at me, and I would have turned back if not for the sight of her prone by the river.

She lies among weeds and roots, fainted or snake-bitten. I've never known myself for such quickness – even on the battlefield I was not so fast. Mouth parched with fear, I kneel by her, straining to see under a moon just half-bright.

Bright enough to see her neck empty.

Not a wound but a bloodless hole where her windpipe should have been. I dare not touch or probe, for who knows whether she will feel? But I've learned the fright-tales of krasue at elders' feet; cut her open now and I will find the shell of Ploy hollowed of organs. Those have gone with her head.

I lack the courage to stay and confront; I lack the courage even to flee. For she knows me, would recognize my scent.

Ploy returns empty-handed this time, and I watch her mouth, her teeth, for flecks of gore and shreds of viscera. None to be seen; she may believe me gullible, but she is not entirely careless.

The army taught me to put on a mask, and I do that now. The slightest change in my regard and she will realize; I address her much as before. Still some hint must have slipped through, for she asks me why I seem to dread homecoming so.

"It's been some time since I last saw them, and of my parents' dreams for me I failed every one."

"Were you a son they would have been proud." She puts her fingers to my jaw. "I say this not to taunt or mock you, but to say: it is not fair. It is not just. With what you've earned, you should be entitled to anything, and in your place a man would've had applause, honor, his pick of a bride."

My betraying body leaps to her touch, longs to lean into her arm. "The world is what it is. The army paid me well, so I'll have something to show for it, something to give Mother and Father."

In Ayutthaya they would have me stay on, to advance from captain to lieutenant, and that's what I would have done if Her Majesty survived. I would have been there simply for her, to protect her even if she would never have glanced my way. I would not have been here, with this creature, this krasue.

Elders' wisdom has it that they inherit the curse, generation to generation. And that may be. It may be true; Ploy could just be the victim of her aunt, uncle, parent. She gobbles up what she must – chicken's blood, Phma innards. She may be as virtuous a woman as any other.

But I cannot bring her to Prachinburi. There will be pigs butchered and she'll hunger. There will be women in childbirth and the blood will summon her to consume mother's insides and infant freshly born. So many things a krasue may not resist, so much evil just one may commit.

Ploy's mood grows tense as we approach Prachinburi, pendulating between elated and anxious. She wants to know if people will be kind to her, a strange widow with no origins; she wants to know if they will disdain her for knowing no letters. I tell her nothing and everything.

Twice I crouch by her headless body, shaking. Twice I fail to kill it and kill her.

"AFTER TOMORROW WE should be in Prachinburi."

She is combing out her hair. It isn't as long as most women's, and uncharitably I think that she must keep it short so it won't tangle up with her intestines when she goes hunting. "Strange," she murmurs, "I'll miss this."

"Sleeping on the ground? Having no roof over your head?"

Ploy swats me on the arm. I should flinch – I should clench my teeth on disgust. "I will miss your company. Just being with you, talking to you."

"We can do that there."

"That's not what I mean and you know it." Ploy ties her hair back. "I wasn't entirely kidding when I said I would have liked to go as your wife."

"I doubt I could've kept up this deception for the rest of my days. Leastwise before my family."

"Not what I mean either." Her brows knit. Oh, she has a way of frowning; before learning the truth of her nature that look would have made me do anything to ease it. "Do you mean to shame me by driving me to say plainly what no woman should?"

Wanting, wanting, that's all flesh is good for. Her hand remains cradling my cheek and I cannot make myself dislodge it. This close I thought she would smell of offal, but there's only a scent of sweat, of her. "What might that be?"

She lets her hand fall; my heart falls with it, to steep and ferment in the bitterness of my stomach. "Nothing. It was only a fancy. It'd profit us both to forget."

"If you like," I say easily, as though none of this has meaning.

I REMAIN AT her insensate shell longer that night. I've heard a krasue's glow is sickly and jaundiced, but what I see is soft, candlelight amber. Innards drift behind her as though the tails of a kite.

Even having seen that, my decision congeals slow, like blood thinned by lymph. Even having seen that I cannot think–

A krasue in Prachinburi, and me its harbinger. She might have children there, and one of them will receive her legacy whether or not they wish, whether or not *she* wishes.

It may be mercy as well as defense.

So I gather wood, as dry as may be found in this weather, until I have more than I need. I gather dead leaves, though some are so damp they are nearly mulch. I moor my thoughts to the pier of Prachinburi; I think of what I will eat there, sweet and sour things, and of greeting friends long unseen. Above the sky lightens.

The lamp oil Ploy and I collected is spent to the last drop. My hands are guided not by thought but by the reflexive process of fire-making, of burying her in branches and detritus. A mound of compost.

It all crackles. Fire is a sound. It all leaps. Fire is an animal. It bursts with smells all pungent. Fire is a feast.

It brings her, as I knew it must. I stand with feet braced and blade bared.

Heart and lungs, liver and intestines, limned in that exquisite golden light the same precise hue of dawn. I would say she is unhuman, but are those not the most human parts of anyone freed from skin, while I hide myself behind the artifice of fabric and armor?

Ploy's face remains her own. There is no bestial rictus that reveals her for what she is. There is only a gaze piercing me like arrows, there is only a mouth parting around words like knives.

"I desired you," she says and her voice is not the hag's croak that I was told would emerge from a krasue's mouth. "I wanted to be with you – and there'd have been no children; I would have been the last."

"You would have killed and eaten." My muscles tremble. My throat is shut and my breath comes fast.

"Wild animals. Pigs. Invaders." Her laughter rings pure and clear while her guts undulate, eelish and glistening. "I've long learned control, Thidakesorn. The Phma cut my nieces apart. There will be no more of us. This would've been the end."

"A krasue would say this." My voice splinters. Beside us the fire grows loud, hungry, the heat and brilliance of it bringing sweat and radiance to us both. "A krasue would say anything to escape death."

"A krasue who wants survival would not give you her trust. A krasue who courts life would kill one who's murdered her." Tears on her cheeks, salt on my tongue. "I despise you."

I kick apart the pyre, plunge my hands into the flames. It is too late; it has always been too late. Beneath the kindling she is limbs gone to roast, flesh gone to broil, her breast bared and red-raw.

Pressing blistered hands to my face I scream, and it's hardly a human sound.

She presses her mouth to my temple, and her guts move against me, coolly wet. I expect them to seek my neck and cord into a noose. But they slide across my shoulders and arms until

I understand this is her last remaining means of comfort. "I despise you," she whispers. "I love you."

We are no kin – her spit will not force her fate upon me – but she could still bite, could still kill. I wrap my arms around her, around a heart that pumps so strong it jolts my bones. My face in her hair and her lips at my ear, she tells me of how an aunt died when she was eleven and passed her this inheritance. Four years later she became mistress of the hunger; four years later she began to dream that she may not have to be her aunt, may live like any other girl save for her forays in the dark. In a prosperous place, a prosperous time, she could fill her belly full by the day, and so need not venture forth every night.

I do not speak. This is her time to be heard. Her words come slower as the sun climbs higher, even though I keep us in the shade and shield her from the day. Her eyelids droop, heavy, and her head lowers to my shoulder as if to doze off.

She crumbles in my arms. It seems unthinkable that she could turn from flesh to husk in a moment; it seems unthinkable that her face should collapse upon itself, her hair drying to twigs, her lips and eyes to sun-baked fruit.

She is dust.

The buzzing of flies grows in my head and I turn to the rising sun, toward home. My arms are full of her, dry flecks collecting in the creases of my clothes and skin.

In the distance I hear war drums. The horizon shines gold with the beginning of fire.

WITHOUT A HITCH

IAN WHATES

I must admit that I was a little surprised at receiving only one hitchhiker story for this anthology. The figure of the hitcher has been something of staple of horror fiction for a while, especially in the movies where we only have to look to Rutger Hauer's psycho or the lunatic picked up by the cast of The Texas Chainsaw Massacre. *However, this being a story by Whates you can expect something a little different, an idea that is thrillingly and unexpectedly resolved.*

"Do you actually *like* this sort of thing?"

Fleetwood Mac were playing on the sound system – a 'Best of' collection that inevitably drew heavily on the classic album *Rumours*.

"Yes. Why, don't you?"

She didn't answer, just looked away, but the disdain was clear.

Ben determined not to turn the music off. This was *his* car and he'd listen to whatever the hell he liked. But his resolve started to crumble almost immediately. It wasn't in his nature to ignore the preferences of a guest and, besides, he found that he wasn't enjoying the music anymore. Her attitude had somehow soured it for him. He held out for one more track and then, without saying a word, reached forward and pressed the 'off' button. She didn't say 'thank you', but he felt sure she was thinking it.

* * *

BEN WAS STILL a little bemused by this girl's – this *woman*'s – presence in the car. He hadn't intended to pick up a hitchhiker, not by a long shot.

It was yet another example of how the day had gone from bad to worse. Too early to say whether or not the trip up north had been a total waste of time, but the meeting with Archibald hadn't gone well, that much was certain. The man was sharp. Some of his questions had wrong-footed Ben, and it was a long while since any buyer had managed to do that.

To top it all off this blasted fog came down. The nights closed in quickly at this time of the year and the meeting had been scheduled later than Ben would have liked – it was already dark and he hadn't even reached the A1 yet. Darkness and fog: a combination guaranteed to make his journey home a miserable one. Perhaps he should have stayed the night after all – the company would have footed the bill for a modest hotel. But no, that would only have upset Sarah. Anyway, turning up at the office early the next morning all bright and breezy was bound to earn him brownie points. He was the oldest one left on the sales force, and couldn't help but feel a little threatened by some of the young pups breathing down his neck – his so-called colleagues. He knew they joked about him behind his back; Gilbert in particular, the smug prick.

Fog or no fog, Ben was going home. Everything would be all right once he reached the A1(M).

He kept reviewing the meeting with Archibald in his head, going over the answers he *should* have given. He was doing precisely that when the girl appeared. Literally. Out of nowhere. One minute he was driving along an empty road, the next thing there she was, directly in front of him. It wasn't just the fog hiding her, he felt sure of it. She *hadn't been there* an instant before.

He slammed on the brakes and wrenched the wheel hard round, grateful that the conditions weren't icy as well as foggy.

In the corner of his eye he saw the girl leap out of the way as he swerved past, narrowly missing her.

The car came to a bone-juddering stop. He *had* missed her, hadn't he?

He glanced in the rearview mirror. She was lying by the roadside, unmoving. *Oh, hell!*

Ben undid his seatbelt and jumped out of the car, hurrying back to where the girl lay prone. *No, no, no! This can't be happening.*

As he reached her, she moved a little. He had never felt such relief in his life. She stirred and gingerly pushed herself off the ground.

"Are... are you all right?"

She looked up, glaring at him. "I think so, no thanks to you. You could have fucking *killed* me!"

Black hair worn in a ragged bob, a stud through her nose – the right nostril – and dark make-up heavily applied to emphasise what had to be the most beautiful eyes Ben had ever seen. She was small, *petite*; easy to mistake for a girl rather than a young woman. How old was she? Nineteen, twenty?

"I know. I'm really sorry."

"*Sorry?* How fast were you driving, for fuck sake? It's foggy, in case you hadn't noticed."

Did she have to swear so much? "I know, I know; you're right." Why was he feeling so defensive? *He* wasn't the one walking along an unlit road in the fog at night dressed in a black leather jacket. "What are you doing out here, anyway?" was all he said.

"Had a row with my boyfriend. He chucked me out the car."

"Out *here*?"

"Obviously. He's a bastard. What's it to you?"

"Nothing... Look, where are you headed?"

She hesitated, as if unsure of a destination. "London."

London? "Well you are going in the right direction, but you're in for one heck of a long walk."

"Yeah, I know. Was hoping to hitch a lift off someone." The look she gave him was a blatantly expectant one.

"I could take you some of the way, if you like." Had he really said that? The words escaped before he could stop them. Sarah would flay him alive.

"Okay."

And that was how he ended up with this taciturn, feisty, spitfire of a girl sitting in the seat beside him; a state of affairs he regretted more and more with each passing minute. Conversation had proved... difficult.

"What's your name?" he'd asked.

"Karen."

"Well hello, Karen, I'm Ben." Silence. "Where are you from?"

"Does it really matter?"

"No, I suppose not." And a moment later, "How old are you?"

"None of your business."

At which point he gave up.

Ben was concentrating on the road and didn't realise what she was doing until he heard the click of a lighter. Then the smell of a freshly lit cigarette reached him and he nearly convulsed. It was all he could do to keep control of the wheel.

"I'm sorry," he snapped, untruthfully, "but you'll have to put that out. We don't allow smoking in the car."

She looked at him for a long second, then lowered the window and flung the still-smouldering cigarette out into the night.

Ben breathed a sigh of relief. Trying to explain away the smell of smoke in the upholstery would have been a nightmare.

Who have you had in the car? A woman, was it?

He was fast reaching the conclusion that the evening's events merited a bit of judicious editing. Best not to mention his giving this Karen a lift at all when he got home.

Just picked up some random girl by the roadside, did you? So what if you did *nearly run her over? That suddenly makes you her personal chauffeur, does it?*

No, far simpler to say nothing. Not that there would be anything to tell. He was simply going to drop the girl off a little closer to London than he'd found her, and that would be that.

He could go home with a clear conscience and no harm done.

Buoyed by this resolve – and the promise of better driving conditions courtesy of the A1(M), which was now just a few minutes away – he switched the music back on. So what if she didn't like it? He did.

For all this bravado, Ben was intensely aware of her presence. She was attractive in a waifish sort of way, no denying that, but he suppressed the thought firmly. She couldn't be more than half his age at most.

As Stevie Nicks sang her way towards the end of "Rhiannon" the RDS kicked in, interrupting the music with a traffic update. Ben only heard the first item. "There are long delays on the A1(M) following an accident involving multiple vehicles. The southbound carriageway has been closed between junctions 35 and 36, and the tailback now stretches all the way to junction 38. A diversion has been put in place, via the A638, but that route, too, is heavily congested. Police are advising drivers to expect delays of up to three hours."

Ben stared at the radio in disbelief. Under normal circumstances he was, what, three hours from home? Allow an extra half hour for the fog and then three more for the delay... That would take him well into the early hours of the morning. "Shit!" He couldn't face driving for that long, not after the pig of a day he'd just had to endure.

Ben was still trying to work out what to do when Lady Luck smiled on him for a change. A sign emerged from the fog, announcing a motel this side of the A1, though it had probably been directly on the road at one point, before the upgrades – yet another business left stranded by the planners. Perfect; it ought to be reasonably cheap then. Evidently he was going to be staying the night after all.

It was only when they drew up in the car park that he spared a thought for his passenger. He'd managed to avoid thinking about her until then.

"Right," he said, "I won't be going any further tonight, what with the fog and the A1 being closed. You can go on if you like..."

She gave a curt but vigorous shake of the head. "In this weather? I'm not crazy or anything. I wasn't out there dodging traffic by choice when you tried to run me over. Next time I might not be so lucky."

He recognised her unsubtle attempt to play on his sense of guilt, but could hardly deny the accusation; and yes, he did feel a degree of responsibility, but not that much. On the other hand she was only a kid, despite the spiky attitude.

"Have you got any money on you?"

Another shake of the head.

Of course she hadn't. So what could he do? His employers would never stump up for *two* rooms... He considered simply turfing her out, or even suggesting that she sleep in the car, but that seemed unfair. Besides, he wouldn't trust her in the car, not unless he confiscated her cigarettes first.

"Okay, I'm going to get a room for both of us – separate beds, don't worry; I promise nothing inappropriate will happen. Would you be all right with that?"

She shrugged. "I suppose."

He wasn't convinced this was a good idea, not remotely, but he was tired and he was angry and it seemed the easiest option. Unless *he* slept in the car, of course, but that was *not* going to happen; it would be his room, after all. She was the interloper here, not him.

"First, though, I want to give my wife a quick ring, to explain what's happened." She didn't move. He gestured towards the door. "If you don't mind..."

After a moment's hesitation she sighed, unbuckled her seatbelt, opened the door and got out.

Ben took a deep breath and braced himself for a difficult phone call.

SHE LIT ANOTHER cigarette and leaned back against the car, smoking and wondering whether he really thought the thin barrier of the car's window would stop her from hearing every word of the conversation – well, *his* side of it, at any rate. The wife sounded like an uptight and insecure bitch.

"No, darling, of course I'm not staying away on purpose... Yes, yes, of course I *want* to get home... Really, it's the weather... Yes, I'll be back in the morning, early as I can, promise... Nowhere nice, just a motel... Yes, the company will pay... Of course I'm sure... All right, then. Kiss Sophie good night for me... Yes, I wish I was there to do it in person too. I'll call you tomorrow before I leave... Well, if it's too early then I'll call when I'm on the way. Okay? Love you."

She wondered if Wifey had said 'love you too' in return.

Thank God he'd finished. It was getting cold standing around out here. Movement from inside the car indicated that he was about to get out, so she pushed herself upright and stepped away from the door. The cigarette was two thirds gone. She took one final drag and then dropped what remained, grinding it out with the sole of her shoe.

THE CLERK AT the desk didn't bat an eyelid when Ben asked for a twin room, but he felt sure the man would be smirking after they'd gone. The temptation to be defensive and say something like 'she's my daughter' almost won out, but Ben resisted.

The room was everything he had expected: small, sparse, functional, and cheaply furnished; but at least there were two beds, suitably separated by a cabinet-cum-table fixed to the wall. He undressed hurriedly while Karen took a shower, keeping his pants on and climbing into the right-hand of the two beds – the one nearest the door. He pulled the sheet up so that just his bare shoulders and head protruded and debated whether or not to turn the light out. He refrained on the basis that she might need it when she came out. This was the first time Ben had been in a bedroom alone with a woman other than his wife in... well, more years than he cared to remember. The sound of a shower stopping had never seemed more ominous, and his nervousness increased dramatically.

Where to look? Should he feign sleep?

The bathroom door opened and Karen emerged with a towel wrapped round her. God, she was beautiful. All his chivalrous intentions went out the window. He *couldn't* look anywhere else. She came across to stand between the two beds, gazing down at him. She bit her lip, as if inwardly debating something, then reached up to untuck one corner of the towel, letting it slide down her body to the floor.

Ben stopped breathing and simply stared. He had never felt such desire for anyone. Small, pert breasts, flat stomach, slim waist... "I'm, I'm married," he said, weakly.

"I know, but Wifey isn't here right now, is she? I am."

She bent forward and kissed him, her lips cool and breath warm. He didn't consciously decide to respond, but before he knew it he was kissing her back, and reaching up to place a hand on her damp skin.

He felt the bedclothes being pulled downward as her lips left his, and couldn't suppress a shiver as a series of butterfly kisses descended his neck and chest. His hand mussed her wet hair as teeth and tongue teased his left nipple. He stiffened as fingertips traced a line downwards to slip inside his pants.

The sensation was electric. Had that groan come from him?

"Wait." He stopped her, regaining sufficient control to take off his watch and wedding ring, placing them hastily on the bedside table beside his phone before pulling her to him again.

BEN LAY IN the darkness, basking in post-coital euphoria. Karen's small form lay curled beside him in sleep, her head resting on his right arm, both of them squeezed precariously into the one bed. She was incredible. They'd made love twice. *Twice!* When was the last time he'd managed that?

One thing was certain, he couldn't let her go. Oh, he would stand by his family, it was his duty, but now that Karen had entered his life he wasn't prepared to see her walk out of it again. Their meeting had been an act of fate, and their lovemaking a revelation.

He'd forgotten how wonderful sex could be. It was as if she had roused him from a state of semi-slumber and opened his eyes to a whole new world.

They could arrange to meet in secret. Perhaps he would help her find a place to live, and then give her regular money towards the bills, an allowance. If he worked hard and earned the sort of commission he used to, it ought to be manageable. Nor would he be overbearing or demanding. If she had other sexual partners, well, that was okay. He was hardly in a position to demand fidelity, after all; just so long as she was there when he needed her...

Ben drifted off to sleep with plans swirling around his head.

SHE WAITED UNTIL the regular rhythm of his breathing confirmed that he was out, and then made herself wait some more. An hour or so later, confident that he was in a deep sleep, she gently lifted his arm and slipped from the bed. A small gap in the curtains allowed a sliver of light from the streetlamp in the car park to slip into the room. The illumination was welcome, but it wouldn't have been necessary. She was an old hand at this game and knew exactly where her clothes had been left. After dressing in silence she worked quickly and methodically, taking what she wanted before leaving.

A PHONE RANG, dragging Ben away from a pleasant dream: his phone. Memories of the previous evening's activity still drenched his thoughts as he came awake. The bed was empty, and the one beside him hadn't been slept in, but he saw no cause for alarm. Karen was most likely in the bathroom, or perhaps she was the type of person who liked to stretch her legs first thing in the morning; perhaps she had tiptoed out so as not to wake him. There was still so much to learn about her, so much to look forward to.

He fumblingly picked up the phone, bringing it to his ear and saying a sleepy, "Hello," without registering the identity of the caller.

"I thought you said you were going to ring me!"

Sarah! He came wide awake in an instant. "Sorry, I must have overslept. It was a difficult day yesterday, and the drive through all that fog just about did me in."

What *was* the time, in any case? He glanced at the bedside table, where he remembered putting his watch, and froze.

"That's all well and good, but when will you be home...? And what should I tell the office if they ring? Ben? Are you still there?"

He didn't reply, hearing the sound of her voice but not the words. The watch was gone. As was his wedding ring. In that instant all the plans he'd so joyously built crumbled to dust, and something inside him died.

"Ben...?"

His wedding ring; how the hell was he going to explain *that*?

"Ben! Don't you dare ignore me!"

"Oh, shut up, Sarah." He broke the connection.

READILY DISPOSABLE ITEMS, they were the key. She had emptied Ben's wallet of cash but left the credit cards – too easy to trace; likewise his phone, though she'd nabbed the watch, which looked to be expensive, and the wedding ring, which was obviously gold. A bit of a meagre haul, but it all added up.

Ben was her third mark of this particular outing and the first that she'd actually had to fuck. Not that she minded the sex, and he'd been okay: a bit quick, but reasonably attentive. She'd had far worse.

There might just be time for one more sting before she was due to rendezvous with the others for the divvy up. Comparing stories and claiming bragging rights were all part of the fun, but she wanted to have a little more in the coffers before that happened.

The morning was a dull one – the sun evidently reluctant to make an appearance. Remnants of yesterday's fog still lingered, though it wasn't as heavy as it had been the previous night.

The air was chilly all the same, and damp. The fog would be among the first things to go, she decided. Concentrating on one small detail to start with – that hedge over there – she walked forward, instigating a process that now came as naturally to her as breathing. She pictured the hedge being smaller, squatter. It changed immediately, complying with her vision and withering by rapid stages, as if viewed via time lapse photography. The effect rippled outwards to touch everything around her. With each step she ratcheted up the rate of change and the world altered, moulding itself to her whim. She loved this, the stepping between one reality and the next, choosing from an infinite number of parallel worlds that were often just a detail or two away. Recognising the many similarities from place to place delighted her almost as much as the differences.

It was a pickup on this occasion: a big red thing with fat wheels and tall radiator grill. There was a shallow dent in the fender and a worn look to the paintwork. She managed to thump the front wing with her open palm as she leapt out of the way, enhancing the impression that the vehicle had hit her – something she'd failed to do with Ben because of the wide swerve he threw his car into.

Lying on the ground, face down, she listened to the squeal of tyres and the opening of the door, careful not to move a muscle.

"God, are you all right?" It was a woman's voice; neither young nor old.

Footsteps approached rapidly. She twitched and groaned at the appropriate moment.

"Are you hurt, did I hit you?" A hand touched her shoulder as she slowly sat up, wincing.

Young thirties; nice eyes; a hint of grey showing in sandy brown hair worn long and loose; full lips that bore no sign of lipstick; dowdy clothes that failed to make the most of a decent figure, and a hint of floral perfume. A wedding ring, so married, respectable, most likely a kid or two. Pretty, though. She assessed the victim in an instant and decided that sweet and vulnerable was the way to play things this time around.

"I... I think so." She lifted a hand to touch her brow, all for dramatic effect.

"I'm so sorry. You came from nowhere. I didn't see you... I couldn't stop."

She noted the woman's pupils, the way her nostrils flared, the rapidity of her breathing. That wasn't just the result of concern or fear; this woman was attracted to her, though she probably didn't recognise the fact and would only have been confused by it if she had.

This one promised to be fun.

"What's your name, sweetie?"

"Emma," she said smoothly, having always liked the name Emma. "I'm sorry, I wasn't thinking... Don't really know what I'm doing at the moment, to be honest. My head's all over the place. My boyfriend's just left me... and I lost the baby..." She started to cry; great tearful convulsions that wracked her body and shook her shoulders.

"Oh, you poor thing. There, there, sweetheart, don't cry."

The woman's arms reached out to comfort her and suddenly they were hugging, her head resting against the older woman's neck, nuzzling.

The tears flowed freely, but deep inside she was smiling.

BALIK KAMPUNG (GOING BACK)

ZEN CHO

The image of Lydia, driving out of hell on a motorcycle, clinging to her demon's back, provides a striking start to Cho's story about a spirit seeking out the cause of her death. This rich tale is full of Malaysian myth and religious custom, a heady brew that brings alive the sights, smells and sounds of this journey towards a hoped-for understanding. I think you'll see from what follows why Zen is already building a reputation for being one of those most exciting and incisive new genre writers around.

THERE WERE A lot of unexpected things about being dead. The traffic was one of them.

Time passed differently here in the netherworld, so Lydia might have been perched on the back of her cheap motorcycle, clinging to her demon, for hours or years or centuries. Every once in an aeon they moved about three centimetres along. The light of the living world shone maddeningly at the end of the tunnel, not so very far away from them – but the intervening space was crammed full of hungry ghosts, using every form of transport they could beg, borrow or steal for their trip up north for the Festival.

"Can't believe the traffic is so bad," she said to her demon. "It's halfway through the month already!"

"You should see this road on the first day," said her demon. "The queue goes all the way back. Like this is not so bad."

Since the dead were only allowed into the living world for one month in each year, the time was precious. Lydia was only so late because nobody had been burning hell money for her, and it had been a struggle to get together the funds to buy some form of transport.

She'd only managed to get the bike by promising to be bonded to a hell official for the next year. It was what they used to call a kapcai motorcycle – a small, aged Honda of the kind hawkers took their kids to school on and Mat Rempits raced with. Fortunately her demon was as bony as most demons were, and didn't take up much space.

The demon had been another surprise. It had appeared the day she arrived in the netherworld. At first she had been too stunned by grief, too numbed by strangeness, to question the strange tangle-haired creature who followed her around hell. By the time she got around to questioning it, she'd grown used to its unvarying calm, its voice that was like the echo of the voice inside her own head. Its answer felt like something she had already known.

"I am your personal agony," it said.

"What agony?" said Lydia.

"You'll figure it out when you understand why are you a hungry ghost," said the demon.

Hungry ghosts were the spirits of the unfortunate, unlamented dead: those who were killed violently; who died burdened by unfulfilled longings; who had been greedy or ungenerous in life; who were forgotten by their living. It was obvious to Lydia which category she fell into.

"I don't care about my parents anymore," she said to her demon.

It wasn't bravado. Lydia had long made her peace with the fact that she was not the daughter her parents had wanted, and they were not flexible enough people to love her in spite of it. Stuck in the traffic jam, she thought not of them but of Wei Kiat.

Thinking about him and their home in Penang made the wait easier. The tunnel leading up to the human world wasn't the most pleasant place to while away a few hours. The rock walls were painted with the inventive torments to which the wicked dead were subjected – disrespectful sons and daughters having their tongues torn out; incompetent physicians being chopped to pieces; litterers being made to kneel on spikes; cursers of the wind being bitten by grasshoppers and kicked by donkeys.

Around Lydia the other hungry ghosts were discussing what they would do once they had got out.

"Bastard, if the fella knew how to do his job I won't be dead now. I'm gonna find his clinic and then that guy better watch out. He better get used to killing his patients."

"It's not like RM5 is such a big deal. It's just annoying, you know? I was dying also she couldn't bring herself to pay me back. Maybe it's too much to possess somebody for that, but if not it's gonna keep bothering me lor."

"Yah, go for the Christians. The less superstitious the better. They're not prepared because they don't believe in hantu all that. Muslim also, I guess, but I prefer to possess Chinese, feels more comfortable... anyway, have you ever met a skeptic Melayu?"

"No lah, I'm not gonna do all this possessing stuff. Die already, no point holding grudges. I'm gonna go home, see how my relatives are doing, smell my ah ma's rendang."

"You're going home to see your family, is it?" said one of the older ghosts to Lydia. She was travelling by bullock cart, and spoke a Hokkien so strangely accented that Lydia struggled to follow it.

"Yes," said Lydia. "What about you, auntie?"

"Hai, I'm too old to have relatives to visit," said the ghost. "I have some great-great-grandchildren in Muar, but they all speak Mandarin and play their iPhones only. Nowadays I only go to the living world to see the shows."

"Auntie must find the shows very different," said Lydia. "Even when I was small I remember there were more operas, puppet shows, that kind of thing. These days you only see girls in miniskirts singing Cantopop."

The antique ghost lowered her voice to a confidential whisper. "I don't mind the Cantopop girls," she said. "After all, the weather is so hot. Why shouldn't they wear something cooling?"

"That's very open-minded of you, auntie."

"Just because you're dead doesn't mean you can't be flexible," said the old woman. "So you're visiting your family har? Where do your parents live?"

"My husband, auntie," said Lydia. "He's in Penang."

IN PENANG. As she sat there in the stinking dark, her arms wrapped around her personal agony, a vision of the small terrace house they had lived in together rose up before Lydia. The low gate, with the patches of rust where the grey paint was peeling away; the narrow front yard Lydia had populated with potted bougainvilleas. She'd had them in every conceivable colour: magenta, rose pink, peach, lilac, deep purple, white. Every day she'd come home from work and exult over the wash of colour spread out before her front door.

She saw her house so clearly she could almost feel the grainy texture of the grille swinging open under her hand. Their living room was floored in fake marble, dim and cool even on the hottest of days. Lydia had furnished it with old-fashioned cane chairs and rag rugs. Wei Kiat had admired her taste.

"You should be an artist," he'd told her. "You look at things so differently."

She was always finding out delightful new things about herself with Wei Kiat. He saw in her depths her parents would never have seen, talents and virtues unsuspected even by herself.

She knew she could not expect her home to have stayed the same while she was dead, but there would be a profound comfort simply in seeing it again, in feeling the tiles cool against her bare feet, and smelling the air in her house: a smell that was a mix of old newspapers, clean laundry, and the curry perpetually being cooked next door.

"We'll have to come out at KL," the demon said. "That's the only exit for Malaysia."

Which was why she'd needed the motorcycle. The dead were disappointingly limited: it was no more possible for her to fly herself to Penang than it would have been when she was alive.

At least, Lydia reflected, the demon knew how to ride a motorbike. She'd never ridden a motorcycle in her life – her parents had thought it unsafe, and Wei Kiat had driven her everywhere in his Chevrolet – but the demon piloted their vehicle with consummate ease.

When they finally emerged into the living world, somewhere behind KL Sentral, it was several hours past sunset. The lights of KL were blinding after the dim red caverns of hell. The starless vault of the night sky seemed too big. Lydia hunched down behind the demon as if it could protect her.

"Hopefully we missed rush hour," said the demon. "Jam out of hell, jam out of KL, everywhere also jam jam jam. If the government stop playing the fool and improve our public transport we won't have this problem."

"Do we have to stay here?" said Lydia. She'd grown up in KL, but she felt no nostalgia for the city. The constant honking of car horns made her flinch. The living, bustling around her, smelt too strongly and felt too sad.

"You don't want to visit your parents?" said the demon. "We can drop by TTDI first."

Lydia shook her head, her hair brushing against the back of the demon's polo shirt.

"Home," she said.

THE FURTHER THEY got from KL, the less populated the roads were. The glow of the orange street lights on the unfolding measures of asphalt, so infinitely familiar, calmed Lydia down.

"When are we reaching ah?" she said.

"You know how long it takes," said the demon. "You sure or not you want to go?"

"What else do people do when they have holiday, aside from balik kampung?"

"You don't want to find out how you died meh?"

Lydia didn't remember how she had died. She hadn't tried to recover the memory. She didn't want to be like other hungry ghosts, clinging to historic grievances, hagridden by old sorrows. As in life, she had managed to get by in hell by sheer discipline: focusing on survival, hope, the image stored inside her of the red-tiled roof of her home, glowing in the sunshine.

"It's not important," she said.

"If you don't even know where you're coming from, how can you understand where you're going?"

"Eh, are you my demon or my feng shui master? Can you please concentrate on the road?"

"It's not like it makes any difference if we have an accident," said the demon grumpily, but it shut up.

THE DEMON INSISTED on stopping off at Kampar. "We should try the curry chicken bread. It's very famous."

"We don't need to eat or pee," said Lydia. "Stop for what?"

"After you're dead for a while you won't need to act human anymore, but you haven't adjusted yet," said the demon. "Might as well eat. You've never had curry chicken bread before. Remember what the auntie said. Dead also still can be flexible."

"Easy for her to say! She got nobody to visit," snapped Lydia. "I only have fifteen days. And I might have to waste time trying to find Wei Kiat."

"Wei Kiat is not going anywhere," said the demon, unmoved. "Come lah, let's make you less hungry."

Since they could hardly stride into a restaurant to order the world-famous Kampar curry chicken bread, it was necessary to hang around the restaurant kitchen and dive at the dishes before they were carried out to the living punters. This made Lydia uncomfortable.

"They can still eat," the demon said. "It's not like we're stealing. We only eat the *spirit* of the food."

"It feels weird," said Lydia. Being a spirit gave her a weird double-vision – on one level, in the material world, the plate of chicken bread her demon had despoiled was perfect, unmarred; in the spiritual world, half of the bun had been removed and the curry was leaking out the side. "Can't we just go outside and eat the offerings?"

As was usual during the Festival, there were offerings of food laid at the roadside: small piles of rice and fruit and lit incense set out by devotees.

The demon was offended. "Fine," it said. "If you want to have cold rice instead of chicken curry, suit yourself."

"Maybe I will!"

"Hungry ghosts I've heard of before," said the demon, "but I didn't know you got such thing as *dieting* ghosts."

It was when they were walking back to the motorbike that they heard the unmistakable sound of the Hungry Ghost Festival being celebrated by the living: the strains of Cantopop, blaring at top volume out of doors at ten o'clock in the evening.

"We might as well check it out," said the demon. "What else do people do when they have a holiday?"

Lydia pretended not to hear it, but she found herself drifting towards the light and noise.

The Festival tents had taken over a whole road. A huge effigy of the King of Hades dominated one tent, flanked by effigies of the guardians of the underworld. An urn full of joss-sticks sent up curls of scented smoke before his stern blue visage.

The tents bustled with people, both living and dead. Food was set out for the ghosts, a much more attractive array of dishes than the roadside plates of rice. Lydia took a pink rice cake. As she drew back from the table she almost upset another ghost's plastic cup of orange cordial.

"Sorry," she said.

"No problem," said the ghost. He was struggling to balance a paper plate loaded with food and his cordial. "You're only eating so little ah? There's a suckling pig at the other table there."

Lydia was going to say she wasn't hungry, but realised in time how stupid that would sound. "Is it? I'll go find it. Thank you, uncle."

"That's right," said the uncle. "Not like when we're alive, can celebrate New Year, Thaipusam, Hari Raya, Mooncake Festival, all that. Now we only get one holiday a year. Better make the most of it!"

Everyone seemed uncommonly cheerful – the dead stocking up on provisions, the living praying at the various altars. Lydia hadn't even known she'd grown so used to the hangdog looks of the other ghosts and the bureaucratic indifference of the hell officials. Despite her sense of urgency, her mood began lighten under the influence of the atmosphere.

She only glanced at the stage set up at the end of the road, but it was enough to tell her that the show would have pleased the open-minded bullock cart auntie. The girls onstage would not have looked out of place at a beach, except for their go-go boots.

As at every ko tai she'd seen in life, the front row of seats was reserved for the ghosts. The only difference now was that she could see the occupants.

But the focus of interest seemed to be somewhere else. She followed the crowd to another tent, where a man in robes was blessing the living. She was about to move away again when the man turned and looked straight at her and the other hungry ghosts watching.

"Sorry ah, good brothers," he said. "I'm almost finished here. Let me drink some water first and I'll be ready."

"He's a medium," said Lydia's demon. "Why don't you talk to him?"

"I thought only the living liked to consult mediums," said Lydia. "Send messages to their relatives all that. Spirits talk to medium for what?"

While she was speaking a queue of hungry ghosts had formed behind her. Lydia paused, embarrassed.

"You think what?" said the demon. "For the same reason lah."

* * *

"GOOD EVENING, SISTER," said the medium. The beads of sweat on his forehead and upper lip gleamed in the fluorescent light, but he smiled at Lydia with genuine friendliness. "Have you eaten?"

Lydia nodded. "The food is very good."

"The Festival committee is run by the local hawkers," said the medium. "So the catering is not bad. How can I help you, sister?"

Lydia had to pause to formulate her question. Despite growing up in KL she only spoke enough Cantonese to order food and watch subtitled Hong Kong dramas. Her parents had spoken Hokkien, and living in Penang had meant that what little Cantonese she had was rusty.

The sentence she produced wasn't the sentence she'd expected, however. She opened her mouth and heard herself say:

"How did I die?"

The medium blinked. "You don't know meh?"

"I don't remember," said Lydia. "Can't you tell me?"

The medium looked confused. He took off his spectacles and polished them before putting them back on.

"Sorry ah, sister," he said. "Usually the living come and ask me questions. The good brothers and sisters just send messages. Advice, life lessons, that kind of thing. You are the ones with the wisdom what."

"I was only late 20s when I died," said Lydia. "It was recently only. I haven't had much time to become wise yet."

"Ah," said the medium. He scratched his head. "If sister gives me your name I will try to find out for you how you passed on. I'll look tomorrow."

"By tomorrow I won't be in Kampar already," said Lydia. Frustration surged in her. She should never have stopped to talk. Every minute she spent here was a minute she could have used to get to Wei Kiat. And she hadn't even asked the right question. "Never mind. Sorry to waste your time, sifu."

"That is not a problem," said the medium. "To contact you is very easy. I am a medium. That's my specialty. You will know what I find out. That one at least I can promise."

"Thank you," said Lydia. She started to get up, but the medium stopped her.

"Wait a minute, good sister," he said. "I have a question for you, if you don't mind."

"I don't have any advice for anybody," said Lydia.

"No, no," said the medium. He looked embarrassed. "I just want to know, what's your birth date?"

THE SIFU'S EYES unfocused, his face twitching. The light of transcendent enlightenment filled his face. His mouth fell open. From the dark depths of his throat issued an awful bellow:

"Eight two one one!"

Even in her impatience this surprised a laugh out of Lydia.

"*Oh*, 4D," she said. "So people can buy lottery tickets, right?"

"Chinese like to gamble too much," said the demon disapprovingly.

The sifu was still shouting numbers to an attentive crowd when they walked away from the lights and smells of the festival.

The demon had parked the motorcycle next to a drain inhabited by bullfrogs, and their importunate moos filled the night air as the strains of Cantopop died out.

"Can we go now?" said Lydia, but suddenly, for no reason, she was afraid.

What would she find when they arrived in Penang? If Wei Kiat no longer lived at their house it would be difficult to find him. He might not even be in Penang anymore. And if he was, would he be different?

The living world seemed suddenly strange, quick-moving, unknowable. Lydia wished the sky was not so large. She wished, for the first time, that she was still safe within the caverns of the netherworld, protected by the rock ceiling from change and inconstancy.

"You'd better sleep first," said her demon. "If not you'll be tired. We can leave in the morning."

"I'm *dead*," said Lydia.

"Then there's no better time to rest, no?"

THE SKY WAS brightening when they set off again, and dawn crept over the country as they sped along the North-South Expressway. Lydia kept dropping off, her face smushed against the demon's bony back.

Every once in a while she would open her eyes to the landscape of the annual journeys of her childhood. The dark green sea of oil palm trees; massy white cumulus clouds in a harsh blue sky; the narrow barren boles of abandoned rubber tree plantations; the occasional water buffalo standing patiently by the road. They zoomed past orange earth stripped clean and levelled flat, waiting for development; temples with elegant roofs curving towards the sky, roof tiles blinding in the sunlight; billboards advertising herbal supplements and massage chairs.

The shape of the green-furred mountains against the sky brought back an unpleasant memory – the first time she remembered really seeing them and noticing their beauty. She'd been eight and she'd wanted to ask her parents why some of the mountains were red on the inside and some white, but they were fighting in a whisper, believing her asleep.

"I told you to ask for discount. These people want to make the sale, ask only they will give to you one."

"Haiyah, bought already," Lydia's father had said. "At most also won't save more than RM100 lah. What for heart-pain over a small thing like that?"

"For you maybe it's not much. Easy lah you, every day come home at five. I'm the one who has to do OT, pay for Lydia's tuition everything. At the end of the day still I'm the one cooking dinner. For some people it's very easy!"

"If it's so difficult marrying a civil servant, why didn't you marry some tycoon?"

"I'm just stupid lah," Lydia's mother had snarled. "That's why, no?"

Lydia had hunkered down in the back seat, making herself small. It had seemed politic to continue being asleep – absent, unhearing.

"What's wrong?" said the demon.

"Just remembering," said Lydia. She told the demon about it. "Dunno why I'm so upset also. They all fought all the time anyway. But Chinese New Year was the worst because they had to be in the same car for five hours."

"Aiyah," said the demon. "Be more *xiaoshun* lah. Your parents what."

Lydia experienced an unfamiliar spike of outrage. "Aren't you supposed to be my personal agony? Whose side are you on?"

"Of course I'm sympathetic," said demon. "But you're dead liao mah. Your parents also were suffering. Angry for what now?"

SOMEWHERE PAST THE Kedah-Perak border, the demon went off-route. Lydia only woke when the bike started jolting over uneven ground.

They were riding over a dirt track in an abandoned patch of oil palm plantation merging into secondary jungle. It was hot and very, very still.

"What's happening?" Inarticulate fury rose in Lydia. "Bastard, always delay here, delay there. You don't realise my time got limit, is it? You think I sold off a year of death to a hell official just to cuti-cuti Malaysia? Where are we going?"

"I'm taking you to the place where you died," said the demon.

They only stopped when they were deep enough that they could no longer hear the noise of traffic from the highway. A heaped black pile of oil palm fruit sat rotting by the path. A lizard ran over the ground by Lydia's feet, lifted its head as if it heard something, and hurried on.

The demon squatted by a tree and looked at Lydia as if it was waiting for something.

"Why–" Lydia realised she was crying, but it was only her demon, after all – only her personal agony whom she had carried ever since she left the living world, only the part of herself she knew best, and she ploughed on: "Why everything has to be some kind of life lesson? I don't need to know what. It's *done* already. This is supposed to be a vacation. I'm not trying to find myself or what. I just want to relax and see my husband. What's so wrong I cannot do that?"

"What's your agony, Lydia?" said the demon.

"My parents lah!" wailed Lydia. "Ask me something I don't know! My parents give me headache my whole life. Even after I die also I still have to deal with them. But I can't forgive, OK? You think I didn't try? I wanted to be a good daughter. I sent them money everything. But you can't control how you feel."

"You're wrong, Lydia."

"What do you know? You're just a demon," said Lydia. "You can't force yourself to love somebody."

"Not *that*," said the demon. "You're wrong about the agony. Look around. You sure you can't remember?"

Lydia looked, but the tears in her eyes had turned the world into a brilliant blur. Shapes lost their meaning. She only saw blotches of vivid green, black shadow, blinding patches of sunlight.

"I don't know–" she started to say, but she felt a warmth in her hand. She looked down.

An orange light was kindling within her palm. As she watched, the flame crept outwards, forming a thin ring of fire. Within it unfolded a scrap of paper. The fire flickered out.

It was a newspaper clipping, its edges burnt black. Lydia had never received a burnt offering before, but she remembered the kind uncle's face, turned to her in puzzlement. The medium in Kampar. He had sent her a message after all.

At first she thought he'd wasted his time. She couldn't read it. It was a Chinese newspaper clipping, and Lydia had gone to a government school. Her Malay was pretty good, her written Chinese non-existent. But she didn't need it in order to understand the picture.

It was a picture of Wei Kiat. She recognised him at once, even though he'd ducked his head to hide his face from the camera. The photograph was familiar – the stern figures of police officers flanking the sullen convict emerging from the court room. She'd seen dozens of such pictures in the newspapers in the course of her life. She'd never known anyone in them before.

"You want me to translate?" said the demon.

Lydia shook her head.

"Do you remember now?" said the demon.

She looked around that buzzing empty space. The only noise was the whirr of insects' wings. You wouldn't hear anything from the road.

It was a good place to have done it.

"No," she said, but there was a hollowness inside her that contradicted the denial. The knowledge settled into her. Lydia knew how it had come to be that she was dead.

She sat down.

"Why did he kill me?" she said.

"I don't know," said the demon.

"I thought he loved me."

"Yeah."

"I loved him so much."

"Yeah."

Lydia stared at her hands. "My family was so... like that... I thought I was so lucky to find Wei Kiat. He was my chance. Before I never knew what it's like to be happy." She looked up. "You really don't know ah?"

"I don't have any answers," said the demon.

"You know how to ride motorbike and read Chinese."

"I'm what you need to find your hunger," said the demon. "Doesn't mean I know anything important. I'm just your sadness. I'm just the fact your true love betrayed you."

"You didn't have to say it like *that*."

She sat with her head bowed, weighed down with grief, and it seemed as if a very long time had passed when the demon's voice broke in on her sorrow. It was as if the voice was merely another strand of her own thoughts; it was a song playing soothingly at the back of her head. It said:

"Now you know. What does it matter? In the next life you won't remember this sadness. You're already dead. Let go lah your attachments."

Lydia lifted her weary head. "Why are you saying all these pointless things to me?"

The demon fell silent. Then it said, "What do you want to do now, Lydia?"

Lydia scrubbed her eyes, but instead of a scathing rejoinder, what sprung to mind was a vision of the sea. A blue-grey expanse seen over the low wall that bordered Gurney Drive. The waves glinting so brightly in the sun that they almost seemed made of metal. Around the bay the dark green hills rising, and against them the prosaic white and grey forms of condominiums and office buildings.

She saw her bougainvilleas crowded together in her little garden, their delicate petals shivering at the touch of the breeze. Her heart clenched and relaxed.

"I want to go home," she said.

"Penang?"

"Yeah," said Lydia. The bougainvilleas, and the sea.

"Not a bad idea," said the demon. "They should still be celebrating the Festival. Penangites really know how to layan ghosts. At least the food will be good."

"Is food the only thing you think about?" said Lydia.

"Somebody has to remember you're a *hungry* ghost," said the demon with dignity.

IT WAS GETTING on for the evening by the time they got to Penang Bridge. The time of what her mother called falling light – the sky a mellow orange-tinged grey, the harsh light of the sun softened by dusk. Over the demon's shoulder Lydia could see the lights running along the bridge, the red backlights of the cars drawing away, the dark mass of the island rising ahead of them. And on the further shore, the lights of home.

DRIVER ERROR

PAUL MELOY

Every time we get in our car and make a journey we're taking a risk. The nature of that risk is laid bare on the news with alarming and stark regularity. Paul Meloy's story takes that thread of true horror and blends it with a metaphysical terror that will stay with you long after you have read the last word.

I WAS IN the car. I was driving down a country road and I had to swerve out of the way of a vehicle coming around a bend towards me on my side. I kerbed the Vectra and felt the car drag left as the tyres bit into the verge and began to pull me into the thick row of bushes lining the road.

I flashed my lights and after a moment of disorientation remembered where my horn was, and leant on it. I got the car under control and felt it slide through the mud. Branches raked the side of the car and clattered against the passenger-side windows and then I was back on the lane. I glared into my rear-view mirror and watched the taillights of the car as it disappeared around the bend. I was raging.

I was on my way to pick my daughter up from a friend's house. Another party, another Facebook crash and another mass fight; and me out after midnight to evacuate Carla from the wreckage.

And then I came fully around the bend heading onto where

the road opened out onto the bypass and saw why the car had been on my side of the road.

I slowed; I had no choice: there were bodies in the road.

I STOPPED THE car and sat there for a moment looking at the dead boys. I had a mobile, but my brain wasn't doing much at that moment other than trying to process the stuff that was going into my eyes, which was awful.

The road was dark. The streetlights didn't start for another half mile or so. My headlights provided adequate illumination. They splashed across the tarmac, throwing the three bodies into relief against the potholed road. They lay, all three on their backs, each with a slick of shadow cast behind them. Their bikes had somehow ended up in a tripartite mangle at the side of the road. A couple of the wheels were still revolving, winding down like the mechanism inside some kind of wrecked and unshelled clock. It was as though they had been riding single file, close together, and had been hit and driven into each other and then passed over and mashed by the wheels of the car.

I glanced into my rear-view mirror again. Nothing coming behind me. All clear ahead. Apart from the bodies in the road. I could drive on. I thought about it.

My mobile rang. I had it rigged to hands-free, plugged into an attachment on my dash. I took a breath and looked at the screen. Carla.

"Hello."

"Dad. Where are you?"

"On the way."

"It's all kicked off here again. I'm scared. Morgan's covered in blood. I think his nose is broken."

"I'd love to do something about that, Carla. I really would."

"Dad? Are you okay?"

I looked through the windscreen at the dead boys in the road. The one nearest me was casting a shadow towards the car as though in defiance of the laws of physics. Blood, pooling around his head. I thought about driving on. I really did.

I wish I had.

"I'm fine. I'll be there in a while."

"Dad?"

"Yeah."

"Hurry up."

The connection died.

I OPENED THE door and got out. I was alone on the road. I looked both ways, but there was nothing coming. This was a well-used road, linking two major towns, and it would normally be carrying a regular freight of late-night traffic. Taxis, lorries on midnight legs, drunks hoping for a cautious run home well below the speed limit. If I hadn't been standing in the headlights of my own car on a country lane at one in the morning looking down at the corpses of three young boys I might have thought that odd. But as it was, I was experiencing a kind of trauma drift, the sort of brief psychic harmony that kicks in for a spell and allows you to process and function in the moments following a major disturbance in the force.

The boy nearest me had been about seventeen. He had probably been at the head of the file. The reason I thought that was that he seemed to be the least damaged, as though the two behind him had been driven into him and had sprung him away from the crush of bikes. He had come down on his head. No helmet. How would a layman like me describe what I could see? I could see his brain. I hadn't been expecting to see someone's *brain* tonight, that was for damn sure. Dreadful sentiments came to me; the last thing he'd expected as he'd set out tonight for a ride with his mates was that some stranger would be looking down at his *brain* tonight; whatever his intelligence, whatever his dreams, whatever his future might have held was bulging lifeless from the top of his head; his catalogue of memories, his personality, his character was as void as the time before all time.

I was starting to panic. My breathing was coming too fast, too shallow. The psychic harmony was fading to be replaced by numbness and dread. I stepped past the boy. His face was pale, bloodless. His eyes were open and he stared at the stars that had made him with terrible, determined senselessness.

The next boy looked slightly older, maybe early twenties. He was at an angle perpendicular to the verge. He was wearing a tee shirt that bulged at his throat with everything his torso had contained. The car had driven over him and forced his guts and ribcage up into his gullet. His pelvis had been pulverised and his legs lay bandy like a spatchcocked chicken.

The third boy lay half on, half off the verge. His arms were twisted behind his back and his legs were tangled together in an unseemly knot. Everything was smashed. His expression was one of absolute surprise. *What's this*? He might have thought. A brief insight as everything within was destroyed and he was flung forwards into oblivion. How quick had it been for him; for all of them? Had there been a moment, as life had been slapped from them, when they'd thought about where they were going next? Not around the next moonlit bend in the road. Not the next town. Not home. But nowhere. Forever.

I reached for my phone, but remembered that it was still strapped to my dashboard. I was about to return to the car, but then something stopped me.

Something I'd noticed. Not a conscious observation, but somewhere my back brain was still processing information freely and jolted a signal through the narrow adrenaline focus I was applying to the immediate situation. It was something to do with the bikes.

I looked at the tangled wreckage. They had been forced together and driven over. Frames were distorted, wheels buckled, handlebars twisted. The wheels no longer turning; all eight wheels were still. All eight wheels.

Four bikes.

* * *

INDECISION GRIPPED ME like a sudden sickness. There must be a fourth body. No. Maybe not a body. Maybe the rider of that fourth bike was still alive. I should go to the car and call an ambulance. My head was thudding. The adrenaline was gone, a lousy fix. My legs began to shake. I squatted down and hung my head, breathing as deeply as I could – the night smelt of the cold earth of the fields the road cut through, and the bitter green scent of the wet trees and bushes that lined them.

There were deep drainage cuttings behind the bushes. They were pitch dark, streams of sodden shadow filled with a sediment of leaves and sludge. I looked up as something moved beyond the tangled line of hawthorns beyond the verge.

I stood up. The hairs on the backs of my arms began to rise. Why did I feel afraid? The lane was deserted and I had three dead boys for company, all staring furiously up into the night. Three separate getaways into eternity. They now know everything, I thought. Everything there is to truly know. If there's a God, they know. If there isn't, they know. It was no privilege; just a right bestowed by the passing bulk of a murderous vehicle.

I walked around the wreckage of bikes and stepped up onto the verge. My shoes sank into the soft earth. There was a half moon high in the clear sky above the fields, and it gave enough light to make the dark red earth of the ploughed fields shine like a broken Martian beach from which the sea had long receded.

And from out of the cutting crawled the fourth rider.

I COULD SEE that there was nothing I could do for him. I stumbled backwards and my hip struck against the pile of bikes. The wreckage rocked in the headlights, its complicated shadow flexing beneath it like a hellish web, and worse, as the fourth rider made it to the top of the cutting and began to push through the dense, thorny stands of the hawthorn bush, a bell clipped to the handlebars of one of the bikes began to ring in horrid elfin counterpoint to the boy's wretched progress through the barbs.

The fourth rider was as dead as the rest of them.

I turned, filled with a sudden and *clear* urge to run. I don't think I'd ever experienced such an autonomic command with the same lucid imperative before. I've read about atavistic horror, often in bad novels in an attempt to tell rather than show the repulsion a situation provokes, but I'd never expected to feel the animal uplift of fear that gave me wings that night.

The last thing I saw before I turned and ran for my car was the fourth rider pressing his shoulders through the lean and twisted limbs of the hawthorn bush, grabbing fistfuls of weeds from the verge as he reached for the open road, as he reached for *me*, with a face that must have turned and taken the full impact of the collision against the grille of that vehicle, blazing with gruesome, white hot dismay.

I ran, and took twelve steps. And stopped.

My car was gone.

DISORIENTATION FROZE ME. I staggered, skidded to a stop on the bend of the road. And then I became aware of headlights behind me, and turned.

And there was my car.

In my terror, I had run off in the wrong direction. I glanced left, towards the sloping verge, and could hear the laboured sound of that dead thing dragging itself up out of the cutting. Clear thought was impossible. It was simply not something I could make sense of; the primal back-up program of denial was already kicking in, that old Trojan put there in the reptile brain to provide us with the ability to shun cold truth.

There was still no sign of any other vehicles. Above the scratching sounds at the side of the road I could still hear the needling, irregular *ting* of the bicycle bell, as if its curved metal surface had been heated and was slowly cooling in the night air.

As the flattened face of the boy rose above the crest of the verge, the shattered bones of his cheeks and jaw and brow, and his teeth like tiny white stones subsumed beneath rising red waters, all wet and gleaming in the headlights of my car, I ran.

I ran past the three dead boys in the road, and their snarl of bikes, and reached my car. I scrabbled for the handle and pulled open the door.

I got in, slammed the door, and drove off.

BY THE TIME I pulled up outside the party, most of the crashers had melted away. They had done their damage, had trashed and robbed, drunk, beaten and terrorised to maximum effect. The door to the house – a spacious detached pile set back at the end of a long, curving drive somewhere in the wealthier part of town – stood open, and lights blazed in every room visible from the outside. I got out of the car and stood for a moment, listening. It was quiet, which I had not been expecting. There was no loud music, no shouts, no sounds of breaking objects or even the panicky post-party clank of bottles being cleared away in anticipation of a parent's dreaded early return. I walked across the drive to the door.

I could hear something now.

Sobbing.

The entrance hall was bigger than my lounge. To the right a stairway curved up to the first floor. Doors stood open everywhere. I went inside and crossed the marble floor. I walked into the kitchen. There was blood on the cream-coloured tiles. It had come from Carla.

My daughter was slumped against a huge American style fridge-freezer. It loomed over her, more like the baleful entrance to a meat locker in an abattoir than the intended high-end designer convenience.

I went over and knelt beside her. She was clutching her stomach, and white, very white, and unconscious.

I remember feeling quite calm. It was detachment, I realise, brought on by overwhelming concern. I had not been expecting this, of course, and now my system was telling me it wasn't really happening, that this was probably just a dream. It wasn't an objectivity that prevented me from acting, though, and I scooped her up and carried her from the kitchen towards the front door.

As I reached the threshold I heard the quiet, insistent sobbing again, and turned my head, and looked into the lounge.

There was destruction in there. The room had been completely turned over. Furniture smashed and upended, mirrors and paintings torn from the walls. The carpet was slashed and burned. A girl was sitting on the floor. She was holding a twisted silver photo frame. She looked up at me and her expression was at once both utterly hateful and full of despair.

"*She* let them in," the girl hissed, and I knew she meant Carla. "We told her not to, but she still let them *in*."

I didn't want to ask, but my momentum was still carrying me out of the door, and Carla was breathing in my arms and her bleeding had stopped, so what I asked was: "Let who in?"

And the girl said, without looking up this time – which saved me seeing the affect it had on her expression – something that enclosed my soul in a sudden mantle of dread.

I carried Carla to the car and placed her on the back seat. I lifted her top and exposed her stomach. There were three long gashes cut into her flesh. They were nasty but not too deep. I found a box of tissues in the glove compartment and wadded them up and placed them on the wound and pulled her top back down. Then I got into the driver's seat and pulled out, wanting to get Carla to the hospital.

As I drove, my speed increased as I thought about the last thing the girl had said, the very last thing – almost missed as I carried Carla off the porch – and it was this that made me speed, because I really wanted to get away from that house and the influence of whatever Carla had allowed in.

"The black-eyed kids," she had said. "I *begged* her not to let them in."

FOR A FEW years I was a lay preacher in our local Baptist Church, before my divorce and before Carla's incremental promiscuity became a problem. After that, my faith took a dive. Well, more of a slow yet uncontrollable tumble down a long, and seemingly endless slope. But I did reach the bottom, eventually, and found nothing there but a plain of indeterminate distance, mostly swamped by a grey mist, across which occasional brief, deceptive sails of sunlight might drift, towing a galleon of false hope on which I had no wish to embark.

I remember my own childhood, which was happy, but my memories of it are tainted now when I found out as an adult, through my mother, how desperately miserable *my* father was. He hid it well, and I had no idea just how deep his sadness was, brought on by a lifetime of failure and loss not even my promising presence could moderate. I thought he was happy, yet throughout he grieved, so what am I to make of life? More denial?

And is agnosticism just denial? I can't reasonably be an atheist because I've seen too much of God's authority to *deny* his existence, and felt his presence, but I can't make any of it stick; I can't make sense of the mind games.

It still causes me sadness, and I still hope, maybe sooner or later, God might resume contact. I still take an interest in the supernatural, and I try to ensure that my interest doesn't take a turn into the paranoid or delusional, but I watch, and I hope a little.

So I still read stuff, and I keep up with things on the internet, and things do seem to be becoming stranger; or perhaps it's just the increasing opportunity for people to expose their madness online that's led to a supersaturation, but my instinct, my *discernment,* somehow rejects that. Something is burgeoning, gaining confidence. I think something is coming.

It may be just an urban myth, or it may be more. It may be as real as people have reported it, but something is happening, and it's worldwide. Many of the people who experience it do not report it, or want to be identified. They are too afraid.

You see, they get visits at night, by black-eyed children. I don't mean they've got bruising around their eye sockets, I mean their eyes are entirely black, with no whites, irises or pupils. They usually come in pairs and they are usually inadequately dressed for the weather.

They visit houses, approach cars, hotel rooms, even boats. And they knock, and if you answer, they ask to come in. They don't engage in conversation, in fact they seem to have a limited range of questions and responses, which they communicate in a demanding monotone. They are insistent and evasive, and appear vulnerable. You get an intense feeling of dread, and panic. These children terrify you. They want to come in. And sometimes they tell you they want to feed. And then you see their eyes and your mind can't cope, because their eyes are entirely black.

There is only one encounter recorded where one of these children was let in and people survived. A woman returning from a shop with her groceries got into her car, having left her young son in the back seat, and saw that a black-eyed child was sitting next to him. Her son said the boy had tapped on the window and asked to come in, so the boy had let him in hoping they could play. The woman grabbed her son and fled, leaving the car in the car park. Later, the boy became ill and fell into a coma. His condition remained untreatable until a member of the mother's church rebuked the spirit afflicting the boy and bound it in Christ's name. He remained weak and sickly for years. Later, the woman's husband was driving the car they had recovered from the car park and he was involved in a near-fatal collision. Evidence seems to point to a spiritual, or interdimensional, element; nephilim hybrids, demons, fallen angels? These children can appear at, and disappear from, various windows and doors around a house in an instant. But they want in, and they seem to want to feed on your fear.

They often appear to people in authority: policemen, nurses, firemen, and once to a soldier in a barracks. Or maybe these people draw on the inner resources available to them that have enabled them to gain such positions, their strength or their will, to resist the cunning presence of these children. It must be assumed they have less fortunate victims. As I said, people seem loath to report these experiences. Denial is, as they say, a wonderful thing.

BUT CARLA HAD let them in.

I drove fast, too fast. Carla was making noises on the back seat. I could hear her moaning. I could hear the sound of her legs moving against the fabric of the back seat. I glanced in my rear-view mirror as I approached a blind bend, just for a second.

She was sitting up and looking at me.

But it wasn't Carla in the back.

Dead black eyes looked back at me.

I LOST CONCENTRATION; I was no longer driving a car at sixty miles an hour, I was gone for an instant. My mind blanked. I heard something, and it was the monstrous whistling dismay of the eternal void. I had preached on Hell, on separation from God, and now I could hear what the damned hear, and for a moment I saw into the eyes of something released for a time from that unendurable vault. There was pressure and temperature in those eyes; what you might experience waking forever in the heart of a collapsed star. It was both cold and immeasurably hot, ever expanding and as massive as a neutron star. All physics was behind those eyes, all the grotesque complexities of imaginary numbers.

And the car came around the bend and I snapped back and saw them, but too late.

A convoy of boys in single file, riding home on their bikes, suddenly thrown into film-set relief in the headlights. And I hit them, and drove through them, driving one into the next and feeling the wheels bounce and smear through them. The noise was awful; like driving through scaffolding.

I swerved, but I had already gone through them, past them. As my car drifted right, into the oncoming lane, another vehicle had to veer onto the verge to avoid me. Headlights dazzled me and then I was past. Moments later, in response to my recklessness, a horn blared from the darkness behind.

I PULLED THE car over in a lay-by a hundred yards down the road. I swung around in my seat, my heart pounding, fists clenched. Whatever had been in the back seat was gone. Nothing. Apart from me, sweating, shaking, terrified, the car was empty. What had I carried from that house?

I put my hazard lights on and in their intermittent orange flash, I got out of the car and stumbled back towards the scene of the accident. My shadow appeared, and then disappeared before me, growing shorter, losing assurance, until I was at the bend and in darkness. The moon was a mist-light behind a streak of delicate, nervous cloud.

I approached the scene. My hands felt like numb weights at the ends of my arms. I flexed them but that just made it feel like more blood was flowing into my extremities, leaving my core cold and hollow.

I stood, wavering, skin prickling, by a pile of broken, twisted bikes. Three boys lay across the surface of the road, dead, still warm; warmer, perhaps, than I felt. Their bikes were enmeshed. Six wheels and a confusion of turning shadows. My memory flickered, stuttered like old celluloid running through a disused projector. Three bikes?

The fourth bike I had imagined; had it been just an adrenaline-enhanced perception? Had it been shadows of wheels I'd seen and miscounted?

I stepped nearer the edge of the road, towards where the verge sloped down into the field and the hawthorns that concealed them.

And saw the wreck of the car.

IT HAD GONE off the road and ploughed through the bushes. It was on its side, the chassis only just visible as the moon broke and reflected briefly off the exhaust. It was a new exhaust; fitted only last month.

I stepped forward, and then I was turning, running in the wrong direction, disorientation blinding me, as I tried to escape the thing heaving itself up that bank, using fistfuls of weeds, labouring out of the cutting of dirt and clambering shadows.

IF I COULD just get up the bank and reach the road…

I could warn him…

Is my daughter dead? Broken in the car wreck I have crawled from…

Is she even there?

If I could get to the top, with what life I still had I could warn him…

But I can never make it…

Footfalls behind me, slow, two pairs, now standing either side…

My hands in the weeds…

Voices, monotonous, insistent…

A cycle I can never break…

A pale face, like plastic in the moonlight, down near my ear…

The last thing I hear before he speaks is the sound of my car, driving away again, at the top of the slope…

And he speaks, and he tells me this won't take long…

But, of course, it goes on forever.

LOCUSTS

LAVIE TIDHAR

Lavie's take on history, real and imagined, is one of the many things that mark him out as a truly extraordinary writer. His alternative world SF novel, Osama, *won the World Fantasy Award and he recently signed a two book deal with Hodder. Here Tidhar takes us on a journey in Palestine in 1915, with a piece that induces in the reader a waking dream state through its unusual and hypnotic form. The history here is real, rather than imagined, though this is as rich as any genre tale you'll find within this anthology.*

IN SAFED ON top of the mountain under a deep blue sky with blue painted walls and doors to reflect the heavens, secretive black clad kabbalists wandering the stone walled streets with wide brimmed hats like horsemen dismounted. Palestine in the year of the gentiles and their god 1915. That night he sleeps in the yard of a stone house belonging to a man who lived in England, lying on his back on the hard ground looking up at a blue black sky and a myriad of stars. In sleep he sees all that is yet to come: first a burning bush and a great fire and men and women and children with yellow Stars of David on their arms herded like cattle in great metal beasts to a place where the tracks terminate. From there through a great gate into a dark place and ovens and black smoke, gold teeth collected in dirty buckets, skeletal moselmen with bare feet in the snow. Then a great cleansing fire and he sees boats on the sea and refugees docking at secret alcoves and kissing the sand, armed men and women spreading out across the bare land. Then later still the roads cut into the earth and the villages eradicated and the new settlers spreading again and again like locusts. New houses, new roads, great cities until of the wild places nothing remains.

But all that is yet to come.

When he wakes it is early and the city wakes around him and he builds a fire and sets to brew his coffee in a tin can. In the distance the call of the mosques to prayer. In the yard a small Jewish boy clad in black, sitting on his haunches by the fire studying the man. His eyes are black. What's your name, he says, and the man answers, and the boy says, Like the king. The man shakes his head but all around him are the Biblical references woven into the land and the air and smoke from the fire and he studies this small boy and wonders what will become of him in the years to come. He drinks his coffee and the boy stands and goes to the horse and pats him. Is he yours, Yes, the man says. He stands up at last and his coat moves aside revealing his handgun and the boy's eyes grow round and he says not a word. The man climbs on top of the horse and man and horse both depart this stone house, the boy staring after them. Where are you going, the boy says, and the man says, There is death on the wind.

He rides for two days out of Safed through the Galilee, camping for a night by the great lake in which reflected are the stars like the eyes of the dead. The air is hot and dry. The crops lie wasted in the fields. He lies alone and is not disturbed. At night he sees the light of fishing boats and hears the fishermen's cries, though some cry in Arabic and others in Hebrew. In the morning he follows the road that leads down, into the Jezreel Valley. There like a bowl of produce but the produce lies dead in the fields and the crows peck at the ground and at stones as if they were eyes. He rides through wasted wheat the gun at his belt his hat shading his face, watching the Arab villages and the Jewish settlements and the empty fields and the empty roads. At dusk he joins horse drawn carts going to Megiddo and he watches the hill, which the gentiles call Armageddon, and sees the fires burning in the settlement there and hears the hard voices of men.

He spends the night there with farmers and agents of the Rothschilds, two men from Paris in the light suits made for the Orient discussing the merits of the young women of that place, who should go to study at the Baron's expense and who should remain. They retire for the night with two of the lasses who are willing or wishing to escape this place for civilized Europe and these men have the power to make it so. He had learned long ago that men have power and he does not intervene for they had gone willingly enough and perhaps he, too, would have gone in their place. In the morning he rides out alone but followed by the carts filled with meagre produce going to the city of Haifa. In the distance he sees a checkpoint and the uniform of the Ottomans and he skirts them and watches from on high as they stop the carts and take away the produce and boot the men away, laughing. He rides on, through temperate hills and gentle forest, the land of Menasseh, until he sees the Carmel mountains rising in the distance, evergreen against blue, and he imagines he can hear the seagulls crying in the distance.

He enters Zikhron Ya'akov at dusk that next night, the town named for the old Baron, and ties up his horse and enters an establishment such as there must inevitably be, even in a settlement of the Jews. They grow grapes in the Baron's vineyards on the mountain slopes and make wine from it and he drinks deeply. It is a rough wine and it suits him fine. He has not much coin but he sits there not thinking much and a man comes and stands at the bar and orders wine and though he is an educated man and dressed in a suit, nevertheless there is a strength about him, a power. Not turning his head he says, I am in need of men.

So, he says.

I am–

I know who you are.

At that the other man does turn his head, and smiles. I'm Aaron Aaronsohn, he says.

A quiet man. A mild mannered man. A dangerous man, with dangerous ideas. We leave at first light, Aaronsohn says. He drinks his wine.

At first light they ride out, fifteen of them, ten Jews, three Bedouin guides and two silent Sudanese. At their head rides Aaronsohn, bottles of samples by his side and his rifle strapped to his back. His round glasses flash in the sun. They ride all day and into the night going north and the wind is dry and hot and the men lick their chapped lips and drink sparingly. They travel first along the coast and when they run into a Turkish checkpoint Aaronsohn shows the soldiers a piece of paper and they are let through with curious looks and the soldiers finger their weapons but say nothing.

The next morning they run into a storm of locusts, the insects come flying out of nowhere in their millions. They grow like a dark cloud on the horizon and the horses shy and the men reach for their guns but they are useless. The insects swarm over them blindly, as if the men and the horses do not exist, are a figment of a locust god's imagination. They enter their hair and their clothes and their mouths and their noses and the horses rear, frightened, and the men curse and one of them cries out loudly and there is the smell of human piss and a dark trickle on the ground. The insects swarm over them and they bat at them helplessly and Aaron roars, ordering them to turn, but the tide of black insects pushes them this way and that and he can no longer see the others in that sudden darkness, that blotting of the sun.

At last he finds shelter against a rock face and watches the locusts swarm past until they are gone and a great darkness descends and where there were trees and fruit there is nothing but bare skeletons and they drift along the road towards the fields and forests of the north. He rides on then and the others join him one by one and at night when they camp by the shore of the Mediterranean they are two men short but Aaronsohn makes no comment. They sleep by their horses and rise with the moon and press on and the next day arrive at Jaffa on the shore of the Mediterranean and there the Turks have their fortress.

Aaronsohn confers with Jamal Pasha while the men go to the harbour where the ships dock and where the oranges come on the back of camels and Arab men run up and down the docks shirtless carrying boxes, as strong and wiry as circus freaks. They drink by the harbour by the train tracks which link the harbour to Jerusalem and they listen to the French and Egyptian and British traders talk in their pidgin and to the Jewish agents and the Arab traders and they watch the few Jewish passengers who come on shore clutching identity documents to their chests and looking around them in what must be shock, at this Oriental town so dusty and ill-formed, a million miles away from the Europe which is the only thing they know.

He drinks wine and arak with the others and they laugh at these new arrivals and wait for the girls to come out parading down the main Jaffa road pretty in their dresses and their scarves and saucy dark eyes looking the men up and down frankly. It is dusty and cool in the shade and the smell of tar and salt from the sea and the injuries of oranges litter the quayside roads and their smell bursts forth like the very essence of the country.

He spends the night with a Greek girl two months now in Palestine but soon to move on, part of a travelling harem of women of all backgrounds all joined together on this mission like fallen goddesses of love. Cairo, she tells him, they will go to Cairo next where she has a family, and where the men are wealthy and pay generously. She strokes the scars on his chest and asks him how he got them and he answers not, but holds her, her wetness and her warmth, and he tries to lose himself inside her. In the morning they ride out, the Bedouins ahead, the Sudanese men leading three donkeys laden with sealed boxes behind them and barred cages from which protrude the dirty whiteness of live pigeons. You must know, the girl tells him, that night, when he is drunk under the moon, the war is coming, the Turks will not hold on to power forever. Why should I care, he says – demands – and she shrugs, You Jews, she says.

You Jews. He remembers other days, other lands, but vaguely, as though they had happened to someone else, and long ago.

He knows only this wild land, where men must carry guns, and he knows the Turks are fighting a war with the French and the English, and that someone must lose: and it is usually the Jews.

At night under the stars skirting the hills of Jerusalem Aaronsohn says much the same thing to him, quietly, as though gauging him out. We need men like you, Aaronsohn says, and he says, Like what?

In the midst of night a great cloud descends upon them from the hills of Jerusalem and the Sudanese cry out in great beats and light a flame. In its light they can see the olive trees stripped of life and the black insects come descending down in a mass in which no individual insect can be discerned. The Sudanese unpack the boxes and the men arm themselves with burning torches dipped into liquid flame, they wave them in the air at the onrushing locusts and the air is filled with the hiss of dry burning carapace and dying insects dropping to the ground until with every step he takes his foot sinks into a crunching necropolis, an insectoid slaughterhouse and the air is full of death. He feels them against his skin and in his hair and on his hands, crawling into his crotch, up his anus, he strips, naked he dances in the moonlight like a crazed person waving torches and the men do likewise, Aaronsohn with his glasses flashing and his pale behind shaking in a dance. None of them make a sound, it takes place in silence, if you had asked him before or after he would have told you it was impossible, yet it was true. It is a circus light show lighting up the dark mountain side and the sweat on the horses' dark skin and the torches are like the crazy fires of a thousand falling stars.

They ride onwards with Jerusalem in the distance up on her mountains like a sagging aged queen, her churches and synagogues and mosques the teats of a cow suckling dusty cowled pilgrims snuggling into her bosom, there the Jewish quarter where Eliezer Ben Yehuda dreams in modern Hebrew a language he is still inventing out of old biblical Hebrew and borrowed words and whole cloth and there too the men of the old Yishuv traders and politicos in the shade of the Ottomans huddled within the walls mistrustful of the new Yishuv these interlopers newcomers in the shadow of their money man the Baron in the north: but they skirt the city clean.

Here they pause, though, while Aaronsohn waits. The Bedouins on their horses scout ahead, the men sit restless, playing cards, he sits apart from the others watching Aaronsohn. At last they see dust rising on the dirt track leading from Jerusalem and an approaching man and horse, riding fast. The rider dismounts and he and Aaronsohn hug. Feinberg, someone says, it's Avshalom Feinberg.

And how much like the king's son he looks, this modern Absalom, how handsome and fetching, born like his namesake on this land, but educated in Paris, a man the girls sigh over, and he and Aaronsohn talk quietly, whispering, and Feinberg delivers onto the expedition leader a small packet of what might be papers, and rides away. In two years he would be dead in the desert, his blood seeping out onto the fine sand, his companion wounded and running, Avshalom like his namesake dead in his prime, it would be fifty years before they found his bones bleaching in that lonely stretch of sand forgotten even by the Bedouins who shot him down.

Aaronsohn goes to the donkeys and opens one of the bird cages and extracts a pigeon, trembling in his hand. When he releases it the bird takes to the air with a cry and there is a metallic container strapped to its foot. It rises into the air and circles and disappears in the direction of Egypt.

They ride on. Beyond the hills the land drops steeply, in seeming moments they have ridden deep into the desert sands. Canyon walls rise above them and the air turns dry and hot, a burning, and he thinks of his dreams of all that is yet to come the ovens and the flames, he can see the future but in the future all that is around them is still sand. They ride down and down and down still as if dropping into the bowels of the earth as though descending into a sort of Christian hell and Jerusalem its mountains its olive groves its broken Temple and its Wall its mosques and synagogues and markets all vanish in the hot dry air like a fata morgana like a thing which did not ever exist.

In the night they are attacked, suddenly and without warning, by men on camels racing through the dunes. He draws his gun and fires, a horse beside him tumbles and falls as its leg breaks with a terrible crunching sound. Its rider drops to the ground, face white in the moonlight, fingers bloodless where they grip the gun. They fire at the marauders men whose faces are obscured by cloth who shoot with old guns but dart close and quick with blades flashing silver and they meet like two primeval armies in the sand, horses and camels clashing, the donkeys braying with a pitiful sound. He fires and kills a man and the corpse rolls still fresh on the sand and blood in bright arcs shoots upwards, collecting within its fading vitality the light of the stars and the moon. The camels run sure footed on the sand but the men riding them perhaps having not expected this opposition drive them away. They disappear as quickly as they'd come, like desert ghosts, leaving behind them the corpse of a camel and three men. On their side one horse dead, one lame, and two men down. He takes his gun and walks to the wounded horse and aims and pulls the trigger. Blood and brain explode on the sand and on his face, wet and salty like tears. They bury the men in makeshift graves. Jerusalem seems to have never existed, the coastal cities are as fabulous and impossible as Ophir.

They move on, through darkness and sunrise, the light suffuses the horizon like a curse. Downwards and downwards still, Aaronsohn making measurements, scribbling in a book, excited. They keep an eye out for marauders, in the sand he sees the droppings of camels, the signs of a fire half-buried in the sand. They push on and crest at last a dune and look down upon the valley and a sea as flat as a mirror in the distance down below, reflecting the sky perfectly. Mountains behind it, all around it the land is bare and rocky, nothing lives, a dead sea.

The Jordan Valley lies before them and across it they can see the locusts migrating in great big apocalyptic clouds like black angels of death but they are alive, hungry and alive, and all

Palestine lies before them, its wheat and orange trees and olives, mulberries, pines, cypress, St. John's Bread, figs, phoenix, za'atar and cotton. He watches them move soundlessly along the land away from the Jordan mountains towards Jerusalem and the coast, an unstoppable hand reaching across vast distances to devour and destroy all in its path. How do you fight it, Aaronsohn says, but it is delight not despair in his voice. They travel on, through dunes rising like camel humps and a sky as black as space in which the stars are numinous. At night standing guard pale coal fire behind him he goes around a dune to piss and a leopard passes, so close he can feel its fur on his skin, the animal padding softly on the sand making no sound, for a moment it turns its head and regards him with eyes like gemstones with an alien intelligence behind them. He holds his breath, somehow he is still urinating, the leopard yawns and walks into the darkness and disappears.

They reach the shores of the dead sea on a day as hot as the ovens which haunt his dreams. Aaronsohn is first to strip off, straight from the horse he slides onto the ground naked, wading towards the water, a stocky man with a dark face and a pale stomach. They run at the water and enter it and float, surprised and laughing, for a moment they are boys again. He too floats in the water of the dead sea on his back, if you attached a sail to him he could be a ship traversing this ancient place. On this sea the Nabateans skimmed asphalt from the surface to sell to the Egyptians to use for mummies, here David hid from Saul, here lay Sodom and Gomorrah, those cities of sin.

Aaronsohn releases another bird into the sky, where do they go, those birds, what messages do they carry? They ride on, following the shore, at night the stars fall into the water in trails of flame.

On the second day the scouts return, the Bedouins confer with Aaronsohn, gesturing to the south. On the third day they reach a temporary settlement of Bedouins, of which tribe he doesn't know. Aaronsohn sits down with their sheikh by the fire, the men stand outside the camp, the children naked run, a drove of goats, a flock of camels. He watches a falcon sail across the skies. A small Bedouin boy sitting on his haunches studying him, saying, in Arabic, what is your name. David, he says to the boy.

At night the Bedouins roast a goat its stomach stuffed with rice the women make flatbread on the fire, under the stars flocks of birds travelling, fan-tailed ravens and Dead Sea sparrows, Arabian babblers, blackstarts, pale crag martins, sand partridges, trumpeter finches, desert larks and scrub warblers, at night the sky sometimes is full of migratory birds fleeing Europe as from a great evil, dark clouds against the waning moon.

Aaronsohn confers with the scouts, again they set off, there is no soul in sight the desert lies silent and vast all about them and the sea as dead, the Jordan at their back. The cliffs rise above them and at night when he sleeps he dreams no dreams.

Author's note:

Aaron Aaronsohn (1876-1919) was a botanist, map-maker and spy. In 1915 a plague of desert locust devastated the crops across Palestine. Aaronsohn was set in charge of battling the invasion by Jamal Pasha, then-governor of Syria and Palestine.

THE TRACK

JAY CASELBERG

Australia is a country more than familiar with the traditions of the road story, especially in cinema – Mad Max, Long Weekend, and Walkabout all explore the form in various ways. Caselberg, an Australian writer living in Germany, sets his story in the desert, on a stretch of haunted road. The harsh environment is as much a character as either of the two protagonists, but there is something else out there in the parched landscape. Caselberg uses a real-life tragedy as the basis for his chilling story, and reminds us of the risks to be found on the road when a long long way from home.

YOU HAD TO do it. Well, that's what he'd said, anyway. It was just one of those things you just had to do – the stuff of legends. Jason tapped at the tiny fan stuck to the dash, sitting there beating at the heat. The car's fan was blowing too, but any extra was a necessity at this point. The car rumbled across the dirt surface, chipped stone and hard packed earth tinged with red stretching in every direction. Behind them, a plume of orange-red dust billowed in their wake, fanning out to obscure the endless nothingness that stretched from horizon to horizon.

"How many did you say had died out here?" asked Kevin.

"What's that?" said Jason, one hand draped lazily over the top of the steering wheel.

"Deaders. How many?"

"I don't know. Countless, probably. It's not what it used to be. There are one or two famous cases, that family in the '60s, but look at it. It's not hard to imagine. Something happens, you break down. It's not as if you can flag down a passing motorist."

"So tell me why we're doing this again?" said Kevin, only half joking.

Jason turned to look at him, one eye still on the line of rutted dirt road that stretched on before them.

"I thought you were up for this."

"Yes, I was, or I am. It's just different once you're out here, I guess. The difference between what you might imagine and the harsh reality."

Jason turned his focus back to the road ahead, if it could be called a road. "Some might call it reality," he said. "The blasted plain. It's like, I don't know, some sort of surrealist hell."

Kevin stretched beside him. Their old wagon, though reliable, wasn't exactly top of the range in the comfort stakes.

"Maybe we can stop in a bit and stretch our legs," he said.

"Here? Are you kidding me?"

"Christ, did you see that?" He was pointing off to the west. "It's a bloody dingo."

"Where?"

Jason eased his foot off the gas and let the car slide to a stop. Kevin was right. In the middle of a stony expanse stood a solitary four-legged creature staring at them from the distance impassively. The car pinged and ticked around them, the only other sound that of both fans labouring against the temperature. Neither of them moved for several seconds, the dingo standing there as if carved from the landscape itself. Then, as if they had been dismissed, it turned and loped away, across the plain, growing smaller and smaller.

"What the hell?" said Kevin. "Surely it can't live out here."

"Well, it didn't seem to think much of us."

"Ha! Would you?" Kevin said with a short laugh. He pushed open the door and the heat shoved into the car like a giant hand, slapping them both in the face.

"Well, I don't know about you, but I need to stretch my legs. We've got more water in the back, right?"

"Of course we have. Shut the bloody door," said Jason, then watched as Kevin wandered off the track a bit, to euphemistically stretch his legs, giving the desert liquid where there was none apart from the deep artesian water below. Their next bore was about thirty kilometres further on, but they had plenty of water with them and shouldn't need it. Jason reached into the back, snagged a bottle and took a healthy couple of swallows, feeling the sweat beading on his forehead even from the brief exposure to the outside air. Hot inside, but even hotter outside, it discouraged the temptation to open the car window and drive, letting the rushing air cool his skin. The dust was enough of a discouragement on its own. You could taste it, you could smell it, and it got over everything – inside your mouth and nose, filling you with that chalky taste that robbed even more moisture from your tongue.

Kevin got back into the car, followed by another blast of heat.

"Geez, it's hot out there," he said. "So tell me why we're doing this again?" He settled back into his seat, and then turned and reached for a water bottle as well.

Jason gave him a pained look and then shook his head. "You know as well as I do. It's just one of those things you've got to do, isn't it?"

One of those things you've got to do…

Kevin and Jason had been friends for years. All of those things you've got to do, like the bungee jumping, the white water rafting, the rock climbing, and now this. One of those things you've got to do.

Kevin slapped his hand on the dash a couple of times and then pointed. "Okay, then, James. Forward!" he said.

Forward into the wastelands.

He kicked the car into gear and pulled out onto the road again. The Track ran from Marree to Birdsville, crossing Cooper Creek and Mungerannie, among others. Jason remembered from one of the guides where someone had written that the main problem with The Track was that it took you to Birdsville, not the heat, the risk, the deaths, or the desolation, but Birdsville itself. Destination Birdsville; nothing much there but the famous pub. In the middle of nowhere and nowhere else to go except on or back, just like the cattle men, the mail carriers or the camel trains from all those years ago.

But it was one of those things you had to do. Even now, he was still telling himself that. He glanced over at Kevin, but his friend had settled into the zone of passing sameness again, just staring out at the featureless plains and fanning himself with an old newspaper they'd picked up along the way.

About twenty minutes more of rumbling dust and nothingness, and one of the regularly placed bores hove into view to one side. Little more than a tin roof over some posts and the pump.

"Should we stop?" asked Kevin.

"No, I think we've got enough," said Jason. "Can't stand the taste of bore water anyway. It's always salty."

"At least they're here, though. Imagine when they were doing the mail route with horse and carriage. Not even a fan, and only the bores to look forward to. They must have been mad. Can you imagine it?"

"Don't think I want to," said Jason. Secretly, he was wondering about their own madness around about this time.

For another twenty minutes, they drove on in silence. Sometimes, between friends as long-standing as Jason and Kevin, you simply didn't need words anyway. Red brown earth stretched in every direction, the pale yellow sky beating down upon them with its palpable heat and glare. Every now and again, there would appear that liquid shimmering: colourless, but bending the landscape behind it as the desert mirage showed them tantalising almost-glimpses of things that were simply not there. Somewhere, somehow in the far, far distance, there might be some reality behind the illusory curtains, but nowhere within reaching. He could only imagine what it must have been like, out here, dying of dehydration, being taunted by some promise of salvation that really wasn't there. It would be the final torture after the realisation of your own stupidity for having left your vehicle in the first place. That's what they always said: don't leave your car, stay with it. People never listened though.

The next artesian bore slowly grew shape as they neared. A pump, a tin shed, some signs, but a promise and the security of knowledge that it was there. It was enough. Nothing else. After their solitary accusing denizen of the wastes had wandered off, there had been nothing more either, just the endless stretch of road and plain in front, reaching to a flat-line horizon smudged by the yellow heat. He tracked the bore as they passed it by, looking up to watch its shape disappear, glinting through and then swallowed by the broad fantail of dust behind them. Even that was difficult, as by now, their rear window was coated with the fine particles.

Kevin had watched the passing bore with a look of almost longing on his face, as if something as simple and unremarkable gave him some sort of inexplicable hope in the bleakness all around.

"What are we going to do when we get there?" he finally asked.

"Well, what do you think?" Jason responded. "There's a pub there. Not much else. What do you think we might do?"

"Yeah," Kevin breathed. "A drink. A nice cold drink. And maybe something to eat. Something decent. But, oh, yeah, I can see that nice cold glass, those beads of moisture running down the sides. You're just cruel, Jason. Simply cruel. I can almost taste it now."

All Jason could taste was the dust and the flat aftertaste of lukewarm water out of a plastic bottle. Kevin started drumming lightly on the dash with his fingers to some rhythm inside his own head. It merged with the thrum of rubber on packed earth and the staccato corrugations across the track's surface.

"And after we've done that?"

"Well, I guess we come back. What else is there to do?"

Really, neither of them had thought that far ahead. Stupid, really, but it was the sort of thing that happened when you did things on a whim.

Isn't that what had happened to those people all those years ago – not thinking far enough ahead? Or maybe it was simply a case of just not thinking. Ernie Page, a British migrant had worked in the area for a few years, knew the risks, but he ignored his own rules when their big old Ford broke down. Two days the family had stayed with the car, but then he left it. The story floated up in Jason's head along with that last note that had been found with their abandoned car:

The Page Family of Marree. Ran out of Petrel. Have only sufficient water for two days. December 24.

What a way to spend Christmas.

"Jesus," he said.

"What?" said Kevin.

"No, nothing, I was just thinking."

Ran out of Petrel. It could happen to anyone couldn't it?

There was another subtle irony to the story, too. Their bodies had been found under a coolibah tree, that particular tree that was so iconic in the old song. *Under the shade of a coolibah tree.* But it had given the Page family little solace on that Christmas or Boxing Day when they'd breathed their last.

Jason tried to shake the thoughts from his mind. Maybe it was just the interminable sameness, inducing a sense of futility, or despair. The bleak landscape beat at his consciousness, sucking away purpose. He cleared his throat. As if to compound his feelings, Kevin asked something else.

"When was the last one?" he said.

"The last what?"

"You know… deader."

"Jesus, Kevin, I don't know. What's with the morbid fascination anyway?"

"Well, you know… it's just…" He shrugged.

Jason turned his gaze purposefully with set lips and narrowed eyes, but Kevin, oblivious, was just watching the road ahead. Jason sighed.

"Actually, it was only a few months ago. I remember reading about it. He was just a kid."

"Really?"

"Yes. He was working as a stockman on some station. He reckoned he wasn't being treated fairly or something, and decided to pack it in. Took off on his own. That was it. They eventually found him, of course. He was only about fifteen."

"You're kidding."

"No, I'm not kidding. I reckon this place just eats people alive."

It was Kevin's turn to clear his throat. "Did he have a horse?"

"Huh?"

"Well, did he have a horse?"

"I guess he did."

"So what happened to the horse?"

"Jesus," said Jason. "I don't know."

"Well, something must have happened to the horse. Did the horse die too?"

"It's not something they exactly write about, you know. I don't know what happened to the bloody horse. Maybe he didn't have a horse. Maybe he took a car." He paused, thinking. "You know, it's a funny thing, though. The Pages apparently had a cat with them. It just wandered off into the desert. They wrote about that. I wonder what happened to the cat."

Kevin turned to look at him then. "A cat? You're kidding."

"Nope."

"Well maybe it survived. Animals have an instinct, don't they? Just like that dingo we saw. It can obviously survive out here. Maybe it's just us humans who don't cut it. The people-eating Track. That's it."

"Well, maybe it's revenge. We're the intruders, after all. Revenge of The Track."

Kevin snorted. "I think somehow, that a cat's a bit of an intruder too. Dingoes, they belong, don't they? But a cat..."

"Hmmmm."

"Well, dingoes belong here."

"Not originally, they didn't. Remember, they were supposed to come across the land bridge with the first, original settlers."

"Oh, yeah. That's right. I wonder how long you have to be in a place before you start to belong. Is it years, decades?"

"Well, I know one thing for sure," said Jason.

"Mmmm? And what's that?"

"We don't exactly belong here, either." He gestured with his chin out the front window.

Both of them turned to watch the road ahead, contemplating.

The last statement seemed to have drained them of further speculation. Jason looked up to watch the retreating dust plume in the rear view as he listened to the drum of tires on earth. He turned back to the road, leaned absently over to tap the fan a couple of more times, knowing that nothing he was going to do would make it run any faster, but doing it anyway, almost like a ritual now. Kevin leaned over into the back and pulled out another water bottle, cracked the seal and tilted it back to take a few healthy swallows.

"Geez, it's hot," he said again unnecessarily, pouring a little of the water into his palm and wiping it across his forehead, leaving a muddy streak where the liquid mixed with dust.

Where would the Pages have found a coolibah tree out here? There had been no sign of real vegetation for what seemed like hours – short scrubby grass, a couple of low bushes, but trees? Jason scanned the unending flatness ahead, but there was definitely no sign of anything even resembling a tree.

The words of a song washed through his head and started repeating over and over.

We're on a road to nowhere...

No, he thought. *We're already there. We can't be on a road to get there.*

He made a low sound deep in his throat and shook his head, trying to rid himself of the lyrics.

"What is it now?" asked Kevin, but Jason merely shook his head again.

"Maybe two, three hours more," he said, changing the subject.

"You think?"

"I don't know. Maybe." He'd lost track of how long they'd actually been driving. "Maybe."

Maybe he ought to let Kevin have a stint behind the wheel too, but at this stage, controlling the vehicle was the only thing giving him some respite from the track unravelling before them.

"What the hell's that?" asked Kevin, peering out through the front window and pointing.

"What?"

"See that, up ahead?"

Jason leaned forward over the steering wheel, trying to work out what Kevin was pointing at. Further down the track, there was a smudged shape, a blur of orange and red, as if a giant thumb had wiped its print across the place where the track merged with the horizon. It made no sense to him.

"Don't know. Maybe it's another mirage."

"It doesn't look like that."

He was right. All it was was a rounded blur of colour. As they drove further, the shape grew larger. Whatever it was, not only were they approaching it, but it was approaching them at the same time and with every moment, its hue was becoming more solid, less yellow and more red. Behind it, there was nothing. It had wiped away the horizon and everything before it.

"Oh, shit," said Jason.

"What is it?"

"It's a bloody dust storm."

And in that instant, it was upon them, over them and all around them. Jason eased his foot off the gas, peering forward to try and see through the stuff. It was as if they had driven into the deepest fog, but instead of being grey, it was red, pastel red and pink, almost orange, and it was all around them. He couldn't see the track anymore; he could barely see the front of the car. He hit the brakes, and the car skidded to a stop.

"What are you doing?" said Kevin, a look of panic on his face.

"What do you think I'm doing? I can't drive in this." He gestured through the windscreen. By now, it was hard to tell how much was dust on the glass itself and how much was outside.

"We can't just stop here," said Kevin.

"What do you suggest we do? I drive any further in this and we're liable to hit something. Break an axle or worse. I can't even see the bloody road. Then what do we do?"

As far as he remembered, that's what had happened to the Page's old Ford as well. The sharp stones of the desert floor had broken something. He let his hands drop from the wheel and he stared out into the blanketing red around them. After a moment, he turned off the engine and then killed the fan.

"What are you doing?" said Kevin again, a disbelieving frown all over his face.

"That stuff gets in everything. The fan's just going to suck it inside the car."

"We'll cook in here."

"Yeah, maybe," said Jason. "But it's better than breathing in that. Besides, we've still got this." He tapped again at the little portable fan attached to the dash.

"Shit," said Kevin and turned back to look into the redness, his mouth slightly open.

"Besides," said Jason. "It can't last forever. We've got plenty of water. We're fine. We'll sit it out and then be on our way. What else can we do?"

The sound of dust against the outside of the car was like a whispering susurrus of voices.

"Shit," breathed Kevin again, turning to look in every direction, and then, with nothing to see, slumped back into his seat and returned to watching the nothingness ahead of them.

Instant by instant, the temperature inside the car was starting to rise. Jason could smell their sweat, their bodies, the dry chalkiness of dust. He reached over to grab himself another bottle of water. This was just what they needed. Outside, the sound of dust, that gentle whispering seemed to grow in intensity, mouthing shapeless words that he could almost decipher, and then faded again. He paused before opening his water bottle, listening.

"Do you hear that?" he said.

"What?" Kevin swung to face him, a slight look of worried panic written in the wideness of his eyes.

"Nothing, just... listen."

Again, the sound swelled, then lessened, swelled, and then faded once more.

Kevin was leaning forward in his seat, his shoulders hunched, staring with narrowed eyes out of one side of the front window.

"I thought I saw..."

"Huh?" said Jason.

"No, look."

Kevin pointed at where his attention was focussed and Jason leaned over to peer through the obscuring curtain as well. He couldn't be sure, but it looked like... it looked like there were shapes, barely visible, moving across the blank redness, shadows in the dust, slightly darker. The shapes became marginally more well defined, loping, long-legged, one coming into sharper focus, followed by another, and then fading into the dust in front. They were camels. Or at least they looked like camels. It was hard to tell. They were little more than shadows. But camels hadn't trod this route for decades, or at least he didn't think they had.

"Hey!" yelled Kevin. "Hey!" He slapped with his open palm against the side window, once, twice and then again. He reached for the door handle, fumbling with it.

Jason grabbed at his shoulder and pulled him back.

"What the hell are you doing?"

"Them. They're out there." He reached for the door again, but Jason grabbed him harder.

"They can't be out there," he said. "You can't open the door. Look at that. Look!"

Kevin turned back to the front, but any sign that there had been anything out there ever was gone.

"What the hell?" Kevin shook his head, once, twice. "I'm sorry, man. I thought..."

He took a deep breath and slumped back into his seat.

"You're right," he said. "It's the bloody Track. It's trying to fool us." He rubbed his hand across his forehead.

The whisper of voices grew loud and then faded. Jason thought he heard words, but they were no words that he could understand. Around them, in every direction, the redness swirled.

Something slapped against the glass beside his head and he swung his face to look. There was something pressed up against the side window, and behind it was a figure, a man, just standing there in the swirling dust. It couldn't be. Jason leaned back from the window, his breath catching in his throat. It was a man, a big boned man with a pale face, his eyes looking hollow, shadowed, filled with despair. He was mouthing words that Jason couldn't make out. His gaze tracked from the man's face down his arm to whatever it was being pressed against the outside surface of the window itself. It was a scrap of paper, block letters hastily scrawled.

Ran out of Petrel.

Jason's heart went cold in the heat. His gaze held, transfixed by those words on the scrap of paper held flat by the man's hand. He tracked back up to the man's face. Thinning dark hair, short, sat combed over the squarish forehead, not moving, unruffled by the swirling winds around him. Jason's attention went to the man's lips, making out the words, the shapes in the whispering silence.

Help us, said the man's lips. *Help us.*

Jason shrank from the window, pushing himself as far away as he could from the glass, but then realised that his belt was restraining him, stopping him from moving any further. He fumbled with the buckle, desperately struggling to release the belt, his eyes glued to that scrap of paper held there against the dusty glass.

Ran out of Petrel.

The belt buckle finally popped and he scrambled backwards across the seat, ignoring the gearshift and the brake as they dug into him. Kevin pushed at him from behind, forcing him back towards the door, but Jason fought against his hands.

"What the hell are you doing?" yelled Kevin.

Jason turned back briefly over his shoulder. "Can't you see? Look!" he yelled, then turned back.

Outside the window was nothing but swirling dust.

Jason, his mouth gone dry, his throat tight, clambered back off Kevin and into his seat.

"There was..."

His heart was still hammering.

"What?"

"I-I don't know. I..."

"Jesus, Jason."

He *had* been there. The man had been there. Jason had seen him. He swallowed a couple of times, forcing his breathing to steady. He hadn't imagined it. He couldn't have. He looked down at his lap, his fingers clasped together, just simply staring down at them.

It was the bloody Track. It was trying to fool them. They always said weird things went on in the desert. He looked up at Kevin.

"I'm sorry," he said. "I guess..." But his words trailed off to nothing. He turned, once more to face the swirling dust.

The Track had a mind, and it was all around them.

Just never leave your vehicle, he thought. *Stay with the car.*

LATER, MUCH LATER, as the dust thinned, it revealed a car, slightly angled, sitting at one side of the Track, coated in fine red dust, the windows obscured. Across the plain, a solitary dingo stood watching. It held its gaze for a minute or more, then silently turned, and loped off across the baking stony expanse.

If there were any to see it, they might have said that it seemed to be grinning.

DAGITI TIMAYAP GARDA (OF THE FLYING GUARDIANS)

ROCHITA LOENEN-RUIZ

When the road comes it has not just an environmental impact, but an impact on the stories the land tells – legends are concreted over, folk tales are exterminated by the march of 'progress'. But some legends simply shrink back into the darkness, there to be re-discovered. Rochita's tale is a story of myth re-discovered, as well as being a warning to the curious about the consequences of travelling with a stranger.

If you go walking and you meet a spirit
Bow your head and pass on by.
Do not meet their eyes.
Do not follow after.

– *Things our Mothers Tell us,*
collected sayings.

THE CALL CAME at dawn on the second day of Arbo's heat. It was faint but clear and shot through him like a bolt of lightning.

How many seasons had passed since he'd last heard that high, ululating cry echoing through the space that stood between him and the possibility of future progeny?

After that summer when he was too young to battle for the one female, he'd thought there were no more females left in the world. But now...

Ruwaaarrr...

Plaintive and trembling on the last note – he lifted his head and scented the air. Perhaps he would catch a whiff of her. Anxiety trembled through him. What if there were others who had heard her call?

He flexed his limbs, his claws tearing away at the fiber he'd swaddled around himself.

He stretched his mouth into a wide grimace and sounded out a reply. If there were any males left, they would hear his claim and his challenge. He was full-grown and well-able to fight for his own.

At once, the jungle fell silent.

His breath came in quick pants and he waited. What if the female's call had been nothing more than a figment born of his rampant heat?

Then, the reply came.

Ruwaaarrr...

The call did not tremble this time. It pierced the dawn with its clarity.

Wherever she was, it was up to him to find her now.

IN THE HALF-LIGHT preceding sunrise, Arbo emerged from his refuge. Before the valley dwellers settled here, guardianship over the forests, the mountains and the creeks belonged to Arbo's forebears. Timayap Garda: the flying guardians – that was the name the first dwellers gave them. Not that they cared what names they were called. Their existence belonged to the wild places and to the wild creatures, not to the two legged beings who infiltrated their world.

But as the number of valley dwellers grew, the world of the guardians shrank. The Timayap Garda's fearsome countenance lent fire to the rumors of their ferocity, and so they had been hunted down, killed and put to the spit.

Arbo's flight had taken him here, to this forest overlooking the valley. Here, amidst the twisting trees and dangling vines, he'd found refuge. When the hunt died down, he'd been content to remain hidden, for the valley dwellers did not like the jungle, and while they sometimes wandered through it, there were not many who lingered long.

Now, he stretched himself to his full height. He delighted in the brush of fresh wind. How long had it been since he'd basked in the open like this?

He cracked his fingers and flexed his wings. Pain rushed through him and he stifled a roar. A hunter's spear had caught him once and there were times when he was still pained by the injury.

Panting, he folded his wings close around himself.

This would not do, of course. To traverse the distance in this form would give rise to fresh speculation. There would be talk of monsters, there would be hunts, and his chosen female and their eventual offspring would forever be unsafe.

A memory came to Arbo as he stood there contemplating transformation.

Once, a valley dweller had come to the grove he called his own – brown-cheeked and brown-eyed, she had looked straight at him and shown no fear. She left a garland of berries and leaves beneath his tree. She would come at random periods and she would sit and babble to him in the words of the valley people.

He'd watched for her until one day she did not return. He heard the gongs and the wailing in the valley, and when the scent of her death came to him on the wind, he realized she would never come again.

Long after she was gone, he'd pondered the absence of fear in her. He'd wondered that she never called the hunters and that she had looked at him and treated him as if he were not different.

His bones bent and folded into themselves. His heart quickened as muscles reshaped and rearranged to fit his temporary form. It seemed to him that such a creature would walk straight towards her goal, never faltering, unquestioned.

KAGAWAN HAD JUST returned from the night hunt when he saw the girl emerge from the forest. He rubbed his eyes because he thought no one dwelt there except the madwoman named Injuti.

He stared at the girl and wondered if he had ever seen the madwoman with child. She was always bundled up in her rags and chanting and throwing dust at passersby. He could not imagine a man being so desperate as to lie with a woman who shouted curses and banished demons all the while.

Where would be the pleasure in that? And could a man endure her stench long enough to lie with her and get her with child?

He examined the girl closely and realized that, slender as she was, there was nothing childlike about her form. She walked past him now, her hair a fall of black swaying behind her. There was strength and certainty in her stride and she looked neither to the right nor to the left.

A feeling of resentment rose up in him then. She was only a girl, he thought. And her mother was a madwoman at that. What did she have to be so proud of that she walked onwards without even a sideways glance?

It wasn't that he was vain. Kagawan understood that the body of a warrior was desirable, but he wanted more than to be liked for his looks. Also, there was something about the girl that called to him. Perhaps it was her straightforward gaze, maybe it was the way she measured out her strides, and then again it could be that he was simply annoyed that she had not turned to look at him.

Nevertheless, he couldn't help but follow her with his gaze and when she reached a curve in the path, he leapt up from where he was sitting and chased after her.

* * *

ARBO SLOWED AS he reached a bend in the road. The smell of the valley was heavy in his nostrils now and he wondered that it had taken such a short time for the valley dwellers to imprint their presence on a place that had once been completely wild.

He heard a rush of footsteps behind him and the clatter of pebbles as the one following him came to a stop.

"I'm sorry," that one said breathlessly. "I didn't see you stop."

Arbo had seen the male sitting at the side of the road, but he had felt no need to acknowledge that seeing. What use was there in trying to wind his tongue around unfamiliar syllables when he would only be passing through?

A presence pulsed in the air, like a lodestone, reminding him of his mission. The path across the valley was not so long that he would need to stop and speak with any of its dwellers. He would simply follow the road that wound down through the rice fields. In his true form, he could have sailed across the deep gorges, but he was restrained by this body and by the memory of the hunt.

"I have never seen you before," the male said now. "You must be Injuti's child. My name is Kagawan. I am a hunter and a warrior."

Arbo stared at him, and after a while the male looked away. Red crept up the male's neck.

"Ah," Kagawan said. "You are proud. Even if you are beautiful to look at, you are hard and cold and without a heart."

Kagawan's words were harsh and angry, but beneath the words there was pain. Remembering his own agony in the time of the hunt, Arbo reached out his hand.

Instantly, Kagawan looked up. The red receded and understanding dawned in those eyes.

"Ah," Kagawan said. "I have been rude and wicked. Forgive me. It's not your fault that you can't speak."

KAGAWAN.

Arbo tested the name inside his head. He thought of the sound it made and of the being it was attached to even as he resumed his journey.

Kagawan strode beside him. Lean muscle bunched and stretched with each stride. If he had been a guardian, Kagawan would have been a formidable opponent. But like this, they were equal. Arbo could not and would not challenge him to battle.

Arbo wondered that this Kagawan insisted on walking beside him, when he had not extended an invitation. But perhaps it was the way of the valley people and so he decided to allow it.

As they passed through the village center, they were stopped by groups of young males and young females. The young males wished to know who Kagawan's companion was, but when they heard whose daughter she was and that she could not speak, their interest dwindled.

The females stared at them, and some of them came up and spoke boldly to Kagawan.

"Who is that?" they asked. "And why do you walk by her side?"

"A friend," Kagawan said. "I met her on the path coming down from Hungduan."

"Where are you going?"

"Somewhere."

"Somewhere? Why won't you tell us, Kagawan?"

The females cajoled with their smiles and their voices, but they could not conceal their jealousy or their desire.

"I am her escort," Kagawan said.

Arbo turned his head and met Kagawan's gaze.

"Going to the river, then?" one of the older females asked. "To the waterfall, maybe?"

Kagawan made a sound that seemed like assent.

The females smiled now and emitted an odor that made Arbo sneeze.

"Oh," said one of them. "But if she catches a cold, she won't be any use at all, will she? Wouldn't it be far better to take one of us then?"

"I won't take one of you," Kagawan said. "I have given my word and I won't break it."

*   *   *

WHILE KAGAWAN EXCHANGED words with those they met, Arbo absorbed the changes in the valley. Metal carriers moved by making put-put sounds and expelling a noxious white smoke. Once dusty paths were now covered with a rough black top that smelled like burnt rubber.

Foliage still grew wild beside the road, but stone walls had been erected all along the edge. Memory rose in him of a time when there was nothing more than a path trampled down by bare feet. A recollection of drums thrumming and voices shouting and the screaming of his kin as they were hunted down and slain—

A hand on his arm drew him back to the present.

"I'm sorry for the delay," Kagawan said. "We can go on now."

He stared at Kagawan and saw uncertainty dawn in the young male's eyes.

"Please don't be angry," Kagawan said. "I won't talk to the girls anymore. Not if it upsets you."

Arbo shook his head. It was not the conversation that had unsettled him. It was the rush of memory and the sudden knowledge that if he was found out, Kagawan would not hesitate to kill him as those other hunters had killed his kind.

He must have made a distressed sound for Kagawan's hand shot out and imprisoned his wrist.

"Don't," Kagawan said. "One more step and you'll fall off the mountain."

Behind him, a piece of wall had broken away and if Kagawan had not caught him he would have fallen into the gorge.

He stared at his wrist and at the hand encircling it. Kagawan's hand was browned by the sun and calloused by years of wielding knife and spear in the hunt. He could feel the strong pulse of something that felt like fear. He looked up. There in Kagawan's eyes was a look that was kindred to that which was mirrored in the eyes of the females they had talked to.

* * *

THEY WENT ON in silence after that. Arbo lengthened his stride, wanting to reach the end of this journey. He was unsettled by the scent of the male who matched him stride for stride. He did not know what to think of the hand that still encircled his wrist like a shackle.

How frail was the hand of the being he'd chosen to transform into. He realized it when he strove to free himself from Kagawan's grip.

"Don't," Kagawan said. "This way, they will understand we are together."

They passed through the center of the town without stopping or being stopped, and Arbo's heartbeat quickened as he picked up a scent in the air. It was very faint, but it was enough. His mate was still at a distance, but she was not unattainable.

Down they went – past a gaggle of ostentatious shelters made out of stone and wood, down along the winding path where dwellings made out of corrugated iron and dried grass stood with their doorways open to the street.

Impatience rose in him. In his true self, he could stretch his wings and float on the wind currents. In his true form, he would reach his female before nightfall. He looked up at the sky anxiously. His heat would end on the third day and with it all hope of producing offspring.

THEY STOPPED WHEN they reached the river.

One of the houses stood open and there were people walking in and out of it. Some were valley dwellers and some had skin paler than Arbo's palm.

He tried not to stare because to stare was to draw attention.

"Aunty Jane," Kagawan said.

A female came towards them. She was slender and small-boned, her skin was wrinkled from the sun and she wore a bright red scarf around her head.

"Aunty Jane," Kagawan said. "Feed us."

"Hungry boy," the female called Aunty Jane scolded. "And who is this? Is this your girl?"

As when Arbo had refused to speak to him, red crept up along Kagawan's neck.

"I am her escort," Kagawan said. "She can't speak, Aunty. But I have decided to go with her and protect her."

"Hm," Aunty Jane said.

Arbo met her stare with one of his own. Even if he wanted to, he could not find the words to speak to her of his own quest. So instead, he bared his teeth and tilted the edges of his mouth upwards as the other females had done.

"Come," Aunty Jane said. "In the back, there is still plenty."

After they had eaten, Kagawan made their excuses. Arbo wondered if Aunty Jane could see the true image of him that lay beneath the transformation. Her gaze was curious though and not at all hostile and so he bowed his head and kissed her hands in the same way that Kagawan did.

"A good girl," Aunty Jane said. "Seek out her elders, you hear?"

Kagawan laughed.

THEY WALKED ON and now that they had rested and had been fed, Arbo felt fresh energy flow through him. They quickly left the valley behind and he raised his head every now and then to catch a whiff of the female's scent.

"Over there is Nasagsagi-an," Kagawan said. "Is that where you wish to go?"

Arbo followed the direction in which his companion pointed, to where a curtain of white was surrounded by the green of foliage and the black of rock. He could smell the female now. She was there, somewhere on the other side of that waterfall.

THEIR CLIMB UPWARDS to Nasagsagi-an was not easy. In some places, the ground was still muddy from the rains and the path was slick and slippery.

Kagawan did not let go of Arbo's hand and even though he sometimes slipped, he never fell.

On they climbed. Above them, the blue took on a darker hue. Wind ruffled the stalks of rice and whispered through the tiger grass and Arbo's nostrils were filled with the sweet smell of Kagawan's sweat. He wondered what Kagawan would taste like. But grown males of his kind never fed on the flesh of living beings.

Night flowed around them and the air grew cool. The path leveled out. Someone had laid stones on the clay paths around the paddies, making it easier to walk. It was full dark now and Arbo stumbled as Kagawan came to a stop.

"We're here," Kagawan said.

Fireflies danced in the glade where Kagawan had come to a stop. Above the cool clean smell of water, Arbo scented her. It was the female he had been seeking. She was very close, and her heat called to him just as clearly as if she had whispered the mating call in his ear.

Excitement shivered through him and Kagawan turned. Even in the dark, Arbo could see the hot light in Kagawan's eyes.

"You feel it too," Kagawan said.

And just like that he drew Arbo into his embrace.

As if sensing Arbo's confusion, Kagawan's lips were soft and teasing. His teeth nipped and his tongue licked until Arbo could not keep himself from opening up.

Heat rushed through Arbo as Kagawan's taste flowed onto his tongue. His female was nearby, she was waiting and yet Kagawan's need awakened a response in him. A whisper of memory came to him, but even as he reached for it, it faded in the heat of Kagawan's urgency.

Kagawan's arms pressed him closer and he could feel a throbbing at the base of his spine. Warmth pooled there, and a sense of waiting.

"Let me," Kagawan's voice was hot in his ear.

They sank to earth, and Kagawan's fingers were plying and playing over his breasts and the length of his legs and the warm place between that was lush and moist.

"Open," Kagawan whispered.

There was a quick jolt and he felt Kagawan inside him. A high keening wail escaped Arbo's lips. Kagawan was a presence that throbbed and pulsed in his clasping heat. He was conscious of Kagawan's breath, of the smell of betelnut on him, of the bittersweet taste of Kagawan's tongue, of Kagawan's mouth on his chest and of something electric passing from himself to where Kagawan's presence was a living thing that pushed and tugged at his other senses.

He inhaled the scent of blooming nightflowers, crushed grass, stirred up earth, Kagawan's sweat and the sweat of this form he had taken on, and then above all that, so strong it drowned everything else, the hot fecund scent of his mate.

AFTERWARDS, KAGAWAN GATHERED Arbo close and spoke promises of rites and sacrifice and pigs and chickens. His words slurred into one another and before long he fell asleep.

Arbo pushed away from the sleeping male. He stood and stared down at the body that had been joined to his. He could feel the wetness of Kagawan's release between his thighs and the scent of their joining still lingered in the air.

But now, an urgency overtook him. His mate was near and it was the height of his heat and hers. With a last glance at Kagawan, he stretched himself to his full height.

Ruwaaarrr. . .

He called to her now and on the heels of his call came her reply.

IT WAS CLOSE to midnight when Arbo found her. She had built her nest in the arms of a great banyan and it was only after he'd taken to the air that he sighted her.

She sighed and opened her arms as he descended. Her talons extended in greeting and he sank into her embrace.

He was overcome by the musk of her heat, and when she pierced his skin, he was too caught up in exaltation to feel any pain. Over and over, she pierced him and over and over he spent himself until her scent changed and he knew with certainty that she would bear his young.

He was still in a frenzy when she split him open. He did not flinch when she tore his flesh to shreds.

This was part of the cycle. His heart and his liver would nourish her and their young. His skin and his intestines would line the nest. His bones, his talons, his wings would become part of her shelter while she waited for the young ones to be born.

In his final throes all he knew was ecstasy.

EARLY IN THE morning, Kagawan arose. He looked around for the girl, but he could not find her. He called, but she did not come.

Perhaps she had gone to relieve herself.

He waited and then he searched all around the waterfall.

When he found no trace of her, he decided to return to the valley. Perhaps she had not understood his intention to marry her. He had never felt such a complete and profound joining as what he had had with her.

For many days, he searched. At first, he went to Injuti, but she looked at him as if he were the one gone mad. And when he asked in Hungduan, they knew nothing of a girl who could not speak. Everywhere he went, he asked, but no one knew anything of her.

"Let her go," they said to him.

"She bewitched you."

"She was a spirit."

"She was Nahipan."

He grew silent and withdrawn and whenever the valley dwellers saw him, he was always headed towards Nasagsagi-an.

"I must find her," became his constant litany.

He didn't notice when the change came upon him. He didn't see the lengthening of his nails, the broadening of his hands, the way his fingers were turning into talons.

I'M THE LADY OF GOOD TIMES, SHE SAID

HELEN MARSHALL

When I saw Helen Marshall reading from her story 'Blessed' at the World Fantasy Convention in 2012, it struck me that she read like a poet – the pacing and voice she employed highlighting the lyrical cadences of her tale. This encounter with Helen's fiction lead me to purchase a copy of her debut collection, Hair Side, Flesh Side *(ChiZine Publications, 2012) which in turn lead me to ask to her to contribute a story for this anthology. What follows is a weird road story filtered through the sensibilities of the poets of the Beat Generation – a hauntingly original piece, marking Helen out as one of genre's fast-rising stars.*

IT'S BARELY PAST midnight on the crumpled asphalt ribbon of Route 66, west of Ash Fork, just past the bridge at the Crookton Road exit on Interstate 40.

We're in an old, beat-up Studebaker Champ, and disaster is playing like a love song on the radio.

Carl rides shotgun.

You wouldn't like Carl much. Not many apart from Juney do, but Juney's got a blind spot for hard luck cases and Carl's the most hard luck case of all, not counting myself. I know Carl. I bailed him out the time he beat up that girl for short-changing him at the 7-11. The cops told me they had to haul him away, screaming, "For a two-buck tip, you better show me your cock-chafing titties, you little whore!"

I never told Juney about that. We aren't much the kind to keep secrets, but he's her brother, and I spent enough nights on the couch in the early years to know when to let a thing go.

The lady of the Ill Wind Blowing, indeed.

So Carl's riding shotgun and I'm in the driver's seat, because I sure as Hell wouldn't let him touch the fucking steering wheel. Even now.

Carl's angry. You can tell by the way he's grinding his teeth – been doing that since he's a kid, I imagine, so's now they're small and smooth like pebbles, rubbed down to raw little nubblins that hurt him to chew, but he does it anyway.

The other way you can tell Carl's angry is the Colt. He's got it trained on me. He's draped an old U of A football jersey (rah rah, Wild Cats, huh?) over the barrel. Only we two know there's a gun under it.

But I know. Yes, I do.

It's my Pappy's Colt. Same one he used to renovate the back of his skull when I was seventeen. I don't like guns. Must be the only fella in Mojave Country who don't, but once you've seen what a Colt does, what it's made for – which is turning a living, breathing human bean into ground chuck – well, the shine goes off fast.

Juney and Carl were raised different. Carl's been shooting beer cans out in the desert since he was five. I seen him at his place with an old air rifle he musta got as a kid. He could pump it just right to pop a fly outta the air, leave him stunned but whole. Kept 'em in canning jars until they suffocated, bumbling like a drunk up against the glass.

Carl knew guns. He knew where I kept the Colt, and I only kept it for Juney. So she'd feel safe. That's a laugh now.

Carl's shifting the gun. I can't see under the shirt, but I can feel instinctively – hair on the back of my neck prickling with sweat – that he's got his finger on the trigger. He's stroking it.

My skin crawls because he could be masturbating for all I can see, that wet gleam in his eyes and his tongue darting out like a lizard's between his chafed lips.

He'd be crazy to pull the trigger now. I've got my hands on the wheel and we're clocking over sixty, it'd kill us both. But that look in his eyes? He don't give a damn. That's what scares me.

So we drive.

I can feel the barrel trained on me. I can see the twitch of his finger. Clutch and release. Clutch and release.

It's past midnight. Nothing but grassland and the odd thicket shape of juniper bushes jumping in the glow of the headlights. The blue gloom of buttes in the distance. Faded neon signs. We pass the ruins of Hyde Park ('Park Your Hide Tonight at Hyde Park!!') and I wonder if that's what Carl has in mind.

I try not to think about that, just feel the road underneath me, the scream of the engine. I am almost relaxed. I can feel my body unspooling the way the road does.

It's a mistake.

Carl senses it, his body goes rigid and he grins a mad dog grin. He's been baking in the sun for too long.

"Enough," he says. "Pull over."

"Hey, man," I try but my lips have gone dry. My throat is raw. "Hey."

"Don't shit with me, Smiley. Just pull over the fucking car."

"I can explain," I start. The line sounds funny in my own head.

"Sure," he says. "Sure." But he's got that grin and I don't think he gives two shits about what I'm going to say. He wants this. I'm used to reading people. You can't sell a man what he don't want in his heart, whether it's God, a Cadillac, or pills for the perfect boner. A man wants what he wants.

I'm releasing the gas and the car starts to shake as we pull off the asphalt. There's nothing out here but sage and sky and the road and us – him with the Colt and me with one shot at selling him something it's clear he don't want to buy.

Otherwise...

Otherwise...

I'll be ground chuck when that damned Arizona sun turns the road into the world's hottest grill.

"I'm the lady of Good Times," she told me. "I am the lady of Turn Up the Heat, Boys."

Here goes.

I DIDN'T MEAN to cheat.

I know that's what every cheater since Eve met the snake claims, but it's no less true. I didn't mean to cheat on Juney. The only defence I got is I'm human, I'm human, and what executioner ever gave a damn for that old song and dance?

Let me try again.

I only saw a ghost once before this all got started. That was the night Pappy died. Don't even know if it was real. When you've seen a man's grey matter splashed over the concrete you're bound to dream any number of things in the small hours.

I was lucky. What I saw was kinder that I had any right to expect. Which is to say I woke up to find Pappy standing at the foot of my bed. Some younger version, it must have been. He still had the head of hair my mammy fell in love with. Whatever bad news come to him later in life – pulling the skin around his eyes with the fish hooks of too much worry – it still hadn't found him yet.

There he was. Some shadow of him slivered by the wedge of light from the hall come sliding into the room.

"G'night, Smiley," he said. Just that. He grinned a sweet old grin at me like he had, I imagine, when I was a babe rolling around in the crib.

"G'night, Smiley," he said, and then he was gone.

I'M THINKING THIS, but somewhere else I am stumbling through sand and cholla. The night smell of creosote is heavy. I don't know where Carl is leading me.

Carl is everything that I have ever been afraid of in the world. Ugly and brutal. A man who comes into the world with his fists balled and plans on going out the same way.

Maybe it's the same for him, though. Maybe I am everything he is afraid of. A man who smiles. A man who had the shit kicked out of him but still knows how to whistle a tune. A man who could make his sister happy – Looney Juney, he called her. God.

A man who could make her cry too. I admit it; I broke her heart more than once. Poor Juney. The only person in the world who had found a way to care for him, and a sumbitch like me has the thread of her love cat's-cradling between my fingers. God, he must have had that hardon of hate for a long time.

And right now I am thinking that maybe I deserve this. That's the thing. Right now I am thinking maybe he has a right to put a bullet in me.

I NEVER SAW another ghost but Pappy until three months ago.

It started off with a sound like crying. Wailing, really. I thought maybe it was a bobcat in heat – some critter, maybe, with tire treads crushing half himself. Nothing left to do but cry his grief to the night.

Juney and I had never had kids. We talked about it, well, years ago, but it had never got much past talk. One of the ways I broke her heart, I guess, though I still think maybe I did her a favour. My parents had got unlucky with me – they couldn't afford a kid, but Mammy had grown up in the light of Jesus so once I had taken hold in her belly there wasn't much for it. But one was enough. Whatever they got wrong that night they never got wrong again.

So I wasn't much used to the sound of babies crying, which is why I'd been thinking about some dying thing.

Juney didn't hear it. She worked the night shift at Dunkin' Donuts, and I didn't ever see much of her til the sun started in.

I didn't think much on it, but then it happened again. This time it weren't crying. It was singing. A drunk's tune. A little of this, a little of that. But sad.

I went into the kitchen. I had the Colt in my hand because wasn't that what my little Junebug made me keep it for? In these parts a man who wanders into another man's house is liable to end up six feet under. Half the folk think they were born from a misplaced squirt from Billy the Kid's cock.

Not me. Sins I have in plenty, but I never thought it in me to kill a man. Not without asking his name first.

Still, I kept my finger on the trigger. I ain't stupid neither.

But the man. Well. When I saw him standing like nobody's business in my kitchen with that sad song on his lips, I knew I recognised him. Not enough to wave, but enough to know I'd seen him before. It took me a moment, but I'm good with faces. I'd given him a dollar or two when I had one to spare. Bought him a Coke outside the drugstore once. Sure enough, I looked down and there were the two bald knuckles of his left hand rapping lightly against my kitchen table. His sign had said he was a vet. He had that half-vacant look in his eyes. True or not, I believed it.

He catches me looking and his lips twitch. He flips me a slow, three-fingered salute, and I swear, just like Pappy, the moonlight takes him. It seemed clear enough whatever I meant to do with the Colt, worse had happened.

He wasn't back the next night, but three nights later he was. I woke with that itch between my shoulder blades that someone was in the house. I didn't say nothing to him, but he looked so sad. And something else too. A sharpish, black-eyed look. I sat with him a while. And the next night too. And the next.

Until he didn't come back no more.

THIS IS HOW I discovered girls.

If you know this, maybe the rest will be clearer. Maybe.

I was sitting with Pappy at the bus station getting ready for my first real haircut. Maybe six years old? Haircuts were a big deal in my family. We were dead broke, but it was my birthday and Pappy was clear. The cut makes a man. I was nervous. I knew this was a grown-up thing and Mammy and Pappy had fought about it. A big ole screaming match. I knew this was Big Boy stuff.

Pappy knew I was nervous. He starts horsing around, trying to let me know that it's no big deal. But I'm this sullen cinderblock. I don't move a muscle. I don't smile.

So he gets down on his knees in front of me, dusting up his best pair of trousers in the dirt. He's pulling faces. At first I won't crack a grin, but the faces get bigger and bigger. And there's Pappy down on that dirty floor with all the other folk starin' and he's yanking at his lips and tugging at his nostrils. Now some of them are laughing, and now I'm laughing too, these giant *yuk yuk* laughs that are half hiccups. My chest is sore from laughing. Now I'm on my knees, half running, half-crawling through the rows of chipped orange chairs because this big ole monster of a Pappy is grunting and chasing after me.

I duck and juke, then I skid to the end of the last row.

I hardly notice someone's *there*.

A woman.

Ten seconds ago I was twisting on skinned knees but suddenly I am transfixed. I am staring straight up the skirt of this young college girl with legs smooth as stripped timber and black stockings running up her perfect thighs.

I have never seen such an elaborate set of machinery as the garter belts that kept those stockings in place. Erector sets had nothing on whatever those were. Nothing.

I'm telling you this because there is still nothing sweeter than those fancy snaps and laces that make a lady a lady. To this day I swear it was seeing the buckle of Juney's garter slipping out from under the hem of her church dress that stopped my breath. That sly sweet smile when she caught me looking.

I was in love. Same feeling at six as it was at twenty-six.

I never meant to hurt Juney. I swear. But women have always been my weakness.

The second woman I loved was Kelsi Koehler. She was a regular feature at the Glendale 9 Drive-In. A scream queen of the highest caliber. The leading lady of every wet dream I had between the ages twelve and sixteen.

Miss Koehler had this thick glossy hair. The most adorable way of shrugging her shoulders and quirking her eyebrows so they almost kissed at the centre of her forehead. The best part was you could find her every other night for the cost of admission. It was Boomtown for the Weissman family during those years – no more fights over haircuts, not then!

It wasn't the hair toss or that perfect little moue that got me though. It was her voice. The super sultry huskiness of it.

"I'm the lady of Good Times," I remember her saying. "I'm the lady of Good Things Coming." When she said that it was like she was speaking directly to me. Her voice low and sexy, cutting the cuteness the way whisky cuts coke.

After that I dedicated every pencil erection my teenage self got to her. She was my queen. My goddess. My lady of Good Things Coming. I worshipped her with paper route money and discount ticket stubs every Friday night.

And three days after the dead vet flashed me his final three-fingered salute, there she was.

The glorious track of red hair. The girlish set to her shoulders. The B-Movie smoulder.

My lady of Good Times. My lady of Love At First Sight.

And then she winked.

HERE'S THE THING you got to know about my Pappy. Billy Weissman was a Bible salesman. It always struck him as funny that a Heeb like him could get work slinging the gospel. He had a big Jew nose just as I've got, but people took him for a cheech. Or a wop. An Apache, even.

He was gone most of the time when I was growing up, but when he was in town, it was always a party. Mammy and I'd get in the car and we'd drive out to God knows where and Pappy would take out a bottle of whatever was rolling around in the back. We'd watch the stars. Sing old Hank Williams songs.

Pappy would drink the road dust out of his throat and get a bit friendly until Mammy gave him that look all men know.

I loved those nights. All three of us together.

What I didn't know was that wasn't his first bottle. It might not even have been his second. Maybe Mammy was happy. I don't know, but you gotta wonder what a mother's to think about being so broke in those early lean years her son has to stitch his shoes together with safety pins while his Pappy's got the cash for whisky.

Well. You know how that ended.

And when it did I got a gun, a briefcase full of the Good Book, and a taste for the bottle.

It hadn't been good between Juney and me for some time.

There were times when I was glad she worked the night shift so she didn't have to see me crawling in at three or four in the morning. But, God, I still remember that girl I saw in church. Her garters slipping out from under the hem. Her stockings drooping.

I didn't know how bad it was though.

I didn't know that she musta been over at Carl's place crying some mornings after her shift, in that trailer of his with its jars full of choking flies. What it musta been like for her to go to her big brother for help.

Even though he was mean.

Even though he could be vicious as a mad dog.

Maybe we all have blind spots.

WHEN I FIRST see Kelsi Koehler I think maybe I'm looking through the thick, glass bottom of the bottle. It isn't real. It could be any woman with her hip up on the kitchen table, her thigh leaving the lightest trace of sweat there.

"Hiya, honey," she says. That voice.

"Hi yourself," I say.

"Pour a woman a drink?"

I nod. Maybe I nod. I find a bottle, anyway, and pour out whatever is in it. Something cheap, I imagine. It's whisky I was drinking that night. I get two ice cubes from the freezer and her eyes are following me as I do that. *Plop* they go. They chime as they hit the glass. I've always loved the sound of ice cracking in whisky.

She takes the drink without saying a word. Makes a face when she tries it.

"This is the best you've got?"

I shrug. She cocks her head and now her eyebrows are doing that kissing thing I remember so well from the big screen.

"Am I dead?" I wonder. It could be. Maybe I've flipped my car on that tricky bend coming out of the canyon. It could be. I guess I'm wondering out loud, because she laughs in that low and husky way of hers.

"No, honey," she says. "I am. Ovarian cancer. It's bin eating away at me for years now. Guess it must have won out." She pauses. Takes a sip of the whisky. "And Nurse said I bin having a good day."

I look again. She must be, what, in her sixties? Not that she looks it. Her skin is flawless, breasts small and perky as apricots. Her thigh is one long, smooth curve. There's a sweet little divot in her dress at the delta where her right leg crosses her left.

"Careful," she says, "you'll catch flies." And she laughs again.

I am thinking, "But what have I caught here?" I don't know. Lord help me, I don't know.

And then she's gone. Fast as that, the moonlight's got her. Fast as the curtains pulling shut. And I am left holding a glass of whisky and water.

Maybe a better man would have told Juney. I wonder that, but I don't think she would've believed me.

I had to know if it was real. If Kelsi Koehler was real. And so I did just about the last thing in the world that I wanted to do. I went cold turkey.

I emptied every bottle down the sink. Every drop of it, gone. And then the mouthwash too. And then the rubbing alcohol, because even though I knew it'd make me go blind I didn't trust myself not to try it if things got hard.

Juney watches me dump it all, and she don't say a word. She's seen this before. But still. I see a little light in her eyes switching on like I haven't in some time.

All she says is, "Will it stick?"

I shrug. What more is there to say?

It's Hell. The shakes get real bad on the second night and I'm glad I dumped the rubbing alcohol. I think I might've tried anything at that point. I stay in the house. I keep the phone off the hook so none of the boys can call.

Because I want to know. I want to know.

And on the third night, Kelsi's back, and this time there isn't a drop of drink in me to cloud my vision.

She has a look to her. Maybe I missed it with the vet because I wasn't paying attention, but on Kelsi it is pretty damn hard to miss. She's paler. Gorgeous? Hell, yes, but now it's a scary kind of beauty. I don't know how else to say it. Just that I know something is off. Maybe she'd been the lady of Good Times, once, but tonight, she was something else. The lady of Bad Things Coming. Even I could see that.

"I'm dry tonight," I tell her when she quirks one of those perfect eyebrows.

"Guess that means I'm dry too, honey."

I stand there staring at her for a while, just making sure it's real. Eventually she gets bored. She stands up. "Got music, at least?"

I switch on the radio. They're talking about the fall of Saigon. They're talking about our boys coming home. Then I turn the dial, and out of the static comes John Lennon crooning about getting by with a little help from his friends. She's nodding her head along. When the jockey comes on during the final fade out, she turns back to me. "Gunna stare all night?"

"No, ma'am," I say.

"Good," she says. "I can't abide a gawper. They were always gawping at me. Well. In the beginning, at least."

"And now?" I say, turning down the radio low so it's just a murmur.

"Honey, I don't know what now *is*. A way station maybe. A pit stop on the Road to Somewhere Else. Who knows how the rules work? I'm just happy to be playin' the game a bit longer before..." She tosses her hair and the copper-red of it gleams in the buttery light. "I'm cold," she says.

The sun has been baking the Arizona desert all day, and inside the house, even though I've got the air conditioner cranked up and it's past midnight, it's still so hot I worry that the windows might crack. It's been known to happen.

But she's cold. And I'm a gentleman.

"Warm me up?" she says.

And I love Juney. I've loved her since the minute I laid eyes on her. But this is something else.

So I go with her. She tastes the way the desert smells after the rains. Like creosote. The black taste of tar. Her skin freeze-sticks like an ice cube, but she's my lady of Good Times.

She's my lady of I'm Only Human.

She is beautiful in the moonlight streaming through the window as I lay her down on the bed. As I kiss the curve of her breast.

She is wearing garters. I know this should mean something to me, but in that moment it don't.

I slide my fingers up the silky surface of her stockings. I can feel the muscles underneath. I dream I can feel her pulse. My thumb catches on the hook.

She's just a way station, I think. Just a pit stop.

She is beautiful, but now her eyes are black. Whatever it was that's underneath her skin, that coldness, that oily sweet smell, it's getting stronger. I don't know what she is. It's starting to scare me. But I can't stop. I don't want to stop. I want to touch her. I want the feel of her stiffening nipple between my fingers, the clench of her legs around my waist...

And that's when the door to the house busts open.

Because I have left the phone off the hook.

Because Juney has been worried. But pleased too. Pleased about me pouring all the booze down the drain. And she don't want me to fall off the wagon. Not this time. Because this is my last chance. I know that. I know I can only break her heart so many times. And Carl knows that too. Carl knows how close Juney is to the edge. How close to breaking she is with that shit-drunk husband of hers.

None of this is a mystery novel. None of this takes much guesswork.

So he hears the noises coming from the bedroom. He knows what those noises mean. And he knows Juney's still on shift at the Dunkin' Donuts.

And, best of all, he knows where the Colt is.

CARL'S GOT A sour smell to him. Like sweat mixed with old bacon. I can smell him.

There's a hot breeze that's tugging at my hair.

I can feel the muzzle of the Colt pressing into my back.

"Turn around slowly," he says.

I am struck because I have heard this line so many times. I want to ask him, "Is this a stick up?" I want him to say, "Reach for the sky, pardner!"

I can't help it. I let out a snort, and he hears it. When I turn – slowly! – his face is running from stunned to hurt to angry.

"I can explain," I told him, but now that we're face to face I know I can't. What do I say? What part of this can I tell that would make sense? Carl is not a smart man. Carl is not a forgiving man. Carl will not buy whatever line of bullshit I want to sell him.

I open my mouth. I close it again. He leans in closer. His teeth are pressed tightly together, the little nubs of them rubbing together. He is angry, but I think he is also curious about what I will say. A dull curiosity. The same look he gives the flies as they bumble around the inside of the jar. How long will this one last?

When my mouth opens the second time, I am just as curious about what will come out.

Because a drunk will say anything to get a drink. And a cheat?

A cheat always has a happy tune to whistle.

"I can explain..." And I surprise myself. "No. I can't. I love her," I say. "I love Juney."

"I know," he says and his mouth twists. There is something that goes across his face – and if I stared hard enough I could catch exactly what it is – but I'm not looking that hard. I don't want to know.

Because by then I am moving. Because, then, I think, he has moved in close enough. There is just enough room. If I am just fast enough I can–

And then there is a noise like a thunderclap.

IT IS LATE when I find myself back in the house. I don't know what time. Close to dawn because Juney has just got in. Her hair is mussed. Silvery-grey strands coming undone from her neat bun. Her Dunkin' Donuts uniform is creased a little. She somehow looks pretty. Worn, but pretty.

My lady of Half 'n' Half. My lady of How Do You Take It?

"Smiley," she says. "Did you just get in?"

I allow that I did.

"And are you sober?" she asks.

"Yeah, Junebug," I tell her. "Sober as a priest."

And it's the truth.

"Good," she says. And then: "You look good."

She's dead on her feet. I can see her swaying a little, her hands on the kitchen table, keeping her steady. But she's smiling and that makes me happy. I'm glad for that.

"Come to bed," I tell her, and take her in my arms. I can feel her weight sagging into me.

"S'cold," she says, but I don't say anything. Somewhere off Route 66 my body is waiting for the sun to scorch it crisp and black. Somewhere Carl is washing the blood out of his shirt. He is careful. Gentle, even. But there is a part of me that is here. Maybe the better part of me.

I take Juney to our bedroom. I help her peel off the uniform.

I kiss her gently on the forehead where she still tastes like icing sugar and cinnamon.

I want to tell her about Carl. About how she must be careful around him. How there's bad news coming for her. I want to tell her so bad it's burning up like bad liquor in my gut, but somehow I can't. Maybe it's cowardice. Maybe it's just that I can't stand the thought of that forehead of hers creasing, that same old fight we spent twenty years on, same as every other fight.

Maybe I shoulda. Maybe.

The thing is, the dead can't see the future any better than the living. They have to drive down that same road. One mile at a time.

And this is just a pit stop for me. Maybe. A way station. I can't stay.

I don't want to.

There is something growing in me. Something cold. Something heavy and black as tar. Is this death? Or is this something else?

And it is cold. And she is warm. I lay down next to her. I do not want to touch her. I can't help wanting to touch her.

"G'night, Smiley," she says.

"G'night, Junebug," I say.

THE WIDOW

RIO YOUERS

Rio has already made his mark on the horror genre with his moving and dark novella Westlake Soul *(ChiZine Publications, 2012) and continues to make an impression with a slew of incisive short stories. What follows is Youers at his best, displaying his horrific sensibility with a gift for characterization that makes 'The Widow' a compelling read.*

"WHAT ARE YOU doing?"

"I'm stopping you."

The man drew whistling breaths and his chest strained against the rope that bound him. Blood trickled from his nose and mouth. Harsh light washed him, emphasizing every bruise and abrasion. Had she thought him immortal... supernatural? Here he was now, weak and bleeding all over her floor. His ancient skin could break, after all.

"Stopping me?" He blinked and shook his head. "From what, exactly?"

She stepped towards him, throwing her shadow like a blanket. A large woman. Not fat, but solid. Her thick arms were packed with toil and angst. She had a prominent brow and square shoulders. Very little could be described as feminine. Not her military surplus jacket, nor her scuffed leather boots. Only her fingernails, perhaps, painted – incongruously – bubblegum pink.

"By my count, you have killed a total of fifty-three people." Cloud-coloured eyes peered through unkempt hair. "Fourteen of them were children. I can only go back to when records began, of course, so the actual number may well be greater."

"Are you out of your mind?"

"And now it ends."

"This is madness." He fought the rope again, twisting his upper body; it chewed into his arms and chest. No give. He pushed against the wooden post he'd been bound to. It creaked, but didn't budge. More blood leaked from his nose.

There was a workbench against the back wall, strewn with tools. Various wrenches and screwdrivers. A handsaw. A nail gun. A claw hammer. She turned and walked towards it, her heavy boots kicking up dust.

"Timothy Peel," she said.

"What? *What?*"

"One of the men you killed… Timothy Peel." Her hand moved from the handsaw to the nail gun. Back to the handsaw. "He was my husband."

"I don't know what you're talking about. I swear I don't."

"We'd only been married eleven months." She selected the nail gun. Cordless, 15-gauge, loaded with two-inch finish nails. Her fingers curled around the handle. "I loved him very much. He was my… my *balance.*"

No one would hear him scream. Not here, in the basement of her house, fifty yards from the road, and a quarter of a mile from her nearest neighbour. And scream he did, looking at the nail gun in her hand. A shrill and desperate effort. Eyes wide. Body jerking. His throat turned dark with the strain, like a bruise.

She let him expend both voice and energy, until he was left rasping and drooling. Tears soaked his shirt. His upper body sagged against the rope. He'd been tied in a sitting position. His legs were splayed. She kicked them closer together, then straddled them. The muscles in his calves tensed, but he couldn't move. Another weak sound, and he looked at her with shattered eyes.

"You're making a terrible mistake," he said.

"Seventh of April, 2009. Almost four years ago. To the day." She pressed the nail gun's nose piece against his left kneecap and he squirmed and struggled, but was held tight. "Timothy wasn't just an accomplished driver, he was a *careful* driver. Yet, mysteriously, he flipped his car one morning on his way to work. Conditions were perfect. No wind. No rain. Good visibility. He died while emergency services worked to cut him from the wreckage."

"A car accident." The man's voice was cracked. His eyes pleading: blue and large and wet. "He died on the road."

The widow smiled. She looped her index finger around the trigger and fired three nails into the cartilage below his kneecap.

He found the energy to scream again.

"But, mister," she said. "You *are* the road."

THERE HAD LONG been concerns about Faye Peel *née* Lester's mental stability, but when she decided to have a house built on Thornbury Road – less than one hundred yards from where Timothy was killed, in fact – her friends and family deduced that she had finally come unhinged. Not irrevocably so, but sufficient to warrant professional intervention.

Her father was a worrisome rabbit of a man with fleet gestures and small eyes. He rarely finished a sentence.

"Your mother and I feel that…" He proffered a sheet of paper, upon which had been printed the particulars of one Dr. Matthew Claridge, MA, MBBS, MRCPsych. His logo was a smiling flower.

"A psychiatrist?"

"We're worried about you, Faye."

"Indeed." She placed the sheet of paper facedown on the kitchen table. Her mother busied herself cooking, humming something, as if she didn't have one ear – or both – on the conversation.

"It's just that, since Timothy…" Her father made half a move to take her hand, but drew back. His mouth twitched. "And all that nonsense about… and now this, with the house…"

"Thank you for your concern." Faye smiled, and it was she who reached across to take his hand. It felt small, somehow, and she noted how it trembled. "I'm fine, though. I feel stronger and more focused than I have in years."

"But the house... do you really...? Oh, Faye, it's just so *close*."

She squeezed his fingers gently. Her smile was sure. Her voice confident.

"I have my reasons."

And she did; the 'nonsense' to which her father referred was her erstwhile assertion that Timothy's death had not been an accident, and her subsequent vow to find the man responsible. These claims were met with sympathy, a great deal of love, but very little understanding. Faye eventually let it slide – even professed a misjudgement, for her parents' sake – although she secretly, passionately, pursued her suspicion.

It began shortly after Timothy's death. The first two months had been an emotional blur. She recalled only damp and grey patches, like fragments of cloud snatched from the sky. The funeral was dreamlike. Red flowers. So many red flowers. Timothy's brother playing 'Let It Be' on a guitar the same colour as his coffin. As many hands as there were flowers, all offered in support. The world revolved too slowly, and with a grinding sound that kept her awake at night. She imagined its ancient machinery full of pain, coughing black smoke, and God crippled by the weight of His dead.

This lassitude fractured, finally, when Faye opened the bathroom cabinet one morning and saw Timothy's aftershave on the shelf. She'd been with him when he bought it, neither of them knowing that he wouldn't live long enough to finish the bottle. It occurred to her – and it was like a hand gently leading her through the rain – that she would never again smell that aftershave on his skin, or the vague trace of it on his shirt collar when doing the laundry. She took the bottle off the shelf, unscrewed the cap, and lifted it to her nose. Her tears were copious, but not without healing. As she wiped the last of them from her face, she felt something give way inside her – an internal landslide that left her partly hollow, but with enough space to exist. She poured the aftershave down the sink and disposed of the bottle. She whirled, then, through the house, not removing Timothy, but clearing those possessions too replete with memories. His reading glasses. His favourite cardigan, threadbare and wonderful. The giant bar of Dairy Milk he'd been nibbling on since Christmas. In the end, a chestful of items that had no place in her half-formed life. And even though she still slept at night with her arm thrown across Timothy's side of the bed, it felt like a huge step in the right direction.

Another step was to visit the site of the accident. Thornbury Road was a seven-mile pencil-line on the countryside, linking the A4301 at Abbotsea to the Paisley Wood roundabout. It often provided a beautiful drive, with raised banks of daffodils in the spring, and clutches of woodland that flared with oranges and reds come autumn. Strings of mist clung to the farmland at dawn, made pink by the climbing sun, and wildlife revelled in the fields that rolled southward, where, on clear days, the English Channel could be seen skimming the horizon. Despite its charm, though, it had, understandably, become a sombre route for Faye. The shadows seemed suddenly denser. The dawn mists obscured secret things. Broken things. It was here – a stone's throw from where Timothy had died – that she first saw the sideways man.

He had a condition, she thought. Scoliosis, or perhaps spina bifida. His back was skewed and his head kinked to one side, always looking over his right shoulder. Uneven hips caused him to *drag* rather than walk, having to correct his direction every several steps. His face, too, sloped to the right, as if sympathizing with his body.

Faye had parked in a lay-by only a short distance away. She looked at the man through the windscreen. He had no purpose, apparently; he circled towards and then away from where Timothy died. Lank black hair covered his eyes.

She surmised his challenges went beyond the physical. The poor man was lost, obviously, and confused. Thinking she could help, she stepped out of her car and onto the road. He looked up, alerted. A breeze blew back his hair and his eyes glimmered. They were notable not in their colour or shape, but in the way they regarded her. She felt suddenly naked, both body and soul laid bare. It was as if he touched – *probed* – her with those eyes, and examined her history. Every smile. Every tear. Every hope and sadness exposed. Faye shivered. She crossed her arms over her bosom and took a step back.

She was about to get back into her car – return another day – when the man dragged himself sideways, onto the bank, and behind a cluster of evergreens. She saw his jacket sway between their narrow trunks, then he was gone. Faye staggered into the middle of the road and waited for him to emerge one way or the other, or to see him shuffling sideways across the field beyond the point where he had disappeared. She adjusted her position and peered through the branches.

Nothing.

"Hello."

Gone.

She shivered again, composed herself. Several deep breaths, focusing on Timothy and the reason she'd come here. She walked to the site of his death. Planted both feet firmly upon it. She thought she'd experience… something. A chill. A vision. A memory. There was nothing. The road felt the same here as anywhere else – as any other road. The broken glass had been swept away. The blood, too. As far as this unspectacular patch of Thornbury Road was concerned, it was as if Timothy Peel had never existed at all.

She cried again, deeply, and with a great pain in her chest. She got into her car and drove away. Too fast. Moving forward, or so she hoped. What else was there to do?

THE NEXT SIX months were better. The pain never went away, but she could fold her hands around it. Contain it. She went out with her friends and smiled more often. She even regained the weight she'd lost after Timothy died. Her parents remarked on how well she was doing, and how proud they were. One morning in December, Faye awoke with her left arm curled beneath her pillow, rather than clutching Timothy's side of the bed. She gasped – feeling both delighted and guilty – and sat up quickly. Early sunlight seeped through a crack in the curtains.

That very day, a family of four was killed on Thornbury Road. Faye saw the wreckage of their Vauxhall Astra on the six o'clock news. Folded in the middle like paper. Roof pried away to get the bodies out. She saw the pulsing lights of the emergency services. She saw the POLICE ACCIDENT signs and solemn-faced officers at the scene. And she saw the sideways man, standing in the background like a large, stooped vulture.

From that moment, everything started to unravel.

SOMETHING THE REPORTER said picked at Faye's mind and wouldn't let go – that Thornbury Road had claimed eleven lives in the last ten years. An interesting choice of words that gave the seven-mile stretch of asphalt a certain character. She imagined it breathing, elongated lungs pounding beneath its surface, occasionally whipping snake-like to send some luckless vehicle spinning out of control.

Ridiculous, but it picked at her. Then it gnawed at her. Then it started to tear. She lay awake, night after night, grinding her teeth and imagining the road moving slickly beneath the stars. She often drove out there, stopping her car every two or three hundred yards, on hands and knees with her ear pressed to its gritty skin …

No heartbeat. No movement. No life.

She researched the road. More particularly, its nature. She was intrigued to find out just how many lives it had claimed over the years. She spent what amounted to months at the library and on her home computer, scrolling through links and news stories. Tracking deaths within the last forty years was easy enough. Most of them got front-page coverage in the Abbotsea *Echo*.

Beyond 1965, though, it became more difficult. The library's files were incomplete, and search engines provided only the more notable stories. She persevered, though, following every thread, however tenuous. Sometimes she worked through the night, with her eyes stinging and her worn body slouched across the desk. When she wasn't digging for information, she was cruising Thornbury Road, daring – almost *willing* – it to come to life.

She saw the sideways man twice. A different place each time. He scuttled along the edge of the road, and always disappeared before she reached him.

"Faye, what's happening? You haven't been…"

"You worry too much, Dad. You always have. Both of you."

"We love you."

"Then leave me alone."

Her parents tried to coax her from her mania, using increments of support that were dwarfed by their lack of understanding. They saw her desk buried beneath notes and old newspaper clippings, and files with headings like NON-FATAL and DRUNK DRIVERS stacked in teetering piles. They saw the magnified image of Thornbury Road taped to the wall, with coloured push-pins marking accident locations. They saw *her* too, of course, having derailed from whatever forward-moving track she'd been riding. Their concern was evident.

"What exactly," her mother sobbed, "are you hoping to find?"

"Connections. Evidence." Faye shrugged. "Maybe a motive."

"But it's a road."

"It kills people."

Her many hours of work were not without reward. She learned that the road claimed its first victim in 1877. Clyde Tummond, forty-three years of age, died of massive internal injuries after being first thrown and then trampled by his horse. Before passing away, he recounted how Dolly, normally so stalwart, had been spooked by a man lurking at the edge of the road – one 'of frightful countenance'. Faye was willing to accept this as a chilling coincidence… and then she uncovered a photograph from 1928. Its subject was a battered Austin Seven lying on its side, with its deceased driver sprawled nearby, covered by a sheet. The caption read, *WEEKEND TRAGEDY. Harold Leggatt, 32, was killed Saturday evening after his vehicle overturned on Thornbury Road*. The photograph was as grainy as one would expect of the era, but the crooked figure standing in a field to the left of the frame was unmistakable.

She searched, then – and with a frantically beating heart – every photo hitherto discovered, studying the periphery for anything she may have missed. She spent further weeks unearthing more photographs, and found three instances of the sideways man. Two were, admittedly, inconclusive – faceless smudges that could be anyone, if not for that crippled stance. One was definite. From a May 1957 copy of the *West Country Voice* (she hadn't found it before because they'd misspelled 'Thornbury'), the grim wreckage of a Ford Anglia wrapped around a tree, with the sideways man hovering in the foreground. He was staring at the camera, perhaps caught off-guard. Looking into his eyes, Faye again found herself laid bare to him, the strands of her life unravelled for him to paw among like a cat.

"Who are you?"

She arranged the photographs on the floor. From 1928 until the most recent: a screen grab of the mangled Astra news footage. She studied the sideways man in each. Never changing. Never aging.

"*What* are you?"

Faye sought reason – an explanation so obvious she would flush with embarrassment. Every lucid argument felt desperate, however... that it wasn't the same man, how *could* it be? Or maybe it was a hoax; photography as fake as that of the Loch Ness Monster. Having exhausted logic, she was left with hypotheses that could only be described as paranormal. She pondered them, and found they had substance. They took root in her mind and grew.

Countless nights were lost to nightmarish thoughts. She envisioned this man – this *creature* – scuttling along Thornbury Road in search of victims. A scourge that spanned generations.

She wondered if every road in Britain had its own sideways man. The idea was ludicrous, but it felt *right*. She couldn't look at a map of the UK without imagining the motorways as arteries, the A- and B-roads as veins, all teeming with infection. A virus in the blood.

"FAYE, SWEETIE, YOU'VE been under a lot of stress lately."

"Don't patronise me, Megan. Just tell me what you see."

Faye had, delicately, taken her findings to her parents, and received the response she expected: a concern so deep it drowned any vestige of open-mindedness. So she called upon her friend, Megan, who deodorised with alum crystals and practised Reiki – an alternative disposition that would, Faye hoped, make her more accepting.

"Car crashes," Megan said, flipping through the photographs that Faye had handed her. "On Thornbury Road, no less. Oh, Faye, what *is* this all about?"

They were in Costa. A quiet Tuesday morning, with few of the tables and chairs occupied, and the occasional sound of the coffee machines grinding and steaming in the background. It was the first time Faye had been anywhere other than the library and Thornbury Road in so long, and she felt self-conscious, decidedly unattractive. She wore a too-big sweater and her hair was greasy. It didn't help that Megan was so pretty, with her swirl of chestnut hair and green eyes, and just a hint of patchouli on her skin.

"Not the crashes," Faye said. "The man. Look at the man."

"Which man?"

Faye pointed out the crooked figure in each photograph, from '28 to '09.

"And?"

"It's the same man," Faye replied.

There was a pause while Megan went through the photographs again, reading the captions, her brow furrowed as she counted the years. She shook her head, set the photos on the table between them, and sipped her rosehip tea.

"Impossible," she said.

"The camera never lies."

"It *can't* be the same person," Megan insisted. "Not with these dates. And honestly, Faye, the pictures are so grainy it's difficult to tell anything for certain. It may not be the same man at all."

"It is."

"Then they're fakes. It's the only explanation."

"I need you to be outside the box on this." Faye sipped her own tea. Twinings Earl Grey. Very normal. "Shouldn't be hard for you."

"I'm listening."

"I've heard you talk about auras and energy signatures. You once said that even inanimate objects have residual energy."

Megan nodded.

"So is it possible for a road to have energy?"

"Yes, of course. Drive down any road where a fatal accident has occurred and it feels... different."

Faye took another sip of tea. Her hand trembled. "A person's energy manifests as an aura. A corona of colour around our bodies. But what if a road's energy – its *evil* energy – manifests as a physical presence? A demon." She tapped the photograph from 1957. The sideways man glared at the camera and his eyes were like probes. "Something cold and hateful. Something that kills."

"It doesn't work like that."

"Outside the box, Megan."

"There *is* no box." Her voice was sharp, touched with impatience. She sipped her tea and the expression in her eyes softened. She reached across the table and patted Faye's hand. "I'm sorry, sweetie, but I can't get behind this line of thinking. It's too negative. And damaging."

Faye tapped the photograph again. "What do you see?"

"It's eerie, yes, but I'm telling you it's not the same man."

"Megan, please."

"You want help from me?" Megan finished her tea, set her mug down too hard, and stood up. "I can recommend an excellent shiatsu practitioner. Failing that, a bottle of Jacob's Creek and a night of hot sex. But all of this..." She waved her hand dismissively over the photographs. "You're still hurting, Faye, and looking for a reason why Timothy died. You're looking for something that doesn't exist."

It did exist, though. Faye had seen it – seen *him* – with her own eyes. Megan had kissed her goodbye and left, and Faye sat for a long moment, feeling both alone and full of resolve. She flipped through the photographs for perhaps the thousandth time. So much twisted metal and spilled blood. But there were no accidents here. There had *never* been an accident on Thornbury Road. The sideways man was responsible for it all. He had killed so many people. He had killed Timothy. And one way or another, she was going to stop him.

THERE WERE THREE lay-bys on Thornbury Road, and she started out parking in one of them and staying there all day, listening to the radio, eating junk food, only getting out if she needed to take a piss in the tall grass.

She waited.

Her rearview and side mirrors were positioned to give her optimum viewing without always having to crane her head. She had 10x42 binoculars with a dandy Mossy Oak camo and the seller on e-Bay said they were the kind used by the SAS. She had 1x26 night vision goggles and sometimes when it got dark she put them on, clambered into a tree where she couldn't be seen, and perched like an owl. She had an elaborate digital camera that she didn't really know how to use, but she could zoom in on a bird's wing from one hundred yards away, and could push the button, which was all she cared about.

She had time.

She waited.

* * *

IT OCCURRED TO her after several weeks of being in one of three places that the sideways man knew her routine, such as it was, and was evading her. She thought she saw him on several occasions – a whisper of something dark in the binoculars, or in one of the mirrors – but by the time she positioned herself for a better look, he (or it) was gone. Maybe just dead leaves lifted by a breeze. Or a large crow taking wing from the hedgerow.

She needed to take him by surprise, which meant rethinking her strategy. Sitting in a car eating pizza wasn't going to get the job done, and she was getting fat, too. No way she could give chase on foot with her stomach bouncing ahead of her, even if he was a cripple. She stopped with the junk food. Switched to raw vegetables and water. She left her aging Mondeo in the Waitrose car park just off the Paisley Wood roundabout, packed a duffel bag with her equipment and supplies, and walked from there. After a few weeks she started to jog. Then run.

She lived in the trees and the long grass, moving stealthily along Thornbury Road, blending in by painting her face and the backs of her hands with green and brown. No one saw her. Not even the deer. She sometimes skulked to within feet of them and they carried on eating leaves, oblivious. During quieter moments she worked on her strength. Sit-ups and push-ups, mainly. At first she could only do three or four of each. By the summer of 2011, eight months after committing to this new way of life, she could do three or four hundred.

She often sat beside the road where Timothy died and talked to him, feeling so desperately alone and with no one else to talk to. She couldn't go to her so-called friends and family. They had no idea what she was going through. And they didn't *want* to know. Not really. Better for them to live in ignorance. Timothy had always been her rock, though. He had always listened, and in doing so could make all the cracks in the world – and there were many – disappear.

"You once told me that I was fragile, like a book is fragile. That it can crumble with age, that its pages can tear and its cover fade. But even so, it remains a thing of beauty and depth.

A limitless treasure that should be shared and remembered. Of all the wonderful things you said in our short time together, this was my favourite. It made me feel... alive."

She wished to hear his voice. Even on the wind. Never did.

"Every breath is a word, and every word has purpose."

She wished to see him again. Just a glimpse. Never did. But one time all the trees around her came to life, flaunting their leaves, and she looked at them with tears in her eyes and pretended it was him.

THE SIGN READ LAND FOR SALE. Faye saw it within an hour of it being posted. By the end of the day someone had slapped a red sticker on top of it and this one read SOLD.

THERE WAS A moment before building commenced on her new house that she really questioned what she was doing. It wasn't the money. Timothy had been paying into a corporate pension since he was sixteen years old, and coupled with a sizable life insurance payout, Faye was able to buy the land and pay for the house outright. Nor was it the fact that she'd be so close to where he died. According to the architect's design, she'd see that strip of Thornbury Road every time she looked out her bedroom window.

It was her parents. Their unending concern. She had told them about the house, showing them the strength in her words and a spine that wasn't cracked at all, yet before she left her father had slipped that sheet of paper into her pocket and she'd found it when she returned home. Dr. Matthew Claridge, MA, MBBS, MRCPsych. That smiling flower. Tears welled in her eyes and she tried to fight them, and then she gave up. She cried deep into the night. Everything hurt.

She had her reasons, yes, but did she really want to live by herself in such a broken part of the world, chasing a shadow? Or did she want to be a smiling flower?

The next few days were spent in indecision. She kept that sheet of paper crumpled in her hand, and on several occasions reached for the phone – even dialled a few numbers before hanging up. She imagined Dr. Matthew Claridge to have a soft voice and a never-ending box of Kleenex that he'd keep on a table between them, and she ached for those comforts. They seemed enough to sway her, and then a cyclist was killed on Thornbury Road and that made fifty-three dead, assuming Clyde Tummond was the first and she hadn't missed any. Fifty-three, including Timothy, who'd told her she was fragile, yet deep, and could make all the cracks disappear.

Faye took a flame to that sheet of paper and watched it burn, and she never saw that smiling flower again.

HER HOUSE WAS built seven months later. Set back from the road, stylish and, though modern, designed to blend with the trees. Faye also had the builders construct a twenty-foot tower in her garden. For bird-watching, she said.

THE CROSSBOW SHE bought had 225lbs of draw weight and, despite her new muscle, she could only cock it with a rope cocking aid. She practised in her garden. To begin with, she couldn't hit a rain barrel from fifty feet away. Within weeks, she could nail an apple from one-eighty.

SHE CAUGHT HIM when the April showers were at their freshest and the evenings had that crisp reminder of the winter passed. She was in her tower, watching the east side of Thornbury Road through the trees. A rustling sound from the blackberry bushes where her land met the edge of Copp Farm. She swept the binoculars in that direction, expecting to see a badger or deer, and there he was, scuttling through the foliage at the side of the road.

She didn't panic. She lowered the binoculars, cocked the crossbow, and lifted it to her shoulder. One second later and his jerky, awkward body filled the sights. She targeted the middle of his forehead. Held her breath.

Pause.

The crossbow had an arrow speed of three hundred and fifty feet per second. The sideways man was a third of that distance away. He'd be dead in the blink of an eye. Too quick. Faye lowered the sights and targeted his crooked right leg. She curled her finger around the trigger.

"Suffer," she said.

He dropped quickly, as if someone had yanked the leafy verge out from under him. He tried to get back up but fell again, and then he started screaming. Faye was halfway to him by that point, sprinting between the trees. When she reached him she saw that the arrow had passed through his leg. He clutched the hole it had left behind, blood flowing between his fingers. His endless eyes were filled with confusion. He pleaded for help and reached for her with one red hand.

She kicked him in the mouth and knocked out three of his teeth. He *still* reached for her, so confused. She kicked him again. Harder. The scream faded on his lips. He fell backwards into the leaves. His body resembled a gnarled branch hit by lightning.

Faye hoisted him onto her shoulder. An uneven weight. A bag of sticks.

She took him to her house.

"You crazy bitch. *Oh, you crazy fucking bitch!*"

Twelve hours later.

Faye had fired one hundred and sixty nails into his left leg. Into his kneecap, his shin, his thigh. Sometimes the nails didn't go all the way in and she had to drive them home with a hammer. After a while he stopped screaming. He fluttered in and out of consciousness. She recharged the gun and fired another one hundred-plus into his right leg. She thought he'd bleed more than he did.

Every now and then she read out the names of all the people who had lost their lives on Thornbury Road. In chronological order, except for Timothy. She saved his name until last. Vivaldi played in the background. Timothy's favourite. He also liked Status Quo, but she didn't think 'Margarita Time' quite fit the mood.

"Crazy... *fucking*..."

Admittedly, Faye was a little surprised to find a wallet in the sideways man's jacket pocket. There was forty-five pounds in cash inside, some credit and store cards. She didn't know what a demon would want with such things. They were props, she reasoned, allowing him to better blend with his current environment. The name on all cards and documentation was the same: Michael Cole. A very normal name. And while it all appeared genuine, it didn't faze her. It didn't stop her.

She selected the handsaw. He hissed and shook his head when he saw it in her hand. His ruined legs twitched, but of course he couldn't move them; they were nailed to the floor. Faye crouched and pressed the jagged blade to his right leg, three inches above the ankle. She started to saw. He passed out when she was halfway through the bone. When he came to – ash-pale and close to death – both severed feet were bundled into his lap.

"No more walking for you," Faye said, setting the saw aside. She was smeared with blood. It was even on her teeth. "Sideways or otherwise."

"Crazy bitch."

She picked up the nail gun, pressed the nose piece to his forehead, and fired two inches of galvanized steel into his brain. He didn't die immediately. His eyes rolled crazily for a little while. Blood trickled from his nose.

Faye walked from the basement, leaving him close to death and with his feet – which had covered so many miles, over so many years – gathered in his lap. She walked from her house and into the pink grapefruit light of early morning. The grass was heavy with dew and the air smelled of new leaves and daffodils. She picked one, then pinched one of its petals between her thumb and forefinger, trying to turn it upwards in a smile. But it only bruised and drooped. A sad face.

MEGAN'S VOICE CHIMED in her mind: *You're still hurting, Faye, and looking for a reason why Timothy died. You're looking for something that doesn't exist.*

Faye saw the sideways man multiple times that day. On a bicycle. Driving a tractor. In nearly every vehicle that passed her on Thornbury Road. She sat in the spot she had come to think of as hers. The place where Timothy had died.

"Does exist," she said.

Her trained ear picked up the rumble of an approaching truck. She counted to ten. Stood up. Looked to her right. The truck – an eighteen-wheeled monster – rounded the bend. She would step in front of it at the optimum moment, giving the driver no chance to brake or steer around her. Not that he would, of course. Faye knew that, in the closing second of her life, she would see his buckled body propped behind the wheel, his timeless eyes reaching deep.

And like him, she would find what she was looking for.

THE CURE

ANIL MENON

*Menon's story echoes one of the earliest road stories there is,
Chaucer's* Canterbury Tales, *with its theme of a spiritual or,
rather, a metaphysical journey. We encounter four travellers,
all heading towards an Indian temple for their own different
reasons. The physical journey is really the least part of the tale,
however. Like the* Canterbury Tales, *the meat of the piece is in
the stories the characters tell each other – and here one story
in particular throws a stark light on the protagonists and their
personal journeys.*

WE HAD ONLY been traveling into the dark for some twenty
minutes but already regret had set in. My back ached, my legs
were cramped. The Toyota Indica could carry a total of four
people comfortably. In a pinch, it could carry five people. I'd
learned shared-taxis in India are always in a state of pinch.
Mrs D'Mello, her daughter Francesca and I were crammed
in the back, the driver, Mani, and his precious cargo were in
front.

Back in LA, Kusum had been studying the Google map.
"Okay, Gabe, the distance from Salem to Dindigul is just over
a hundred miles, so let's say, a hundred-and-twenty miles in all
to reach the Muthuswamy temple. Basically, we're looking at
about two hours by car. If we–"

Then I lost my cell connection. Notwithstanding my wife's brisk, stoutly cheerful tone, I knew she missed me. Kusum always turned aggressively plural. *We'll need to do X. If we take this road Y. We should probably make sure Z.*

Miss you too, cuddly-cakes, I thought. But I'd have to wait till I got back to Chennai or Madurai to tell her that. My American cellphone worked everywhere except where it needed to work. And it wasn't because I was surrounded by tall hills, part of the Palani range in rural Tamil Nadu. The place had nothing to do with it. Everybody and their great-grandmother had a cellphone in this part of the world. Mrs D'Mello and her daughter certainly seemed to have no problem with their connections. I was the primitive here.

The word invoked a twinge of white-guilt. Primitives and heathen cultures, heart of darkness and oriental exoticism. Old toxic frames were hard to replace. I missed Kusum even more. She would tell me I hadn't gotten everything wrong.

I suspected I'd picked the wrong driver. Mani was being so damn careful with his precious – a seat-belted, restrained and amply-padded LED TV set – it was likely the journey would take three, not two, hours. At this rate, we would reach the temple well past 2 AM. Sucked toads.

"Lean back, you'll be more comfortable," said Mrs D'Mello in her motherly manner. "Francesca, shift just a bit, look at how Gabriel is sitting."

"Pasty white thighs squashed together," intoned Francesca, "mid-forties belly bulging shyly over his Ralph Lauren belt, his pink face sweaty with the effort to be amiable, his mind churning–"

"Don't mind her," said Mrs D'Mello, with a very quick flash of teeth. "Francesca, just shift a bit. A little more. Francesca, this is not right. You're not being very nice."

"And whose fault is that?" hissed Francesca.

"No, no, I'm fine," I lied. Pasty white thighs? *What the fuck?* I smiled at Mrs D'Mello, to show I hadn't taken offense. "It's the car's low roof that's the real problem."

"We're lucky to have gotten a taxi, Gabriel," said Mrs D'Mello, looking relieved. "If you hadn't come along, I don't know what we would have done."

"Well, same here. I'm glad it worked out."

Actually, I hadn't been bothered by the sudden railway strike that had grounded all the trains at Salem's famous junction. Perhaps it's always the natives who are thrown by sudden local events; the stranger has fewer illusions. I'd expected to reach Namakkal by four in the morning, relax, get some breakfast, maybe even check out its famous rock temple, where the mathematical genius Ramanujan had supposedly communed with the Goddess Namagiri. I'd wanted to check out this Goddess who was into elliptic integrals and partition functions. I'd planned to hire a taxi to Dindigul later in the morning. When I heard about the strike, I'd figured, no big deal, find a local hotel, get a drink, hunker down for the night, travel onwards the next day.

"Oh, I knew it would work out," said Mrs D'Mello, smiling. "The Good Lord helps those in need. He sent you to us, Gabriel."

"Oh, it's not *God*," said Francesca, in that knowing, notes-to-self tone she used. She tapped her nose. Twice.

Poor girl. I was beginning to see why Mrs D'Mello might have become religious. Still, the God bit made me uncomfortable. I was an evangelical atheist, compelled by my faith to spread disbelief.

Besides, Francesca was right. God had nothing to do with it. Mrs D'Mello had looked totally lost at Salem railway station. Francesca was a pretty twenty-year-old, but a pretty twenty-year-old who clearly had something wrong with her, and there'd been something predatory in the way the just-standing-here types were looking at her. The panic on Mrs D'Mello's face had been impossible to ignore. But as I approached, Francesca folded her arms and turned her back to me. It had almost made me change my mind, walk past them.

However, Mrs D'Mello had been approachable. Perhaps over-approachable. Mrs D'Mello seemed to lack the blanket of suspicion with which most Indian women, quite understandably, seemed to wrap themselves.

"Have you made arrangements to stay once you get to the temple?" I asked.

"Yes, yes. There's a small guest house. My sister's husband knows the local collector. Arrangements have been made. What about you, Gabriel?"

Mrs D'Mello obviously liked saying my name. I already knew quite a bit about her. The D'Mellos now lived in Mumbai, but had migrated from Nevalim in Goa. They had family all over the place. She was proud of her heritage, and far from resenting Portuguese colonialism, she seemed to instinctively understand it had given her the gift, perhaps accidentally, of setting her apart in a country where standing apart was how one belonged to the main.

"Info dump," Francesca had muttered, as her mother outlined a wonderfully complex story of relatives, migrations, family ups and downs.

Francesca was a tall slim girl with a pale face that wouldn't have been out of place in a Victorian sanatorium or in some ruined white mansion overgrown with weeds. She had inherited her mother's hazel eyes, a light green with an admixture of brown. She seemed out of it all, sometimes jerking her head, sharply, once, twice, and at other times standing distracted, head tilted, as if listening.

"I'll be staying with the temple manager," I said. "One of the descendants of the original Muthuswamy. My friend Venkat–"

"You know the manager of the temple!" Mrs D'Mello's hazel eyes gleamed in the car's dimly lit interior. "Gabriel, can you do us one more huge favor and introduce us? It'll mean so much to me and Francesca. There'll probably be lots of people, and I am very worried about not getting enough time at the temple. Oh, dear goodness, you truly are a godsend."

"Sure, I'll do what I can. Not a problem. Must warn you though. It's my friend Doctor Venkateswaran who knows him personally, not me. So I'm not sure how much I can help. How long do you plan to stay there?"

"Two weeks."

"Only?" I was a bit surprised.

Most people stayed for six weeks. Venkat's paper had mentioned some stayed for as long as a year or more. Legend had it that towards the end of his life, Muthuswamy, more or less a nobody in the village, had been able to cure the mentally ill merely through his touch. True or false? It didn't matter. Muthuswamy had died, a temple had been built over his grave, and the legend had become fact.

"We first want to see the conditions," said Mrs D'Mello, and though she smiled, her darting eyes revealed her anxiety. "Who knows? Francesca also has to like the temple."

"There is no Francesca," said Francesca.

Mrs D'Mello smiled, shifted her head slightly to block her daughter's face.

"Venkat told me the place has helped a lot of people over the years." It was awkward to pretend Francesca wasn't there. "But there shouldn't be much of a crowd at the temple. In three months, he observed about thirty visitors. It's not like the Mehandipur Balaji Temple in Rajasthan."

"Oh, we went there." Mrs D'Mello shuddered. "The place is a disgusting shame. Gutters overflowing, people treated like cattle, full of crazy people. I told Francesca, forget it, let's go back to the hotel, this is not for us. I was so upset. Now I see why it didn't work out. We were meant to meet you."

"I don't know about that. But I'm glad we met." I once again marveled at the ecumenical nature of Indian belief. Mrs D'Mello saw nothing paradoxical about relying on a Hindu temple to cure her mentally-disturbed daughter. "It's a nice coincidence."

"Nothing nice about it," muttered Francesca. "Stay tuned, buddy boy."

As Mrs D'Mello put a warning hand on her daughter's arm, Mani suddenly pulled over to the side of the road.

"What's the matter, Mani?" I asked, in Tamil. Then noticing Francesca's inexplicable terror, I added, "Such sudden stops, please consider there are ladies in the car."

Mani didn't bother to reply. He got out, went around the front of the car, opened the passenger seat. Tug, check, adjust padding, close door. There was something obsessive, even crazed, about the way he worried about the TV. When he'd agreed to take us to Dindigul, he'd been really taking the damn TV to Dindigul.

Mani got back in and started the engine.

"Mani, I don't think you take such good care of your child even," I joked, again in Tamil.

Mani half-turned his head, and I caught the gleam of a gap-toothed smile. "Sir, all this is to take care of my child only. From where did you learn such pure Tamil?"

From Kusum. But I didn't want to discuss my wife. It would merely reinforce the fact I wouldn't get to see her for another three, maybe four, months.

"A previous life, from where else, Mani? Now tell me, why this comedy with the wretched TV?"

"Aiyyo, not a comedy sir, a complete tragedy. My whole life is a tragedy." Mani launched into a Father India saga, complete with floods, bandits, item numbers, countless taxi rides, two deeply cherished daughters. The younger daughter had fallen ill, the older daughter's in-laws had paid for her care, she'd died nonetheless, and now the in-laws wanted their money back. Or a large Samsung LED TV. They'd sent the older sister back to demonstrate their seriousness. Seven months had passed, she had to be sent back, Mani was desperate to send his daughter back before things really spun out of control.

Once, such a story would have made me furious. But after twenty years as an economist, after twelve years with Kusum, I had become a little smarter. Mani's actual life probably didn't bear much resemblance to the story. Indians used stories to hide themselves. Every living inch of this world was barnacled with stories. The stories said one thing, meant another.

The legend of the Goddess Namagiri was a case in point. The mathematician Ramanujan may have credited her for his brilliant intuitive leaps, but in myth, she was wedded to

Vishnu's fourth incarnation, Narasimha, the Lion That Devours All Categories, also Indian logic's traditional term for extreme skepticism.

At one point, as Mani described his daughter's death, Francesca shook with silent laughter. It was unlikely she was understanding a word of Mani's Tamil, so it had to be the driver's dramatic inflections and gestures. I decided to ignore it. But Mrs D'Mello didn't. With an almost absent-minded motion, she drew her daughter's head downwards to rest against her shoulder. Francesca quietly acquiesced. The Madonna pose did something funny to my heart.

I wished I had recorded Mani's story. My aching body, the Indica's cramped interior, the alert hazel eyes of the anxious woman next to me, the pale repose of her troubled daughter, the unexpectedly smooth road, the indifferent darkness streaming by our mobile campfire of a billion years: the only witness of this moment would be my unreliable memory.

"Liar," whispered Francesca, her eyes still closed.

"What is the driver saying?" asked Mrs D'Mello, anxiously. "Does he want more money? Is there a problem?"

"No, no. He was telling me about his daughter." I gave in and sank back into my seat. My thigh pressed solidly, indecently, against Mrs De'Mello's thigh, but I simply couldn't care anymore. "Sorry, Mrs D'Mello."

She patted my hand. "What are you doing here, Gabriel?"

"Info dump. Dimensionalize character."

I'd become used to Francesca's little outbursts. And I was dimly beginning to understand the pulsing, black, tentacled nightmare in which she lived.

"I'm here for a project. I do a lot of contract work for World Bank. I'm an economist. I'm looking at community-based palliative care. My wife, Kusum, she makes documentaries. Educational, inspirational stuff. Kind of a mix between TED talks for villagers and short movies. She was making a documentary and I got interested in the topic. I have a team in Bangalore, we're studying palliative care, and we're excited because we think it's going to be at least as big as microfinancing. Mental health care" – I didn't glance at Francesca – "doesn't scale well, so it's costly, at least in the US, and when I read Venkat's paper on the Muthuswamy temple, I thought I'd come check it out and see if we should set up a data collection unit here. So that's why I'm here."

After I'd finished, a small silence filled the cab. It was one of the reasons I resisted explanations of what my wife and I did. Our project-driven lives offered little purchase for those with real careers. But even if Mrs D'Mello had nothing to say, Francesca did.

"Your wife," she said, hesitantly, "Kusum, she's a movie director?"

Mrs D'Mello's face broke into a delighted smile. I took it to mean that by speaking to me directly, Francesca had just paid me a huge compliment.

"Kusum's a lot of things. She works with small budgets, so she's whatever she needs to be." I laughed, remembering. "Once, she even roped me in to act."

"She made you act?"

"Yes."

"In a movie?"

"Well, an educational movie." I couldn't see what Francesca was getting at.

"It had a story?"

"Oh, yes." I smiled. "I played an evil western capitalist. British, of course. She made me sport these ginormous sideburns and say things in a villainous Hindi. My Hindi is pretty good, actually."

"Was there a Gabriel the Economist in that world?"

"Pardon?"

"In the story world, was there an economist dude called Gabriel who's into saving brown people?"

"Francesca!" Mrs D'Mello managed to smile apologetically and bark at her daughter at the same time.

"No, it's all right. It's a good question. You're asking about metafiction, aren't you Francesca? I'm afraid it was just a straightforward morality play. And I wasn't trying to save brown people. Quite the opposite. But my evil plans are foiled by plucky villagers led by a brave maiden who'd studied economics and played by none other than my lovely wife. Kusum made me gnash my teeth at the end. It's harder than you'd think."

"So there's no Gabriel the economist?"

"Nope. It wasn't relevant."

"Oh, but it is. Your wife played an economist? If Gabriel the economist isn't there, it means all the papers which cite your work aren't there. Ditto for the economists who wrote those papers. Do you think Adam Smith would exist in that world? So how can your wife play an economist? *The Butterfly Effect*, have you seen it?"

I waggled my hand. "Interesting point. But not necessarily. In an alternate world—"

"Have you seen the movie?"

"*Butterfly Effect*? No. Ashton Kutcher is in it, right?"

"No. Some guy who looks just like Ashton Kutcher. Weird thing is, no one tells him, oh, my god, you look exactly like the famous actor Ashton Kutcher. There are no Ashton Kutcher fans in that movie. Or take the *Silence of the Lambs*. I watched it thrice. I think I watched it thrice. I am told to say I think I watched it thrice." She jerked her head, twice, as if shaking off a restraining hand. Then she resumed. "No one tells Hannibal Lecter, man, you look just like the actor Anthony Hopkins. The FBI doesn't think that's relevant, for some reason. For that matter, no one's bothered that the FBI agent looks like Jodie Foster. Nobody's going, isn't this bizarre, we have an FBI agent who looks just like Jodie Foster going to interview a master criminal who looks just like Anthony Hopkins."

"Well, you got to suspend disbelief."

"Or else what? The characters will realize they are just characters?"

"*The Truman Show* did tackle this topic."

"No it didn't! The movie is a joke. Truman doesn't ask why he resembles Jim Carrey. It doesn't occur to him even once. He pretends he's living in a world without Jim Carrey." She jerked her head. "He continues to pretend he's not Jim Carrey even after he realizes his whole life is fake. Why does he do that?"

"It's just a movie," I said, helplessly. "Kusum is the literary one. She's hip to these postmodern twizzlers. I'll intro you two once I get back to Chennai."

"She doesn't even exist, you poor fool."

"Oh, Francesca," said Mrs D'Mello, sounding exhausted, "please don't start. Don't bother Gabriel. Go to sleep, be a good girl now."

Francesca's face underwent an extraordinary range of expressions. It was strangely inhuman to watch someone shift from rage to fright to humor to doubt to sorrow. My heart went out to the girl.

"I'm the only sane person in this car. But nothing is mine, not even silence." Francesca's voice trailed away and she once again rested her head on her mother's shoulder.

Mrs D'Mello turned to me. "You can't win arguing with her, you'll only go mad. I've tried everything. She's tried everything, poor baby. So many doctors, they just reduce her to a vegetable, that's all. I'm praying the temple will help. God doesn't care about religion. Didn't Jesus help the Canaanite woman? People get cured in the temple, don't they, at the temple? What do you believe, Gabriel?"

What could I say? I nodded. I tried to imagine Francesca's life and failed. She was being consumed by the Lion That Devoured All Categories. It wasn't wise to approach the beast.

I felt the car hit a stone, shudder. I instinctively grabbed for something, felt living hands grasp my own. The LED TV lurched, threatened to slip free; it was safe enough, but Mani extended his left hand to stabilize it. The car turned savagely to the right, again hit something, a grinding metallic sound, hung suspended for a terrible second, started to fall, over the side of the hill, gently, such a long hopeless fall, the fall of all doubts, all hopes, all sins, all plans, until only one crystal clarity remained: it was over. Yet my mind wouldn't let go. I sensed my mind cry out for Kusum. Kusum, Kusum, beloved wife, my Kusum. I began to weep. Francesca's hazel eyes, luminous in the forest of screams. She was cradling her mother, smiling.

"Don't worry, Gabriel," I heard Francesca say. Or was it another? And we fell.

THROUGH WYLMERE WOODS

SOPHIA MCDOUGALL

Readers familiar with Sophia McDougall's story, 'Mailer Daemon', in Magic *(Solaris, 2012) will be delighted to encounter two old friends here, though both stories stand alone. This is both a prequel and an origins story, an exploration of Morgane and Levanter-Sleet's complex relationship. The road here acts as a conduit for power and a path into the unknown. McDougall writes brilliantly about empowerment and identity, making 'Through Wylmere Woods' an extraordinarily heartfelt story about a journey into self-discovery.*

CHAINSAWS ARE SHRIEKING against the sky as she runs into the woods. It sounds as though the road crew are somehow suspended in mid-air, their blades carving out blocks of cloud, rather than down here biting into oak. Even when she's stopped sobbing, curled up and hidden at the base of a tree, the roar almost drowns the usual sounds of Wylmere Woods. The birdsong, the noise of the stream, and the woman's voice she sometimes hears chattering and yelling in the water, the whispering among the leaves.

This isn't the first attempt at escape, but it is the most premeditated. This time she has supplies: inside her school backpack there is a change of jeans and underwear, *Tales of the*

Round Table, her sewing kit, embroidery silks and some stolen swatches of velvet, an art-deco hair slide, a packet of fig rolls, and a twenty pound note from her mother's purse, which she hopes should pay for the bus fare to London.

Her seeing stone is clutched in her hand in case she needs it, but for the time being it seems safest not to use it. It's always a difficult balance: the things are blurry and indistinct when she doesn't use it; she can't always see what they're up to, but it's also easier to pretend she hasn't noticed them. A lot of things know when they're being looked at and get much more interested in her, and much more dangerous when she puts the hole in the stone to her eye.

She uncurls, cautiously, but carefully avoids looking up, or forward, or at anything. Around her, shadows leap and rattle. Rust-coloured wings twitch overhead. Eyes blink at her in the dark places between roots. But there will be things in London too. Perhaps the things here would get used to her in time, and she could live among them here, eating berries and mushrooms, like people in stories.

But you would have to eat an awful lot of berries to actually get full. And there never seem to be any berries in Wylmere Woods.

She is aware all the time that what's really going to happen is that she will be found and brought back to the house, and everything will be even worse. She's thirteen, she can't pass for any older (in fact the idea of passing for, *being,* older makes panic boil in her gut). Thirteen-year-olds do not actually succeed in running away to seek their fortunes. They cannot actually start embroidery businesses in London, or live off the land in the forest. It's pathetic she's even trying, running away with her stupid King Arthur picture book; it's like something a six-year-old would do.

Nevertheless, she puts her hand into the backpack and draws out the flapper-girl hair slide. It's beautiful, real mother of pearl, it must be seventy years old. She found it in a box in one of the shut-up rooms they can't afford to heat or clean. It might be worth a lot of money, but not enough to actually repair the roof or pay off the mortgage, so she hasn't told anyone about it. She's never worn it outside her bedroom before, but until they catch her, she might as well escape as fully as she can, for as long as she can. Her father has taken to growling about how long her hair is getting, but as actually getting it cut is supposed to be her mother's job, it hasn't happened. She parts her hair on one side, and pushes the slide in beside her temple, enjoying the little glow of tension on her scalp. She still doesn't let her eyes focus too precisely, but she lifts her head with something like defiance, wipes her eyes and plods onwards through the woods.

There's a banner spread between trees, sagging a little under the weight of rain. It reads, 'THE END OF THE ROAD'.

There are people in the trees. Human people, who are obviously not aware of the shadows that crawl and leap in the undergrowth, the eyes. Trees festooned with people like Christmas baubles stand like wayposts all along the imaginary line that is the route of the A3012 through Wylmere Woods. They're singing into the rain.

The line is the shortest possible route to Delchester, that's why it's there. From Delchester, she might be able to get to London.

"Hello."

There's a girl, maybe a year older than her, chained to an ash tree like a maiden sacrifice left for a dragon. She doesn't have quite the desperate, martyred expression suitable to her position, however. She looks matter-of-fact and slightly bored. She's wearing khaki combat trousers; her blonde hair, knotted messily with coloured thread and beads, straggles over a rainbow jumper.

"Are you here to join in?"

She hesitates. She's been ambivalent about the new road so far. Her mother has decided the A3012 cannot come soon enough, it is the valve from which their revived fortunes are waiting to burst. It will bring a flood of day trippers who will pay to visit the gardens, and buy tea and sandwiches in the cafe she wants to set up in the gatehouse. George and her father are both against it, but for reasons the protesters would probably not find sympathetic.

As one would expect, the things in the woods are against the road. Is she on their side? She can tell they're agitated, even when she's not looking at them, she can sense the jaggedness in their movements, the flashes of disorder they leave in the air. The wood-things are not benevolent, but nor have they ever actually harmed her, which is much more than can be said for the things in the house.

And maybe if she stays and doesn't talk much, she'll be absorbed into the protesters and they'll forget she wasn't there all along and take her with them when they leave. It's like running away with the gypsies, only more modern. *My mother said I never should play with the gypsies in the wood,* she thinks, with a small thrill.

"Yes," she decides.

"What's your name?" asks the maiden sacrifice.

She ducks her head and wishes after all she'd left the slide in the bag. What must she look like? She thinks of the names she sometimes whispers in front of the mirror at home, *Vivien, Lynette, Rhiannon,* but what if she says one of them aloud and the girl laughs? She is too cowardly to do anything but mutter the horrible truth so quietly it won't be heard.

"What?"

She mumbles it again. All that's audible is a breathed half-syllable "*...tin...*"

"Christine?"

Warmth floods her chest. Though she's dressed in shapeless jeans and an old blue jumper of George's under her mac, though there's nothing but the slide in her hair to say she isn't a boy, this girl has looked at her and seen a possible Christine. It's not a name she particularly likes, there's no resonance in it, but it's infinitely better than her real one. She thinks of St Christina the Astonishing, and the name becomes more palatable still. She can be Christine if it means she can stay.

She grins helplessly and nods.

"I'm Amber," says the maiden sacrifice.

"Do I have to be chained to a tree too?" asks Provisionally-Christine. It doesn't seem safe. The wood-things might not realise they're not really being sacrificed to them.

Amber shrugs. "Don't you want to?"

Provisionally-Christine looks up at the people perched impossibly high in the canopy, the walkways strung between boughs, the treehouses. "Can I get up there?"

"Are you sure? We're not very health and safety. We haven't got enough hard hats. And some people are scared of heights."

"I don't mind. It looks really cool up there."

"Okay. I can't get out of these chains without help."

Christine scrutinises her. "Can't you? What happens when you need the loo?"

"We thought the pigs would've come by now," says Amber philosophically. "I'm bursting for a pee, actually. Give us a hand."

There doesn't seem to be a key to Amber's chains, all she can do is yank at them until Amber manages to wriggle out from underneath. She scurries off into the undergrowth and comes back, still hitching up her combat trousers.

"So, are you here with your folks, or what?" she asks. Christine is dismayed to find herself torn between admiration and vague disapproval of the casual Americanism. Her parents are not anybody's folks.

"They don't know I'm here."

"What, you just walked here on your own?" Amber considers briefly. "Cool." She leads Christine over to a tall oak which supports a small village of platforms and tarpaulin, and yells amiably at a man with dreadlocks. "Jed, can you get me and Christine up to Lothlorien?"

Christine, charmed by the name, tries not to be too pleased at how easily Amber says 'me and Christine', like it's normal, as if she's meant to be there.

"You ought to have a hard hat, we don't need any more trouble," fusses Jed vaguely, but he seems to feel that he's done his duty by having said that, so he helps Christine into a rope sling and hoists her swiftly into the tree.

She sits on the edge of a platform, her legs dangling. The tree breathes and sighs around her. She feels weightless, as if she's part of the lacework of branches, as if she's left her awful body down on the ground.

Amber scrambles up beside her and says "What music are you into?" Christine almost answers *Chopin,* but just in time says, "Radiohead."

Amber smiles approval and says, "I like Supergrass."

Christine can see the empty space the A3012 has already gnawed into Wylmere Woods, an invisible worm with chainsaws for teeth, crawling through the valley. There's an encampment on the ground at its nearest edge, more banners and signs rising to greet it.

"It's awful, isn't it?" says Amber. "We were down there overnight planting acorns in it, but..." She shrugs. She has, Christine realises, no expectation that the protest will actually succeed. Christine is saddened, but it's a bright, enlivening sadness that sings in her chest. She says a silent prayer in her head to St Jude, the patron saint of Lost Causes and her favourite. Christine looks above the scar in the valley, up to the wooded ridge the A3012 won't touch. There's something strange up there; a quiver in the air that says *Things,* but something else...

A tall pine tree among many. But when you look straight at it, you realise the trunk is a column of steel, spray-painted brown, the branches are green metal fins, arranged in too-tidy circles to disguise the array of antenna.

It's the mobile phone mast they put up last year.

Christine puts her stone to her eye and looks at it.

"What's that?" Amber asks.

"It's a seeing stone." She's never said this before, to anyone. She thinks of telling the story of how she found it on the beach when she was ten, the chilly glow it gave off even before she saw the hole in it, but decides that's going too far.

"You should show it to Mum," says Amber, indicating a woman in jeans and a damp purple velvet top, bisected by a bulging utility belt. "She's a white witch."

Amber's Mum is called Rachel. She tramps over, introduces herself and looks kindly at Christine's stone. "Oh, are you interested in Wicca? You want quartz or beryl for scrying. Though of course, you can make do with a bowl of water."

Christine tries to keep her eyebrows from rising. "Can you see that?" she asks mildly, nodding at the mobile phone tower.

Viewed through the stone, the mast wavers and shimmers as if obscured by a heat haze that thickens into a boiling black column, fraught with electric quivers. From within it a pair of brilliant lights glower out over the trees.

She's never seen a Thing living in something so modern.

"See what?" asks Rachel.

The eyes in the blackness meet hers and she puts the stone down quickly. "Never mind."

Rachel is certainly not a witch. But she passes Christine a thermos of cocoa, so Christine doesn't hold it against her.

Rain soaks her hair. Bulldozers and cherrypickers are crawling closer from the edge of the scar, flanked by men in acid yellow jackets. There are terrible shouts from people on the ground, dragged out of the machines' path. "Save our trees!" a man with a megaphone is booming from a sycamore fifty yards away. "Save our trees!"

She starts shouting along.

"Eruga!" shouts Rachel, instead.

"It's a Celtic battle cry," Amber explains.

"Eruga!" echoes Christine, who thinks she has never been so happy in her life.

THE DAYS ARE still short. The yellow-jackets have dragged or chased off everyone on the ground they can and have settled into a siege around the foot of the tree by the time the sky darkens. Some men in blue boiler suits have scaled one of the other camps, but the protesters fled across highwires and are now catcalling their foes from other trees, though they look colder and wearier now.

But the chainsaws have advanced. The vanguard of the A3012 is closer now, its progress laid out in white, raw stumps.

The wood-things are getting very anxious now. They trample and lash out in the undergrowth. Christine saw a man carried away by the police, blood pouring from his head. Amber huddles against Rachel's side, pale-faced, while Rachel exclaims at the brutality.

"I don't think it was the police," says Christine. She wishes she hadn't, afterwards. Amber looks at her oddly.

She doesn't want to do it, with Amber looking at her like that, but the case is urgent: she begins drawing a pattern on the platform in chalk, a complex labyrinth of lines and pathways, like a fingerprint. Sand or flour or salt would be better, but even if she had any, it would all blow away up here.

"Is that a *spell*?" asks Amber. Her tone sounds, if only very faintly, unnerved and censorious; presumably this is not the kind of spell Rachel does. Christine knows it's not a very good spell, having made it up through trial and error. She has no idea if there are better ways out there. All she knows is that *sometimes,* drawing a certain kind of pattern and thinking about it in a certain kind of way, letting her attention run through it like the silver ball in a maze puzzle, *sometimes* holds off bad things, when praying to St Jude or St Monica doesn't.

(Praying to God or the Virgin never works at all.)

The pattern is not like a protective wall around them – how she wishes that were possible – it's more like a camp fire to ward off midges, and in this case it doesn't seem to be working. No matter how carefully she tries to pour her mind into the gullies and whorls, she remains aware that the thing up on the ridge is moving. It separates itself from the phone mast, organising itself into something crudely bipedal, and comes striding down the valley, condensing as it walks so that in the blackness she catches glimpses of its inner structure: bones, claws, teeth. Christine clenches her fists – the thing is heading for *her,* she knows. She hunches lower over the pattern, whittling her attention away from everything outside it; she senses rather than hears Amber whispering something to Rachel but does not look up–

"Oh, sweetie," Rachel says. "Don't your parents know where you are? It's been lovely having you here, but you'd better go home."

Christine draws her knees up under her chin and doesn't take her eyes from her chalk pattern.

The thing is beside the tree now. It glowers down at her, curious. The chainsaws and loudspeakers blare below.

It's still better than the house. "I want to help stop the road," she says.

"It's fantastic that you're so passionate, but you know you can't stay here overnight all by yourself."

"I'm not all by myself."

"Your parents must be worried sick. Where *do* you live?"

Christine shrugs again, gestures vaguely, coughs a monosyllable. She knows that pretending she doesn't know the answer to questions she doesn't like isn't a very good strategy, but it's all she has.

"You can come back tomorrow," offers Amber, relenting.

"Yes! Give us a call tomorrow," Rachel soothes. She takes out a mobile phone, and a little notepad and pencil from her utility belt. Christine looks up, slightly interested. (The thing is still staring, but isn't doing anything to hurt her). No one she knows has a mobile phone apart from George. His is more modern, a little bit smaller and it has a cover at the bottom you can flip open. He takes transparent pride in flipping it open.

"Need it for organising," says Rachel.

Then a voice bulls its way through the mess of sounds. It's hard to gauge whether it's really as loud as it seems to Christine, but to her it's already the grind of the chainsaws. It's shouting her real name.

She freezes, panicked,

George has grabbed one of the loudspeakers and her name blasts up at the tree as if flung from a flamethrower.

"*QUENTIN!*" George bellows. "Quentin, get down from there at once."

It's physically painful. She feels the blush seeping across her skin like a spilled acid. She shrinks on herself, helplessly. Rachel and Amber are looking at her, baffled, reassessing her face, her flat chest, her jaw-length hair.

"Is he talking to *you*?" asks Amber, as Rachel says "*What* did he call you?"

"Quentin, am I going to have to come up there and boot you down?" George roars up at the tree, a trace of angry laughter in his voice now. She knows without looking there's a little crowd now, of police, cutters, stewards and even some of the protesters. "I will if I have to."

She can't answer Amber and Rachel, she can hardly even breathe. She stares into the bright eyes of the Thing and thinks for an instant of hurling herself down from the treehouse; maybe the drop would be enough to kill her, maybe the dark thing would *catch* her.

Instead she reaches in silence with damp and shaking hands for the harness, slides into it with her eyes half-shut, and someone lowers her down into the grimy heat of the onlookers' attention. Once on the ground, she lurches, her legs won't stop shaking.

George grasps her shoulder. Her brother is only nineteen, but somehow the image of himself at forty: hearty and pink with immunity to doubt, his chestnut hair as solid as his firmly-packed flesh.

She sees his eyes go to the slide she'd been too dizzy with horror to remove. "What the fuck is this?" he demands, yanking it out along with a clump of hair.

"...playing," whispers the child.

"Playing at being a poof," says George, resoundingly, flinging the slide into the undergrowth without noticing what it is. "Come on, for God's sake, you've made enough of a spectacle of yourself."

He doesn't let go of her arm, even though it must be obvious she's not going to run away; sinking to the ground is more of a risk. He reaches into his pocket with his free hand and pulls out his mobile.

"Hello, mother," he says into it. "I've found him."

GEORGE DRAGS HER, shaking and sobbing, to the pitted track that is for now the only road through Wylmere Woods, packs her into the ancient Range Rover, and drives her home.

"Father's talking to the BBC," says George. "They'll be sorry they missed your performance. Why don't you give them an encore?"

Quentin stares at silvery trails of rain on the windscreen and says nothing.

"Go on, Queenie, give us a turn."

Queenie is his favourite name for her, though he has others – Fifi, Lulu – always names that carry a vaguely dated impression of jutting bosoms and frills and high-kicks. She can see those things in the names although she doesn't know why they are there.

Somehow George has always *known*, even when she didn't herself.

They round the turn of the drive and their home emerges from the copper beeches. Quentin has never found Wylmere Hall easy to look at; lacking the blandly even surfaces of brick or cut stone, the untamed flint rubble sparks dangerously at certain angles of light. It is too transparently an assemblage of fragments, on the point of flying apart. Even though, as their father never tires of telling people, it has been here a very long time indeed.

In every season but the depths of winter, it always seems to be colder inside than out.

No one is waiting for them in the kitchen, except the plaster-pale and twitching Thing on the ceiling, so she twists free of George and runs.

The house is dark. They are trying to save money on electricity and gas, and the light bulbs in the Long Gallery are all dead anyway. It's too dark for her to *see* the Things, beyond a horrid peripheral impression of shifting and shuffling; clicks and titters that remain, for now, on the edge of hearing.

There's a slice of light under the door to the library, though, and a rumble of voices from within. It's not surprising her father has chosen to be interviewed in there, even though they've sold all the important books. The stained glass windows with the family's coat of arms are still there.

"They can't buy something that isn't for sale," Sir Randall Sacheverell-Lytton is saying. "I haven't touched a penny of their filthy money and I won't. *All* these people are trespassing, *none* of them have the right to be there. Neither the hooligans with the chainsaws *nor* these hippies with the silly hats; they're not there out of altruism, you know; what they really want is to be able to wander in and build wigwams and so on whenever they like. But I've been here five hundred years."

He has a way of saying that, as though he has actually lived all that time.

Something slides up her ankle, snags and scratches at her shin under the denim, and she trips, falling headlong on the uneven floorboards, with a crash that echoes through the house.

Her father bursts out of the library into the gallery: George a little scaled up, large and red, giving off a dangerous glow like heated iron. "For God's sake, what are you doing now?"

Quentin stares past her father at the woman from the local BBC news, hoping her father will remember she's there. The woman is poised in a shoulder-padded suit, her expression curious, her hair preternaturally shiny. He won't go too far in front of her, she hopes.

It works, at least for now. Randall growls only, "Idiot boy. If your mother ends up in a mental ward..." and slams back inside.

She hurtles onwards, towards her room. She hopes it's just possible that the television people will have effectively distracted her family to the point of their forgetting her escape – her mother might be lying in a stupor that will last till morning. She skids to a stop on the landing and stands paralysed, because the grand staircase offers a quicker route, but the darkness hanging in the stairwell is so thick and grimy and she's afraid to breathe it. She turns at last to the servants' staircase, where the electric lights are still bright on peeling white paint, but it takes longer, this way, gives the things more time to notice her presence.

It had been very bad, the night before. An hour or so after midnight, she'd run down to the kitchen and returned with a bag of flour. It was an hour and a half before she'd completed the pattern filling the floor of her room, and another hour before she'd charged it with attention enough that the things drew back and quietened a little, enough to buy her a couple of hours of sleep.

Randall or George would have just thought it was a mess, a stupid game; her mother knows, unfortunately, exactly what it is. She'd hoped for at least a few days, maybe enough time to think of something better, before anyone found it.

Cecily Sacheverell-Lytton is sitting on her bed, straight-backed, swathed in a moth-eaten cardigan and a Liberty scarf, waiting for her. Her eyes are unfocused, her fine cheekbones streaked with trickles of mascara, a chapped bluish stain on her full lower lip. "For all I knew, you'd been taken by paedophiles," she says.

At some point during the day she's kicked her foot through the pattern, ruining it, but hasn't actually cleaned up the flour. A hoover stands beside her.

Quentin does not have anywhere further to shrink inside herself, any deeper recesses of silence.

And now they know; they know she tried to scare them off and then she ran and now she's back, the whole houseful of things know, she can feel it.

"What happened to you?" Cecily asks. "You were so good. You used to be such a sweet little boy."

Quentin looks at the wreckage, and can't think of anything to do but offer part of the truth. "It's the only thing that helps, Mummy," she says.

Cecily springs up and seizes her by the shoulders with painful force "Help!" she cries. "It *helps* to bring this filth into our home? You're going to clean that up." She's almost screaming. "You're going to clear up every *grain* of it, and then we're going to *pray* for you."

She crushes Quentin close. She smells of stale Chanel No. 5, red wine and sweat. She doesn't wait for Quentin to clear up the pattern to begin praying.

"Spirit of our God, Father, Son and Holy Spirit, Most Holy Trinity, descend upon me," she says. "Purify me, mould me, fill me with yourself, and use me."

Quentin frees herself with some difficulty and turns on the hoover, but she can still hear Cecily, chanting under its drone.

"Banish from me all spells, witchcraft, black magic, malefice, maledictions and the evil eye; diabolic infestations, oppressions, possessions; all that is evil and sinful."

"It doesn't *work*," she says mutinously. If anything, the pressure gathered around the room is getting worse. She wonders if it's evidence of her spiritual sickness that she's often suspected that praying to St Jude (lost causes) or Monica (abandoned maidens) does sometimes help, only because the saints are really just a different kind of Thing.

She didn't mean to be heard, but Cecily lunges at her again, dragging the hoover from her hand and knocking it, still whirring, to the ground.

"Because you *don't want it to!*" Cecily wails, "You *want* the darkness. Why are you like this, what *are* you?"

As if Quentin ever stops thinking about that question.

Cecily whirls out of the room, weeping. "I can't *do* this!" And Quentin looks at herself. She's always both tempted to and afraid to, whenever she's near a mirror – it's hard to resist the dread things will be worse than last time she looked, the lunatic hope that somehow they'll be better. *What are you?* She feels the urge to strip off her clothes and punish herself with the search for thickening hair, coarsening flesh. But she can barely see her outline in this dim light, under the mirror's velvet coat of dust.

The dust thickens as she looks at it.

The things in the house are not really ghosts, she is sure. But some of them are mimics. Their thuds and bangs caricature Randall's heavy-footed stride, they warble in the Long Gallery in parodies of Cecily's sobbing, and sometimes there are traces of others she hasn't known, horribly human turns of expression or tones of laughter that she suspects must have belonged to long-dead Sacheverells and their servants, priests, persecutors.

The shape in the mirror is her size, her shape, but the wisps of dust and cobweb stir around it in a mocking suggestion of skirts and floating hair. The face that grins back at her has a child's proportions, the skin knotted and puckered in on itself under the dust.

"*Mould me, fill me with yourself, and use me...*" echoes the thing, in a piping, little-girl lisp, as it drifts from the surface of the glass.

"Please, don't," she says, though she knows it's no use.

It crams itself inside her and stays there.

POSSESSIONS, INFESTATIONS. THEY'RE not the way Cecily thinks they are. When you can't hold them off any longer and they get inside you, things don't actually make you *do* anything (she shudders – not yet, anyway). They're just there, smearing themselves over every thought, burrowing into every crevice you most want hidden. The thing presses dirty hands against her from the inside.

She doesn't know why the word *she* slides weightlessly over her skin like silk while *he* constricts and rubs like hemp rope. She doesn't know if it has anything to do with the things (the *demons*, she admits wretchedly in her head, and hears the creature inside giggling approval at her), but she's certain Cecily would tell her it is. It's an aspect of infestation, a sign of the ruin of her – *his* – soul.

She can feel the thing sucking a little filthy nourishment from her, but not enough to kill her. Not fast, anyway. She sleeps, dreams of rotting flesh falling in clumps from her bones, and the boys from school chasing her naked through the mud of Wylmere Woods, while chainsaws roar.

AT BREAKFAST, CECILY isn't speaking to her, though when Randall grumbles, "When are you going to get that boy's hair cut?" she does snap, "*Soon,*" so at least she hasn't gone as far this time as pretending Quentin doesn't exist at all.

Quentin stirs cereal, trying to kindle up the energy to lift the spoon to her mouth. There's a constant taste of rot and dust in the back of her throat.

THEY ARE GOING to be installing the World Wide Web at Wylmere Hall today. "The *Information Superhighway,*" says Cecily reverently, whenever she mentions it. A man from the village is going to help her build something called a site or a page for Wylmere Hall. And this will bring in the money to repair the roof and heat the rooms and send Quentin to Ampleforth instead of the local comp.

"But *how* does it make money?" asks Randall.

"People will be looking for ideas for days out," says Cecily. "We're going to take them on a *virtual tour* of the house."

"And then they'll come charging here up that road. That's the plan, is it?"

"*Yes,*" says Cecily. She stares fiercely at her bowl for a moment. "If you would only take that money...!"

"It's all a fantasy, you know," Randall says. He looks around the table, as if for agreement, as if expecting more people than are actually seated there.

Cecily says nothing.

"First prize, a day at Wylmere Hall!" says Randall darkly. "Second prize, two days at Wylmere Hall."

Cecily lays down her spoon with a sharp little clink. "You constantly undermine me."

"There's a lot of people making money in dot-coms," says George.

Cecily talks much more about dot-coms and much less about malefices or the evil eye in front of Randall or George. There's an awful intimacy in the fact she only really shows that side of herself to Quentin.

Quentin dreams vaguely about the Information Superhighway, imagines climbing inside the computer in her mother's study and blazing away down a road made of light.

THE HOLIDAYS WILL be over soon. She wonders if the thing will accompany her, whether it'll let her go each day at the gates and wait to greet her when she returns home. She'll have to let Cecily get her hair cut soon, or school will be even worse.

She says nothing, she acts as much like everyone else as she can, but so many of the boys are like George; they seem to *know*.

Five more years, she thinks. In five years, it'll be over, she'll be able to go wherever she wants.

In five years it will be 2003 and the world may very well have ended.

In five years she might look like George.

She sprawls listlessly in the drawing room, staring at *The Round Table*, but turning the pages is so hard and it makes no difference to anything when it's done. The chainsaws screech in the distance. "It'll be like that all the bloody time when that road's built," says Randall, stomping through. For a moment he looks desolate. He's not supposed to admit it's going to happen.

She heaves herself up and picks up the phone. There's a weird trilling full of clicks and whistles, which unnerves her before she realises it must be to do with the Information Superhighway. Evidently it stops the phone working.

In the same moment she sees George's mobile lying abandoned on the sofa, and on impulse grabs it and runs back to her room and dials.

"What?" says Rachel. "Who is this? You're breaking up."

You're breaking up, agrees the thing.

But at last Rachel works out who she is and what she wants, and Amber's voice comes on the line. "Is that... Quentin?"

She manages an affirmative cough. There's a long, oppressive pause.

"So, you're actually a boy?"

She steels herself. Makes herself breathe, "Yes."

"Wow. I mean, wow. I really thought you were a girl," Amber marvels. "Do you... often do that? Pretend?"

"Kind of."

"So, is it like a gay thing, or something? I mean, that's fine, if you are, but the pretending to be a girl thing's a bit weird."

"I know," she breathes. "I wanted to say sorry."

"Look," says Amber, awkwardly. "You can come back, if you want. It's okay. Just, be normal, you know?"

Her voice warps oddly, static sings and roars on the line.

"All right," agrees Quentin, without knowing why. Because she can't go back. There's no question of that. She presses the little red button to end the call.

Something comes boiling out of the phone. Quentin drops it, but it's too late, the thing seethes it way through, gathering into black vastness, filling the room like a gas, two white-hot eyes in the midst of it. It condenses into something perhaps nine feet high, something all black blade-edged bones and claws and teeth.

She cowers back. Without hesitation, the thing stabs her through the heart.

THERE'S A SPIDER dangling above her head. It's so tiny, but has cast a huge swag of web across a corner of the ceiling. She never noticed before. She breathes. The inside of her feels bare and spacious, as if heavy furniture has been cleared out and the windows left open; it feels *clean.*

She lies on her back, one hand resting over her chest. Nothing hurts. She sits up, and disturbs a veil of dust that was apparently lying over her; she's lying in a pool of dust, not blood, dust spread around her as if blasted outwards. She lets a handful slide through her fingers. She peers, cautiously, into herself, she finds no one else there.

The dark thing from the tower is crouched in a brooding heap on her ragwork rug. It makes no move to come any closer. They sit in silence on the floor, watching each other. Minutes pass.

"Hello," she says, at last, her voice just a thin creak.

The thing glowers in silence. She notices that she cannot feel the proximity of any *other* thing, glorious emptiness stretches out around her in all directions. Wylmere Hall's unofficial occupants have all fled *this* thing's presence.

"What do you want?"

No answer.

She rubs her chest. "Thank you," she manages.

The thing expands enormously, fills the room while somehow at once ricocheting off every surface. She squints, the windows flash, dark, bright, dark – as the thing darts to and fro, blocking the light, letting it through.

George's phone, which she had forgotten, chimes, and keeps chiming. She ignores it, staring at the thing swilling like liquid around her bedroom, but the phone chimes and chimes and suddenly the thing stops by the windows, looking for a moment more like a smouldering skeleton at a martyr's stake than anything else, and points one clawed hand at it.

She picks up the phone. There's an image on the screen like a little envelope, the word 'open'. She presses the button in the middle of the phone and there's the text message (she's never sent or received one before, but George has). The letters seems larger than anything she's glimpsed on a mobile before, filling the screen.

DO

That's all.

"I don't understand," she whispers, and the thing resumes its frenetic motion; the bedside light flashes on and off, the walls seem to quiver faintly. It occurs to her that she's awed, dazed – but not frightened. "Do what?"

It stops at the windows, almost man-shaped again, and lays its claws on the glass. The traces remain there of a spell she drew in spit; Cecily didn't see it.

MAKE

says the phone in her hand.

"That?" she asks. "The patterns? Things... ah, people like you... don't normally like those."

LIKE

the phone asserts, obstinately.

She hesitates.

MAKEMAKEMAKEMAKEMAKEMAKEMAKE

demands the phone.

In common politeness, how can she refuse?

SHE SHAKES THE ashy remains of the dead Thing off her clothes, and scrabbles in her desk for something suitable. She finds her geography exercise book under a box of coloured pastels. She tears out a sheet of paper and folds it in half, scoops up a little load of dust and carefully pours out the first line. The thing stills, squats on the floor beside her and watches her work. It should be impossible to think up a pattern under its gaze, but then, she's managed in far more oppressive circumstances. She tries to think about this web differently, to adapt the meaning of its spirals and angles; not a deterrent, a sort of... welcome.

Before she even thinks she's finished, it springs up eagerly and sinks into the pattern like black ink into a sponge. It courses through the pathways she's drawn and she has the impression it's *revelling* in the convolutions, the connections. It emerges after a moment, larger, brighter, more full of sparks. The eyes blaze at her expectantly and she expects the phone to beep again, but instead the thing plunges back into the pattern, and she lays her hand on it, pouring her attention along its inner pathways as she always does, to meet the thing, to *touch*. . .

But it's a touch, a courteously light pressure, like a handshake, not the invasion she's used to.

A word sounds in her head, heavy and weightless at once, like thunder.

WHAT

It's awkward at first, getting beyond single words. She has the sense of it clearing its throat, frowning, fumbling for language it once knew.

WHAT DO THEY CALL THEE?

She grimaces. "Quentin Sacheverell-Lytton," she says, unhappily. "What... what do they call you?"

There's such a long pause that she's sure there is no answer, or it has forgotten whatever name it once went by. She can feel her own name turned over and over in the thing's hands, fingered like a stone from a beach, hear the syllables of the preposterous double barrel separated out and weighed.

LEVANTER-SLEET

She's oddly touched. It's no coincidence, she's sure – the thing has named itself in mimicry of her. Her own name feels a little less absurd and ill-fitting alongside it.

"Pleased to meet you, Mr Levanter-Sleet," she says.

That's when George bangs through the door, looking for his phone. He sees it on the rug beside her at once, then takes in how she's crouched over a new pattern of dust.

He flattens her easily. Her immediate instinct is to freeze, go limp, not to fight back. He shoves her face-down into the pile of dust and rubs. Too late (it was always too late) she begins to struggle. "I knew it was you," he says. "You thieving little freak, how dare you." He knots a hand in her hair, scoops her back up to see her face. "Do you think I want you running up bills chatting to your little friends about dolls' tea parties? God, look at all this hair, look at you, Queenie."

He shakes her by the hair like a puppet. She can just see herself, in the mirror, her face coated white with dust.

"You look like a... a dollybird," says George, absurdly. She cannot remotely see why she looks like that. But he lets go of her and she thinks it's over, scrambles up and makes to run out of the room.

But it's not over and he slings her back to the floor. He was grabbing her box of coloured pastels from the desk, it turns out, and he sits on her, his heavy bottom hot on her pelvis, and holds her head down with one hand while the other scrubs a pastel across her face. She claws at his hands but he slaps her and she's scared of the scraping of the pastel near her eye, scared of his weight. He hasn't gone this far before.

"There. Now you're a *pretty* girl, aren't you?" he pants, oddly breathless. He lets her up, not completely but enough to see the mirror again.

She looks, if anything, less like a girl than usual. A wild-haired boy with a toddler's approximation of a clown's make-up scuffed across his face stares back at her. And yet, yes, she can see what George means now, the white face powder, red lipstick, rouge, eyeliner.

Something goes hard and clear inside her, like an icicle. She looks back at him.

"I'm not just a girl," she says. "I'm a *witch*."

He opens his mouth to laugh, raises his hand to hit her again. Then she sees something change in his face, as Mr Levanter-Sleet's shadow falls across it. George can't exactly *see* him, of course, but some motion in the air, some shred of darkness must have drifted through his awareness, because he starts back. He mutters, "Fucked up little creep," grabs his phone and slams out.

She sits holding herself. She can't stop shaking, she's uttering reflexive, breathless little sobs. And yet, she discovers, she's not actually crying. She stops making sounds. She looks at her reflection again, the colours smeared over it, and waits for the agony of humiliation to come, and somehow, it doesn't.

She is *furious,* though perhaps not as angry as Mr Levanter-Sleet, who is surging about the room again, making the lights flash. She can't make out what he's saying. George has left the pattern in ruins. She reaches out and draws a line in what remains. She's still trembling too hard for anything complicated, but it doesn't seem to matter:

WHO he demands savagely in her head.

"My brother," she sighs.

ILL-NURTURED LOUT, growls Mr Levanter-Sleet. *PRATING COXCOMB.*

He considers for a moment, then adds: *DICKHEAD.*

She doubles over laughing, tears squeezed out of her at last.

"Yes," she says. "Yes, he is."

HATE says the thing, HATE, HATE, SWAGGERING ROUSTABOUTS, LADS, YOOFS, DUDES, HOODIES, BOYS.

"You don't like boys?" she asks. She hesitates. "But you like me."

Mr Levanter-Sleet peers down at her with more affection in his phosphorous eyes than she can remember seeing in a human face. *THOU MAK'ST THE LINES,* he says. *AND THOU ART BUT A LITTLE MAID IN TROUBLE.*

She catches her breath. "You think I'm a girl?"

Amber thought she was a girl. George has been calling her one since she was six. The boys at school are all the same. And she, she has felt like this so long, she still feels the same now, even with nothing gurning at her from inside.

Maybe everyone's right.

GIRL confirms Mr Levanter-Sleet, sounding faintly puzzled, as if he had no idea there was any question.

After that they're always together.

CECILY MANAGES TO take her into Delchester and have her hair shorn close to the scalp without speaking to her. It's not a record. Her silences can go on for weeks. Quentin thinks about the lives of the martyrs and endures, endures.

They sit for twenty minutes in traffic on the way home. Cecily smells faintly of wine again, and she bounces in her seat and pounds the horn. She forgets not to talk to Quentin, exclaiming, "I wish they'd hurry and finish that bloody road!"

Quentin decides that just because Cecily's talking to her doesn't mean she has to speak to Cecily. She grins privately at Mr Levanter-Sleet, who is filling the back seat with darkness.

On the way out of Delchester you can see the A3012, boring right to the heart of Wylmere Woods. Most of the protesters have been heaved out now. There are only a few encampments left; specialist climbers are coming in to pluck them down from the trees.

Mr Levanter-Sleet comes with her to school like Mary's little lamb, and hates all the boys and teachers so extravagantly that they can almost feel it, and more often than not, they keep away. So it's a little better; everything is a little better. On the rare occasion that incautious things come close, Mr Levanter-Sleet stabs them. Sometimes he stabs people too, and usually they don't feel it, but sometimes they do; sometimes their faces go pale and they snatch a hand to their heart, they quiver and rush out of rooms and do not soon come back. This happens more and more often. Mr Levanter-Sleet is getting stronger and fiercer, her patterns are charging him up like a battery, and she can do more, too. Now she isn't always occupied trying to warn off things, she has attention to spare. For instance, she can't actually make herself *invisible*, but she can make it so no one notices or thinks to question her when she stops going to rugby lessons. It helps if you build things with power into the patterns, she discovers; her seeing stone, the skull of a mouse, small fires.

And blood. Blood helps with everything.

But mirrors scorch her, worse than ever now she doesn't have her hair to hide behind. She wants not to look, but she can't help it, to check whether her exposed jawline is growing fuller, whether hairs are appearing on her upper lip. She doesn't want to know what's going on under her clothes and can't bear not to strip off and see. She finds a few dark strands between her nipples and spends an hour curled up under the bed.

She tries to think of a spell but isn't sure where to start.

When she sleeps, now, her dreams are beautiful. Labyrinths of camellia trees, stairways through the clouds, and Mr Levanter-Sleet is always there beside her. But she still sleeps very lightly, wakes easily to creaks in the household or the echo of shouts from the woods.

She's taken to wandering the house at night when she can't sleep, now she has no need to be afraid of anything that might occupy the dark. One night, she goes into Cecily's office.

Mr Levanter-Sleet plunges eagerly into the computer as soon as she turns it on, while she spins idly in Cecily's office chair as the internet twitters and rattles into life. First of all, she searches 'Radiohead' just to make sure she's doing this right and in case the internet is somehow watching her. Then she types 'witchcraft' and finds some people talking to each other about spells on Usenet. Most of them are no more authentic than Rachel was, but one or two of them are saying things that have a certain ring to them; they feel recognisable, like something she'd always known but forgotten.

She takes notes on how to spot soil with a high iron content and why this is important. She takes a break to find out if the internet has more on Morgan le Fay than *Tales of the Round Table*. It does, and she learns that you can also spell her name *Morgane*. The word gives almost the same sheen of recognition, it glows so beautifully she just has to say it aloud.

Morgane, Morgane, she chants, like an incantation, and the name slips over her like ointment, sinking in through her skin and smoothing the old name away.

It transforms even her unwieldy surname into something darkly splendid: *Morgane Sacheverell-Lytton,* she whispers to herself, to Mr Levanter-Sleet, who seems to approve.

And then she digs deeper into other Usenet threads. She types 'boy feels like girl' into Alta Vista. She searches for hours, bouncing from link to link, and comes back the next night to search again. Mr Levanter-Sleet always comes too; he *loves* the internet, he emerges each time sleek and solid and crackling with energy as if from one of her best patterns. And he learns things, too; he never becomes exactly articulate, but his vocabulary does become much more modern.

"Can you change my body?" she asks him one night.

She doesn't think he can. But at least she knows now that she's not the only person in the world with the reason to ask the question.

Mr Levanter-Sleet shifts and growls and doesn't emerge from the computer.

Without looking at herself, she thinks about her body. There are several fundamental things wrong with it. But she's still no taller than Cecily, her face still a neat heart shape. There's a faint crack in her voice sometimes that terrifies her, but it hasn't actually broken yet.

"Then," she asks, "can you keep it the same?"

MAKE says Mr Levanter-Sleet on the screen in front of her. *LINES.*

It would take a lot of work, she thinks. A very big complicated spell. She's not quite ready for it yet, but soon. Maybe she wasn't a witch when she told George she was, maybe she still isn't one, but she's getting close.

Then two things happen: Morgane Sacheverell-Lytton comes home from school one day and finds the house full of bailiffs, and Cecily discovers something on the internet called the 'search history'.

AFTER THE FIRST brunt of it, the crying and screaming and violence, Cecily leaves her locked in her room. Morgane is glad enough to stay there, where it's quiet, at first.

But the others are still in the house somewhere, still shouting. She can feel it, even though she can't hear them. She uncurls, wipes her face on her sleeve.

The lock is no trouble to her at all now; it just takes a simple sequence of lines sketched with her finger on the wood. She walks out silently, paces down the empty Long Gallery, stands in the shadows outside the drawing room.

It's May, but the house is still so cold.

"Actually, Father," George is saying, "running this place is supposed to be my career, too, so it *is* my business."

The bailiffs are gone, it only took two hundred pounds to make them leave for now. But apparently Randall, who has not paid any tax in a long time, wouldn't take the money from the compulsory purchase for the A3012 because he knew it wouldn't be enough to make a difference.

"You both carry on as if I am somehow deliberately *withholding the money*," Randall says. "Where is it, this fortune we possess, do you know?"

"You deliberately *didn't tell me*," screams Cecily.

"Oh, well, we know your idea of a helpful contribution, my dear. Ten prayers to St Whatsit or crawling into a bottle."

"How *dare you*. How dare you insult me when it's me you expect to clean up your mess!"

"Of course, it's entirely my mess, it has nothing to do with you burning cash in one fad after another. What is it now, five thousand to ship Quentin off to America?"

Morgane turns to Mr Levanter-Sleet and stares. For a moment she pictures walking down a gangplank from a ship at Ellis Island, a suitcase in her hand, all America before her, alone except for Mr Levanter-Sleet. It doesn't sound like an entirely bad idea.

But that isn't what Cecily wants to do:

"They have people who know how to *deal* with this," says Cecily. "The Emmitsburg Prayer Warriors – no, don't roll your eyes at them when you don't have the first idea how to help him yourself; it's not just prayer, they do aversion therapy, it's all researched. Don't you realise how serious this is, how he's going to turn out if we don't do something?"

"Then *you* do something about it. Sort him out, that's supposed to be your job. Can't we sling him into a few cold water baths for free?"

"Maybe if he actually *had* a decent male role model," Cecily spits out.

George volunteers instantly: "*I* can spend more time with him, at least until we find somewhere for him to go. And what about the ACF? Military training, like Donald's brother had. They're a charity."

"That's just treating the problem from the *outside*," says Cecily.

"He doesn't need anything *mystical,* Mother, he just needs to get it into his head that he can't flounce around in a tutu."

"Don't you think," says Randall, "that anyone who isn't paid to keep a kid like that around will kick him out?"

This, briefly, silences everyone. "I don't know how we're going to handle this if we're all turned out in the streets," Cecily quavers.

George says, "There has to be something we can sell."

Randall laughs.

It would be unbearable to listen to all of this, but Mr Levanter-Sleet is there.

It is going to have to be a very big spell, Morgane thinks. It is going to take a lot of work to make everything better.

THEY WALK THROUGH Wylmere Woods together in the dark, Morgane and Mr Levanter-Sleet. She turns on her torch and breaks off a stick of beechwood from a sapling as she goes and the things flutter nervously and shrink back into the wet trees. The earthworks have begun in earnest, Morgane skids down a loose bank of sidecast soil onto the flat bed of the A3012.

The earth is damp and raw beneath her, they have laid nothing new down yet. And she has the space she needs to work.

She digs the point of the beech staff into the earth and draws a line as long as she's tall, then, as she pulls it into a sharp curve, scatters blood from the back of her hand on the bend. She works the pattern along fifty yards of road, and she focuses different desires into different parts of it (diamonds, mandalas) and seals them with blood and flames, and then she tries to knit them all together.

Not to be sent anywhere terrible. Money for Randall and Cecily. To stay the same. To be left alone.

But it gets harder and sometimes she realises she's just stumbling through the mud, sore and shivering and half-asleep, unable to focus on anything more elaborate than *Everything to be better.*

And at last it's done, the pattern, but the spell isn't, it still needs something more.

"Be very small, Mr Levanter-Sleet," she whispers. "Be so small nothing can see you."

Mr Levanter-Sleet obliges at once. Even she can't feel him at her side, for the first time in months. The loneliness of it weakens her knees and she has to lean on the beech staff. And there isn't limitless time, dawn is coming and the rain is getting heavier; it will wash away her lines, in the end.

Gradually, the things re-emerge from what remains of the woods. But they're not like the things in the house, they're not so vicious, so half-human.

But she needs one to approach.

She is sick of hurting herself, but she grits her teeth, pokes the little knife from the kitchen into her arm again and draws in blood on the palm of her own hand. And this time instead of desire or intent, she loads the pattern full of the pain it cost to make. She fills it with loneliness and defencelessness and hurt.

And still it takes so long that when it finally happens, she looks up to see something ragged and green inches from her face, peering at her, and realises she was crouched on the ground, barely propped upright on the staff, asleep.

(It's possible, she has to admit later, that the thing didn't want to hurt her. It's possible it was only curious, like Mr Levanter-Sleet was at the beginning.)

Mr Levanter-Sleet explodes out of nothingness. The thing has only time to emit a thin shriek as he stabs it and drags it down into the labyrinth Morgane has made. The ground beneath Morgane rocks as he surges through its passageways and turns. Then he erupts out, the force of it knocking her onto her knees, roaring like a black geyser into the air, and goes streaming away towards Wylmere Hall.

Morgane stumbles after him, through woods that are utterly silent around her. She climbs the dark and silent stairs to her room, and falls asleep. Mr Levanter-Sleet is not there to bring her sweet dreams, but nothing else comes near her, and for once she sleeps heavily. She doesn't hear the sirens.

*   *   *

THE INQUEST INTO George's death fails to reach any very satisfactory conclusion on what he was doing down at the construction site at five in the morning. As he was barefoot and still wearing pyjamas, sleepwalking seems the only answer.

But one of the last protesters, cold and wakeful in the upper branches of an oak, claims to have seen a man *running* away from Wylmere Hall, shouting for help, scrambling over roots and sawn-off stumps in the first glimmer of dawn.

"Like he was being *chased,*" he insisted. "As if the devil was after him."

But whatever brought George there, he was not responsible for the Highways Agency's contractors failing to follow proper procedure before finishing work for the night. All heavy machinery should have been left securely parked and firmly turned off, keys should have been in key safes. It should have been thoroughly impossible for the excavator to trundle down a slope of loose earth and topple over.

The construction firm, with surprising alacrity, offers Cecily and Randall two million pounds. They accept at once.

There would be plenty of money to send Morgane to the Emmitsburg Prayer Warriors now, but somehow no one gets round to it.

Cecily cries in her room a lot and Randall broods in the library or the drawing room. But they both did that anyway and now they do it with the lights on and the refitted central heating comfortably blazing.

She asked for everything to be better, Morgane supposes, not for everything to be perfect.

"I DIDN'T ASK you to kill anyone," she tells Mr Levanter-Sleet in her bedroom. On one of her midnight walks around the house, she found a trunk in an attic and inside it a beautiful oyster-coloured flapper dress. She's repairing some patches where beads are missing; no one tends to burst into her room and interrupt her, these days.

She feels she has to say this. She should be devastated, eviscerated with remorse.

Though when she imagines George stricken with guilt or grief over her, she doesn't get very far.

"He was a human being," she tries. It sounds rather flat.

Mr Levanter-Sleet, bunched in inky cumuli on her bed, just stares at her. He does not seem to feel any need to defend himself.

She stares back.

She says, "Well, try not to do it again."

SHE WALKS AMONG the skinny saplings on the banks of the A3012, planted in waist-high, beige plastic tubes, to replace the seven thousand trees felled.

"Save our trees," Amber had shouted.

"Actually," George would have said. "They're *our* trees."

No one has mentioned it, but she supposes she's the heir to the whole estate now. *Morgane Sacheverell-Lytton of Wylmere Hall.* She has to admit to herself, she likes the way it sounds.

But not enough.

Mr Levanter-Sleet nudges her attention towards something shining in the grass. She bends and picks it up. It's the art deco hair slide, it's silver grey and tarnished, but the mother-of-pearl is still gleaming. It has waited for her, lovely and intact, while the landscape transformed around it.

The A3012 was completed just before she turned fourteen. She wanted to wait that long, to be sure. And she isn't a millimetre taller or broader, there is not one additional hair on her skin, not a note in her voice has changed. "I'd have thought you'd have had a growing spurt by now," said Cecily drearily.

In her backpack, there's a change of clothes (and the beaded dress), a toothbrush, her sewing things, a packet of Jaffa Cakes, and twenty thousand pounds in cash. She has emptied a Delchester cash machine with Cecily's credit card and the assistance of Mr Levanter-Sleet. She thinks, in the circumstances, that's fair.

Her hair is still very short, but she jams the slide into it anyway. She skids down onto the hard shoulder, and sticks out her thumb. Children are warned not to do this, she knows, especially girls (*my mother said I never should play with the gypsies in the wood*). But she is in no danger at all. And she has already done a small spell, which she thinks will discourage any one from following her.

It doesn't take long at all to flag down a car, and then (she times it by the dashboard clock) it only takes six minutes and twenty four seconds to drive the length of the A3012, through what remains of Wylmere Woods. They charge towards London, Mr Levanter-Sleet churning in the air above a green Ford Fiesta, like a plume of black smoke.

> *I was up on his back and away with a crack*
> *Sally, tell my mother that I shan't come back.*

"Eruga!" whispers Morgane.

BINGO

S.L. GREY

You never know who you are going to meet on the road at night, who is behind the wheel of that car or bike in front of you, whether or not a momentary lack of judgement on their part will lead to you being involved in an accident. That potential for catastrophe and violent death is explored in the following story – an incredibly bleak but powerful tale by a writing duo who are at the cutting edge of horror.

4 A.M. THE only time the N2 highway ever sleeps. He coasts to the inside lane, leans the bike in, then rolls on the throttle as he comes out of the corner. He should be careful – with the roadblocks packed up for the night, this is the time the coked-up kids drive home from the clubs – but he's irritated, restless; the night hasn't gone as he'd planned.

The road is his. He pushes the Ducati to two hundred and imagines the city disappearing behind him: all of it – his work, the years he's invested in trying to fit in, the Bingo Club, this latest girl. He can't remember her name, and that bugs him. In the six months he's been playing the game, he's always tried to keep it civilised. It's been a means to an end: finish his card and he'll be with the inner circle at the brokerage; he'll be a made man, offered all the massive accounts. This is what they told him, and he believes it – he's seen it happen. James de Wet, Phil

Malope were kids from nowhere like him, and they skipped a few rungs on the ladder to the big leagues. Now they've got flats in Camps Bay and Bugattis in the garage.

It was a squalling winter evening when he first heard about the club, so unlike the dry heat of tonight. He was standing outside the office building, smoking, trying to figure out an imbalance in one of the pension schemes, one of those cut-fee, low-risk packages for ex-schoolteachers who were hoping to get enough back to stay in cat food until they died. This is what a scholarship boy out of government school and with no contacts has to handle at Levine Botha: twenty-hour days, for barely any commission. The boys from the Bingo Club – he didn't know it was called that then, just knew they were the rich kids – came out of the lobby elevator, already drunk. He was surprised to see De Wet and Malope among them.

"Willems! Pulling another all-nighter?"

He shrugged, sighed out the smoke.

"There's another way, brother," Malope said.

Eventually he got an audience, doesn't like to think about the humiliation, but back then anything seemed better than being stuck in a dead end at the company forever. Then he was put on trial – that's what they called it: not initiation, not probation. Just fill the card and he'd be in.

So for the last six months he's been checking the boxes, different types of women: a geekishly obsessive list of races and sizes, hair colour and physical attributes. It seemed quite simple at the time: bed them, take a picture for proof, and get out.

There's a wink of a single red tail light far ahead of him, then a double flash as the driver touches the brakes. He slows the bike just a little. The last couple of months, he's been wondering about the Bingo Club, why they do it. He's been wondering whether it will actually get him into the inner circle after all, or if it's just a bunch of kids playing a practical joke. The doubt, the idea that he's just been played for a fool, the fact that he's still dealing with cut-rate savings schemes, has made him frustrated, has made him angry; and last night, he supposes, it sort of came to a head.

He's come up fast now behind the car – a black Beemer – with the broken tail light. As he overtakes it on the left, it drifts across his lane. He instinctively leans left, correcting immediately to stay on the road. He barely avoids going off onto the hard shoulder.

Shaky, flushed with adrenalin, he pulls to the side of the highway, where the concrete barrier is scarred with red paint (it's always red, as if red cars are the only ones that ever crash) and drops the stand. If it wasn't for the ABS, he'd be fucked. He flips up his visor, breathes in fuel-tinged air, flexes his fingers to stop his hands from shaking. He's been in bike accidents before; he knows only too well how the time slows in the moment just before impact. How details come into sharp focus.

He replays the moment as the clutch on his heart loosens. He was way too close to the Beemer for that frozen second. He sees a still of the back of her head as she bent to fiddle with the radio or fish something off the passenger seat, oblivious that he was even there. And the snapshot reminds him of how he left the woman less than an hour ago, faced pressed down and crying into her pillow.

He's got three more slots on the bingo card, but he doesn't know if he can finish. He doesn't know if he *should* finish. It's only making him feel smaller. He doesn't believe them anymore, that after the game it will be done, and he'll have earned their respect.

That's what it's all about, isn't it? Respect. And the bitch in the Beemer didn't even fucking see him. He's shunted by a shaft of fury, peels the bike with a scream back onto the highway. He's not sure what he's going to do if he catches the car – let the bitch know that she nearly wiped him out, maybe. Make her see him. He speeds up, hoping that she hasn't exited somewhere up ahead.

No – he sees pale tail lights ahead, just past the airport turn-off.

Then, as if he's done it with his mind, the car swerves, its back spins out, clips the middle barrier, and then it flips over once, twice, landing right-side up, its front crashing into the concrete wall that bolsters the hard shoulder.

He slows to a chug, then pulls up, the anger shocked away, sober. A silver sedan screams past, its horn blaring.

He considers driving on. Someone else will help, surely.

But he knows no one's going to stop. Not on this dodgy road: the barbed-wire fence doesn't keep the hijackers and vultures off the highway.

The car has come to rest perfectly within the bounds of the hard shoulder, neatly behind the yellow line, the front caved in, the windows smashed and spider-webbed. It's an old off-white Toyota, not the black BMW. He's not sure whether this makes it more or less of his business. The wreck already looks like one of the orphaned vehicles that clutter up the side of the highway, their owners unable to afford the cash for a tow truck. He takes off his helmet, rests it on the seat.

He approaches the car cautiously. Another vehicle whooshes past. When the sound of it dies, he hears a snatch of music floating out of the wreck, some millionaire wanker crooning, "You're beautiful." The music cuts out. The engine tick-ticks. The tyres are flat, twisted to a broken angle.

He tells himself he isn't squeamish. You don't travel South African roads without experiencing carnage. He's seen bodies flung across the highway like toys. Once, a torso like a bin bag dumped on a dark road.

The street lights bathe the scene in a yellow glow, turning the car's dirty white exterior a muddy gold. He crunches over glass. The bodywork is patched with old putty and scratches and dents. The bonnet is folded in half like a paper castle. On the back seat there's an empty baby seat, encrusted with filth.

He doesn't want to look in the front seat, doesn't want to see what he's going to see. It's been a long night already, too long. He can just go. The night started with so much promise. The woman seemed genuinely interested in him, out on the prowl, just like him, on a Friday night. Why can't he remember her name? The cocktails were working; she was feeling him up on the sofa. If it weren't for this bloody game... It could have been a perfectly pleasant night, but when she took him up to her place, he couldn't get the image out of his head, of the boys of the Bingo Club leering over them as he tried to fuck her. Saunders snapping his braces, watching too closely with his moist stare. He couldn't manage; he pushed his softening dick against her. She laughed at him.

The blare of a truck going by, then silence, then a whimper draws his attention to the wreck. The driver's side window is smashed, and as he bends to look into it, he catches a whiff of something. Smoke? He sniffs. An acrid electrical smell.

"Help me," the driver whispers. There's a diamond of glass embedded below her eye. She's twisting her body, writhing. No air bag – it's not that kind of car. The steering wheel is practically in her lap; he tries not to look too closely at that, concentrates on her face. He thought she'd be younger; the car made him imagine a student, but she's older than he is – way past her sell-by. Flabby, sweat-shirted, he can see the lines on her face even in the flattering light. He wonders what she's doing on the road alone at this hour.

He yanks the door handle – it doesn't budge. She's locked herself in. "Ug," she says. "Legs. Can't..." She wriggles again. "Hot," she says. "Hot."

The acrid stink is getting stronger. There's a loud crack on the car roof. Something breaking? Someone lobbing stones from the slum over the fence? Her eyes swivel, panicked.

"Oh God please help me I don't wanna die I don't wanna die."

She tries to tug herself from the seat, but she can't move. As she thrashes her head around, he can see her left cheek is masked with blood.

He should say something like: "It's fine. I'll get you out of here." But his instincts are screaming at him to step away, just leave. Something's telling him not to use his iPhone to call for help. They can trace calls, can't they? "Do you have a phone?" he hears himself say.

"Uh. Bag."

He knocks out the last bits of jagged glass in the driver's side window. He can't get to the other side, the car is concertinaed against the crash barrier. He has to reach across her, feels the soft mush of her body against his. Rubbish is scattered everywhere. Old McDonalds bags, coffee cups. "Ah," she moans. "Ah, hurts." Another vehicle rushes past, doesn't even slow.

He scrabbles wildly into the junk in the passenger seat, his fingers catching a strap. A bag? He hauls it out, tips it up, gets another lungful of that smoky stench. The car won't blow, will it? Doesn't that only happen in movies? But then… why are there always burnt-out cars on the side of the highway? The fire has to be coming from the electrical system, but he can also smell petrol and he doesn't want to be caught in an explosion. That could happen, couldn't it? Cars aren't his thing – he doesn't even maintain his bike himself, gets some dude from Durbanville to pick it up every so often to service it. Another luxury he can't afford.

He roots through the bag, but there's no phone, just a confetti of receipts, an old lipstick and a child's drinking cup.

"Something's burning," the woman sobs. "Please! I don't want to die like this. I don't want to burn to death oh God please help me." And then, "Please," she wails. "Please! Help me!"

He yanks at the driver's door again, leans in, fiddles with the inside catch. It's jammed, and even if he could open it, she's really trapped. The engine block has been pushed forward, pinning her hips, crushing her legs.

He could just get back on his bike, roar away and pretend he was never here.

"Mister," she whispers. "Mister. Don't go." Has she read his mind?

He needs a fire extinguisher, he has to somehow dampen whatever is causing the smoke that's leaking out of the vents. But this is some old jalopy, not a Merc fresh off a showroom floor. He knows, even without looking, that there won't be one in this car, but he snatches the keys out of the ignition anyway – the woman batting at his hand as he does so – and runs around to the boot. His gloved hands are trembling and it takes him several tries to fit the key in the rusty lock, and it opens with a creak. He blocks out the sounds coming from the car's interior – the muffled cries of the woman, as if someone's trapping, pushing her face down, taking out his rage on her – they hurt his ears. He surveys the junk filling the boot. He hauls out an overpacked suitcase, the sleeve of a purple silky blouse hanging from its seam. There's also a tote bag filled with all sorts of shit. He scrabbles through the stuff, chucks it onto the tarmac – an old iron, a plastic kettle, a hairdryer, a photograph album, a half-full jar of Milo, a pair of child's sneakers, shoelaces knotted together, a balding teddy bear. What the fuck was she running from?

"Mister!" she screams from the front. "Mister!" she's coughing now, sounds like she might be choking. "Burning! I've seen it happen. I've seen it happen, I've seen people die like this on TV."

He makes himself walk to the front of the car. She whips her head back and forth. "Mister," she says again, "Please!"

"What show was it?" he says. As if that will calm her. As if it will calm him. As if he was just back at home and he was never really here.

"Discovery," she says. "I used to…" She starts to cry now. A regretful cry; not fear, but sadness.

"I'll try and flag someone down –"

"Mister, I don't want to die like this."

She's starting to annoy him. What the fuck is he supposed to do? This isn't his mess. Another car whooshes past. Then another. It's as if he's cut off from the real world – a world where everyone else just gets on with their shit, goes home – trapped behind an invisible barrier, behind their massive barbed-wire fucking fences. The light is changing. It will be morning soon, then rush hour. The highway will be teeming with people.

"It hurts, mister! Get me out, mister!"

She stares into his eyes and he remembers the woman from last night. She looked at him the same way: that mixture of pleading and betrayal. Then she laughed again, as if his fists were as soft as his dick. He steps back. The booze and the anger churn in his stomach. He wants to be sick.

And then she says it, the hysteria gone from her voice. "Then kill me. I don't want to burn to death. Kill me," she whispers. "Make it quick."

He looks into her eyes, the thick wisp of smoke drifting between them. She means it. He's never been looked at like that before. No woman has ever looked at him like that before.

He steps away woodenly. Limbs moving of their own accord.

"Don't go, don't leave me, mister! Please! Please!"

He rounds to the back of the car and picks up the steam iron, feeling a trickle of cold water running down his wrist – she didn't bother to empty it when she packed it up.

He approaches her window. "Do it," she screams, flapping her hands towards her crushed legs. "I'm burning. It hurts. It hurts so bad, mister it–"

The angle's all wrong, and the first swipe only glances off her forehead, and she screams again. He braces his left shoulder against the side of the car, swings his arm back and in the split second her eyes lock with his, he sees something in them – doubt? betrayal? – then lands the first real blow with a hollow thunk, and her noise stops. He shuts his eyes and keeps swinging. *Thunk, thunk, thunk*. He thinks he can feel something give. He keeps going until the muscles in his arm spasms.

He drops the iron. Draws in a shuddering breath. Realises his eyes are stinging. He wipes his gloved hands across his face. They come back sticky.

Get away. Get away from the car. But he doesn't move.

He doesn't allow himself to look at the woman. He doesn't want that imprinted in his mind. Breathes in again.

It's then that he realises he can no longer smell smoke. Makes himself look past the thing in the driver's seat. Not even a wisp of smoke floats out of the vents.

The fire has gone out of its own accord. Hasn't it? There was a fire, wasn't there?

He backs away, is only aware that he's stepped into the road when a car horn screams past him, followed by a muffled yell.

He imagines himself getting back on the Ducati, riding away, the blood on his gloves slipping on the throttle; getting his grip, eating up the road, the sirens washing towards him, heading for the scene he's just left behind, increasing his speed, becoming a roar and nothing else. He sees himself taking his exit, heading past the 24-hour Engen garage on the corner, the place where he usually stops for a Coke and a packet of smokes after one of his nights out. The pictures come clear and fast, so clear that his right hand clenches, as if he's squeezing the accelerator.

You can't take it back. You can't jump back to that moment and wish it away.

Ahead, the N2 and freedom beckons, but he doesn't make a move towards the bike. He waits. He wants to tell the police when they come what happened. That there was a fire, that she begged him, that he did what was right. That would be the respectable thing to do.

But the sky lightens and the kids come to the fence to look at the new wreck. They're talking loudly among themselves. They're calling the adults who start shouting across at him, clashing their fists against the fence. Still the police don't come.

The kids start throwing stones: idly, he senses, not with any purpose. The traffic is thickening on the highway. The car is still; what's inside is still.

He takes out his cellphone, thumbs through the photos. Sees the woman from last night at the bar. She was good-looking. Then the one of her in bed, just before. She was turned on, drunk, smiling. She really liked him; it was just a minor setback. He slides through the other photos, the nearly complete card. It's a beautiful set, and he feels pretty proud of himself. Maybe he wants to complete the card – he's a collector, a prospector, after all. Maybe it's not about earning the boys' respect after all, but his own. If he just finishes what he started.

He stands up, stretches, dusts himself down, and gets on the bike. He kicks up the stand, turns the key and hits the starter button. He thinks of the woman's smile, blends into the encroaching rush, and is gone.

PERIPATEIA

VANDANA SINGH

The roads taken and those not taken, the paths before us and the possibilities they can lead to – all these are considered in Vandana's story blending scientific speculation and personal discovery. Here the road leads Sujata, a scientist trying to come to terms with loss, to a realization about the true nature of the universe.

IT OCCURRED TO Sujata that what she was experiencing was a kind of life-after-living. Veenu's abrupt and unexplained departure three days ago was a clean dividing line between what she had thought of as her life, and the inexplicable state of being that came after. A phase transition as fundamental as that of water boiling in the saucepan, turning to steam, she thought, stirring in the tea leaves. The brown ink spread through the water the way pain seeped through every part of her being. She'd become, in her post-life, a sponge for metaphors, a hammer to which everything was yet another nail in the coffin of that earlier existence. The other day she had found herself wandering disconsolately through the park between frolicking, screaming children, staring at Lost Cat notices on the utility poles, and she'd thought of posting a notice – Lost: The Ground Under my Feet.

It was getting dark; she left the tea steeping in the pan and turned on the kitchen light. The brightness hurt her eyes. White walls, white counters, the potted coriander on the window-sill, a small dining table piled with sympathy cards. The fridge snored like a polar bear. On a shelf to its left was a little altar from the time Sujata's mother had visited last year; it held a smiling Buddha and a Nataraja, a somewhat garish print of Lakshmi, and a Jehovah's Witness pamphlet showing an equally garish Christ. Sujata's mother didn't really have any basis for believing in God, a fact she would readily admit, but she liked to plan for contingencies. She'd put Jesus up there with the others, as she said, "just in case." The wall across from the window bore witness to Sujata's own probabilistic approach to the universe: it was covered almost entirely with sticky notes in yellow, green and pink, fluttering in the breeze from the window like so many prayer flags. Here, in Sujata's tiny, neat hand, were maps of possibility, random thoughts, and notes on a variety of subjects that had caught her interest. In the middle there was a large sheet of paper with a graph showing two world-lines, hers in purple, Veenu's in green, two lines crawling across the white space, close together and more or less parallel, until three days ago when Veenu packed up and left. Since that time the purple line had crawled forward, tentative and alone.

The latest series of sticky notes was an exercise in possibility. Imagine a phenomenon, and write down all possible explanations and descriptions. Then some time-dependent weighted combination of these was (maybe) an approximation to the ever-changing truth.

Who or What is Veenu?

An idea. A beginning and end in one, a snake chasing its tail. A lover, a partner, a friend.

An offspring of the mind's deepest sigh.

A neural implant, an AI that enables us to network with others at a thought.

Defined by my existence, the way Veenu's existence defines mine.

A traveler through the whorls and eddies of space and time, whose world-line sometimes intercepts with mine.

An imaginary friend who didn't go away when I grew up.

She picked up the last one, which had fallen off the wall, and stuck it back next to the others.

"You're so *weird*," Veenu used to say, in an indulgent tone. She approved of eccentricity as a matter of principle, but was the more practical of the two of them. "Why don't you go back to your paper on the Higgs field?"

The paper on the Higgs field had been sitting in Sujata's laptop for three months. The trouble, she had said to Veenu – goodness, was that just a few days ago? – the trouble was that the paper was straightforward and eminently publishable, and therefore not very interesting. She'd rather write a paper entitled 'The Higgs Field Considered as a Metaphor for the Entanglement of Matter in Time', or 'Alien Manipulations and the Unfinished Universe'.

She was sipping the too-bitter tea when the road appeared. As always, the apparition came without warning; the only hint of its impending arrival was a dull headache and a slight visual aura. Then the wall, the one with the sticky notes and the graph, began to shimmer and crackle like an old television set between channels. After which there was no wall at all, just the white and dusty road.

She dropped the cup. Bits of china crunched under her shoes as she walked through where the wall had been, and stood on the road. It smelled vaguely of burning insulation, with a hint of cinnamon.

She had developed a ritual by now: look to the left, into the past first, a check for accuracy. Yes, there was the misty bulk of the university building where she worked, and the coffee shop where she and Veenu used to hang out most evenings until the impossible happened – and beyond that, a sloping green hill from her undergraduate days, and then the trees she climbed as a child, and the chai shop she frequented in high school. The order was a little muddled, and the images vague and shifting in the mist, but she could recognize each thing.

She steeled herself to look to the right, toward the future.

There was a deafening beat in her ears. Would there be any indication of Veenu's return?

On every previous sighting the future had appeared as a turbulent dust haze, a shifting cloud bank, through which vague images were sometimes discernible. On occasion these were visions of the road itself, flowing like a dark river through an unfamiliar green land, branching and bifurcating into the horizon. This she had interpreted as some kind of probability graph, a reassurance that the future was not determined, that she could choose her path. Sometimes other, more mysterious or terrifying silhouettes emerged from the cloud bank – a decrepit house by a river, a figure on a sloping roof, a sadness that was without shape or form, but recognizable as a sharp jab in the ribs, a sudden breathlessness. Once there had been an incongruous white tower like one of the minarets of the Taj, but she had never encountered it in real life, and it had not been there in subsequent sightings of the road. Her hypothesis was that some futures were more likely than others, and that the future with the white minaret had simply been eliminated through the games of chance.

She closed her eyes before looking. When she opened them, she saw, to her complete astonishment, that the road ended to her right. No mist, no vague shapes, no branching paths into a semi-determined future, but just a clean line where the road abruptly stopped. There was nothing beyond it but a blank wall. She was so astounded by this that she staggered toward the demarcation before remembering that it was never any use walking on the road, left or right. It was the sort of road where the destination maintained a constant distance from the traveler, no matter how fast or far she walked. She rubbed her eyes and looked again, but nothing had changed. She thought: this means I'm going to die.

Abruptly she was back in the kitchen. The lower part of her left trouser-leg was cold and wet with tea, and there were bits of china on the floor everywhere. The air was still. The familiarity and emptiness filled her with foreboding. She looked at the wall she had walked through – it was solid again, and a few more of the sticky notes had fallen off.

There was no sign of impending death. Perhaps it would come tomorrow, or the day after. Or maybe there was another interpretation for that clearly demarcated finish line. *Something* had ended. But what, exactly?

She stayed up half the night, sipping tea and munching on dry crackers, thinking about Veenu and waiting for death. When death refused to oblige, she went to bed.

NEXT EVENING, AFTER a day at work in which she felt as though she was swimming upstream through a bewilderingly swift river, Sujata returned to the house, exhausted.

There were more cards in the mailbox. She picked them up and threw them on the dining table in the kitchen. The house was silent as a tomb, except for the refrigerator's constant purr. She stood in the dark by the window. The neighborhood was quiet, lights on behind curtained windows. There wasn't a soul in sight. The neat lawns and fenced backyards of suburban America – every house a prison unto itself. Her reverie was disturbed by the cards falling off the table. A fury took hold of her then – she picked up a mass of cards in her hands and threw them up into the air. They were all around her like a pack of predatory birds. She was finally going insane, or so it seemed; the cards flapped away at her, calling out what was written in them in high-pitched voices. *Thinking of you, wishing you strength for this difficult time.* Theater tickets. People trying to be kind, without actually getting involved, people trying to mask their shock at the unthinkable: Veenu leaving, without warning, without a word! As though what had happened to Sujata was something shameful, something that might infect their own blessedly ordinary lives or threaten the security of their relationships. She batted at the cards, tearing them from the air, tearing them into little bits. At last the cards fell silent, lying torn and tattered on the floor, and she knelt down, sobbing like a child, pleading with the universe for some kind of explanation. The universe, not being obliged to reply, remained silent.

At last she gathered the torn cards and put them in the recycling, and washed her face. Three of her sticky notes had fallen off the white wall. She picked them up and stuck them back on.

Alien Manipulations in an Unfinished Universe: an Anti-Occam's Razor Hypothesis

The neutrino was predicted by Wolfgang Pauli in 1930. It took until 1956 to discover that it actually existed.

One of the great predictions of particle physics, from considerations of symmetry, was the omega particle. Predicted in 1962, discovered in 1964.

In an effort to distract herself, Sujata made some tea, set out a plate of cookies, and began to complete the list. Pink sticky notes on the prediction and discovery of the tau neutrino, the top and bottom quarks, dark matter, the Higgs Boson.

When Sujata was in graduate school, she had founded the Anti-Occam's Razor society. Membership varied between one and four. Occam's Razor, a guiding principle of science, posited that the simplest idea that explained a phenomenon was most likely to be correct. She had always found this a dull notion, a surrendering of the imagination to the tyranny of the mundane. She liked to invent complicated explanations for straightforward phenomena, a kind of intellectual Rube-Goldbergism, just to thumb her nose at William of Occam. It was a joke, of course.

Over the years, as an extension of the long joke of ideas, she'd come up with the Alien Manipulation hypothesis. This is how she had first explained it to Veenu:

The universe is a massive quantum-mechanical relativistic Rube Goldberg machine in continual need of adjustment by a bunch of super-intelligent aliens. Suppose an intelligent species comes up with a theory, and a prediction. The aliens then adjust the machine in order to make the prediction come true. One reason why interstellar civilizations cannot meet is because contradictory predictions must be avoided. There is bedrock reality – you know, Pythagoras theorem, gravity, not falling through floors. But beyond bedrock reality there are multiple ways to explain the universe, and the duplicitous alien manipulators ensure that we are taken in by our own illusions. But – if everything we predicted was exactly right, we would become suspicious, or worse, even more arrogant than we are now. So they throw in the occasional surprise result – accelerating expansion of the universe, stars at the edges of galaxies moving faster than visible matter would entail.

They had laughed about it, she and Veenu. That the universe is an illusion had been suspected by many a mystic in many a tradition, but to construct an argument based on logic and physics was truly fun. Every once in a while Sujata would get a feeling of a feather (or antenna) being drawn slowly down her spine, and she would shiver. It was as though the alien overlords of the universe were warning her not to think (outside the box) too much. Because however indulgent these entities might be toward the intellectual inventions of human beings, the one idea they would not want people to take too seriously was this: that the whole thing was a goddamned magic show; that all laws were ad hoc, imperfect, made-up, inelegant. If the Standard Model was so messy that even particle physicists called it the sub-standard model, then better to let people believe that it was only a part of a greater, more elegant truth, instead of accepting that reality itself was a mess.

Veenu: How would you know that the universe is one giant theater performance, with your hypothetical aliens running the show? I mean, if it is all show, how would you get to go backstage?

Sujata (after a week): I think you'd have to bump up against something that was irrefutably there – a phenomenon or an artifact or a prop – that didn't fit anywhere on stage. Something that couldn't be explained in any schema.

Veenu: So you mean you'd have to catch the aliens napping?

Sujata: Yes. Yes, I know. Sounds unlikely.

Veenu (accusingly): And you wouldn't know whether your unexplained phenomenon was just a really hard problem you were up against, or whether it was something that violated all explanations of reality... I think your idea is full of shit.

Sujata (unreasonably annoyed): Well, of course! Can't you take a joke? Of course it's full of shit!

It was at that moment she realized she sort-of believed the shit. Despite all reason, all sensible feeling, it rang true, at least in a coarse-grained way. There were details to work out... So far, for each phenomenon in her life she had found a schema, a scaffolding in which things fit, made sense. When they didn't, it usually meant that there were other schemas to be invented and elaborated. An essential element of science was the faith, after all, that the universe was comprehensible.

Until the day Veenu walked away.

Furiously she began to scribble a new series of sticky notes, in green:

Hypotheses for Veenu's Departure

Schema One: I am a terrible person who did something wrong. I am so stupid that I don't even know what it is I did wrong. Stupid, naïve, what's the difference? (Unless she has amnesia, she can't recall anything that could cause Veenu to leave.)

Schema Two: There's been some misunderstanding. (There've been misunderstandings before and they've always managed to work through them.)

Schema Three: Veenu left because there was something urgent that needed doing, nothing to do with me. (An attractive idea, Veenu as a secret agent with some kind of covert agenda, but there are no supporting pieces of evidence – although if the agent was really secret, would there be?)

Schema Four: Veenu is insane and irrational. (Veenu is one of the most clear-headed and rational people she knows.)

Schema Five: Veenu is not what I thought she was; despite these years of knowing Veenu, I really don't know Veenu. So I am blind as well as naïve and stupid.

She stayed up that night coming up with seventeen more schemas, researching each, and coming up empty. The facts didn't fit the hypotheses, although there were some facts that fit some, if only slightly. Of all of them, only Schema Five had a somewhat higher probability than the others.

To know something, or someone, is to be able to see them without the cloud of pre-conceived notions, prejudices and paradigms that we carry around with us. But is it even possible to lose that cloud? Everyone goes about with such a cloud, and inevitably their world-view is distorted, refracted, diffracted. It's as inevitable as an electron carrying around with it its cloak of virtual particles. Nothing in the frigging universe is naked.

The interesting thing was this: Schema Five was consistent with her half-in-jest notion that the universe was a sham controlled by crazed aliens. As the dawn light poured in through the kitchen window, she remembered another conversation she had once had with Veenu.

Veenu: So tell me more about your idea.

Sujata: Well, there are the deadjims.

Veenu: The what?

Sujata: It's an old *Star Trek* joke... did I tell you I used to watch *Star Trek* all through graduate school? Well, I made up the word from something to do with *Star Trek*, for the people who've figured it out.

Veenu: Figured what out?

Sujata: You know. That the universe is a sham run by aliens. They know there is no point trying to come up with grand unified theories of the physical universe. Or of human nature. The aliens did a shoddy job of putting together a foundation for the universe, and they take our ideas and improvise with them to do the finishing touches. Take the Higgs boson...

Veenu: Never mind the Higgs boson. You already told me how it took so long for the aliens to construct the evidence for it. Tell me about the deadjims.

Sujata: There's this homeless guy who hangs around outside the grocery store, looking for a handout. Big, smelly guy with a salt-and-pepper beard. Used to be a brilliant physicist. All he'll tell me is that it doesn't mean anything to him anymore. There's this look in his eyes, like he's seeing through everything. You know, from the parking lots and the walls to the scripted conversations between people – he sees what's under it, what's real. And it's not a grand unified theory he sees, it's a mess.

Veenu: So he's a deadjim?

Sujata: He's a deadjim.

Veenu: Is there no other choice? Confronted with your hypothesis a person could become a nihilist, an existentialist, even a bodhisattva!

Sujata (annoyed): Not necessarily. There are different reasons why people become nihilists or bodhisattvas. A deadjim is a person who's seen through the façade, the surface illusions… oh, I see your point. Damn!

Veenu (consolingly): Still, it's a damned cool idea. The aliens-at-the-controls is nothing new, but the deadjims! Nice touch.

Sujata (growling): Stop mocking me.

Veenu (thoughtfully): Tell me something else, though. If I dream up an idea, something totally crazy, like 'the distant stars are made of cheese', does that mean the aliens will have to scramble to make it so?

Sujata: It doesn't work like that! That would be stupid. See, ideas have to have weight. Weight comes from internal consistency, and how much in line the idea is with the bedrock, the foundation the aliens have already laid. Weight also comes from how long the idea has lain around, and how many people believe it.

Veenu: You really believe this, don't you? So why do you keep publishing papers in physics?

Sujata: One, we have to eat. Two, I don't want the aliens to suspect that I'm on to them, do I? Plus it's fun to have a role in the construction of the universe. Hey, don't look at me like that! I don't really believe this shit! I like making things up, in case you haven't figured it out by now!

* * *

OVER THE NEXT few days Sujata went about her life doing what was expected of her, in a blind and oblivious fashion. She had to play the game for now. That's was everyone else did, didn't they? Step around each other in polite little circles, mouthing scripted lines, as though from a play. When the actor realizes it's just a play, what can the actor do but continue to repeat her words? When there are no words she can come up with as a substitute?

In the evenings she wrote furiously on sticky notes until she ran out of room on the white wall. She stuck some around her mother's little altar, so that they formed colorful haloes around the Buddha, the Nataraja, the garish Lakshmi and Jesus.

Sujata's Cosmic Censorship Principle: All material objects are surrounded by clouds of ambiguity – which may be virtual particles or prejudices or paradigms. Nothing in the universe is naked.

Sujata's Cosmic Uncertainty Principle: The Universe exists as a superposition of unformed possibilities for theorists to speculate about, and experimenters to discover. The alien technicians set things up so that the 'discovery' causes a possibility or a combination thereof to become 'real'.

She submitted her paper on the Higgs boson (the straightforward one) without bothering to review it, and began work on 'The Higgs Field Considered as a Metaphor for the Entanglement of Matter in Time'.

Just as the Higgs field gives mass to matter through coupling with various particles to different degrees, so does an analogous field tangle us in linear time, like a leaf carried by a river.

De-couple from that field, and you can wander outside of linear time. Aliens do not want you to do this because then you can see what they've been up to.

The thought came to Sujata then that the people she called deadjims must be able to do such a thing, that if she was turning into a deadjim too, she should be able to walk off linear time and see what the aliens were up to, if they were really there.

Sujata had been fourteen when she had first realized there was something strange about the universe. It happened when she began to notice that whenever she drew a graph, within a day or two she would see the shape of it in the real world: a city skyline, the planes of a face, the curving of a stair railing in a tall building. When she drew her first world-line, in her relativity class in high school, the road appeared before her for the first time. It took a few of these ghostly visitations for her to realize that the road was nothing but a world-line, her world-line, her path in life through space and time, made real, or as real as a vision could get. After that first time, the road appeared at random intervals, without warning. She had learned early in life that the universe was more than the notions of theorists and pundits.

As she remembered this, a thought came to her. She had been chewing the end of her pen; she set it down on an untouched plate of fish tacos. She marched up to the white wall and glared at it, and demanded silently that the road appear. This had never worked before. Her head hurt; the sticky notes swam before her eyes. There was a shimmer and a crackle, and the smell of hot plastic and cinnamon. There, before her, was the road.

THIS TIME SHE did walk up to the demarcation, the place where the road ended. At first the road seemed to make a half-hearted effort to maintain a distance between Sujata and the clean finish line, but her fury carried her forward until she was at the blank wall where the road stopped. She took a deep breath, tucked a stray tendril of hair behind her right ear, and walked through the wall.

She found herself on the lawn outside her house. The neighborhood was simultaneously familiar and different. She could tell that everything around was a hastily put together construct. She didn't know how she could tell, because it looked the same. But some inner eye had opened within her. She had wandered backstage at last, and she could see, in a manner of speaking, the supports for the stage-sets, the gantries, the unpainted cardboard backs of the façade that made up reality.

She walked around like a child, eyes round with wonder, and saw that her own life was nothing – all her theories and assumptions, her hypotheses about particles or people, were as intangible and meaningless as the cobwebs you brush away from your face when you enter a dark, abandoned room. Even meaning had no meaning. It was all a goddamned sham.

The *why* of it bothered her, though. Why would the aliens take all this trouble to deceive? What was in it for them?

The kid next door waved to her from his front porch. Bright little seven-year-old with a mop of copper colored hair – she'd help him with mathematics problems sometimes. She could see him with her inner eye, the atoms and molecules ghost-like, great voids of emptiness between them, the forces and reactions clear in places, fuzzy in others, where the processes had not yet been determined or invented. He was a ghost, a hastily put-together construct, needing and awaiting constant tinkering. She stared at him, at the maple trees, whose branches nodded at her as though in agreement. She saw the door of her own house. How had she gotten outside? Oh yes, she had walked through the wall. That meant she was probably locked out, not that it mattered. The road had ended for her because world-lines were part of the illusion of pattern and order. Once you saw that, no need for the illusion. The world swam before her, unfinished and awkward and imperfect. So that is how the homeless man at the grocery store had seen it. She knew that if she looked into a mirror she would find in her eyes the same look. She was a deadjim, and it was funny, and not funny at the same time. Veenu's bizarre behavior had been the thing you could not explain away. Who, or what, was Veenu, then?

She caught herself. There she was, constructing another schema. It was an endless obsession. Humans were so desperate for pattern that they had to invent it, construct it, even where it did not exist. Were other animals like that? Other aliens on other worlds? She thought of the gulf of space and time, and the impossibility of two species meeting and understanding each other. Different schemas might simply tear the cosmic fabric apart, shoddily constructed as it was.

She began to wander through the neighborhood. Although everything was as usual – the cars in the driveways, the shuttered windows, the guarded expressions on the faces of the few people she passed, the formulaic greetings, the sun beating down on the parking lot in front of the grocery store – she was suddenly frightened. "A nightmare," she said to herself. "I'm in a nightmare, and I'll wake up and have tea with Veenu and everything will be back to normal." But it wasn't. She passed the place near the store entrance where the homeless man always sat in a dilapidated heap, and as their eyes met, he seemed to solidify, to come into focus. A look of recognition passed between them that terrified her. She turned to go home.

The kid was still there on the front porch of his house. He waved again. Something occurred to her. She went up to him in desperation. Looking at him deliberately made him clearer, more real. She said,

"Peter, who else lives in my house?"

Peter's eyes went wide.

"Nobody, just you," he said. He smiled a little tentatively.

"Why am I getting sympathy cards then?"

"Because... your mother died." He stared at her.

She rubbed her hand across her face. She stumbled away to her house and sat heavily down on the front steps. She scratched absently at an itch on her left calf, where a mosquito had bitten her. She sensed its fat little body, replete with blood, its hum in her ear as it sailed away. For a moment she could see, through its compound eyes, the crazy, patchwork, swaying world.

There was a pad of sticky notes in her pocket. She had no pen. She plucked a blade of grass and began to write in invisible script.

The Universe does not need a bunch of control-freak aliens. The aliens are among us. The aliens are us.

The universe is a giant quantum-mechanical relativistic Rube-Goldberg patchwork construct, knit by interactions of its constituents, changed and ever changing through these interactions.

All we ever see are shadows cast on the wall of our limited understanding, and the shadows change depending on how the beast of reality mutates, and which way you shine the light.

She half-smiled. She was caught in her net of schemas just as much as before.

She looked up. The bright day was fading. She saw the familiar neighborhoods of middle America, the green lawns of Indrapal University, and the hornbills sailing awkwardly through sunset skies. She saw the tree she'd fallen off as a child. The scar was still there on her knee. She saw the people with whom she'd shared her life, so distant now, separated by space and time and more.

Then she saw Veenu striding through all the jagged pieces of reality, the backpack flung carelessly over one shoulder. She thought of calling out, but then she saw the serenity in Veenu's face, the way her arms swung as though she might take off into the air at any point. In her eyes was the same curious, interested, engaged look that Sujata knew so well. Long after she had gone, Sujata sat on the step, thinking about her choices. Before anything, she had to call her uncle, book a flight to Mumbai. The empty space inside her was filling up slowly with sorrow, like rain. She felt it as surely as she'd felt the mosquito's bite. She would go for the funeral. After that... after that, who knew? She'd have to think about it later.

ALWAYS IN OUR HEARTS

ADAM NEVILL

Adam is one of those writers who is as at home with the short story as he is with the novel. He's already proven himself with several stark, white-knuckle, visceral horror novels – Banquet for the Damned, Apartment 16, The Ritual and Last Days – and continues to produce short fiction on a regular basis. His story for House of Fear (Solaris, 2011) was short-listed for the British Fantasy Award and he has appeared in many anthologies. What follows shows Adam at his very best – a hit and run driver faces the consequences of his actions in a tale of terror that is gradual in its build-up and devastating in its pay-off.

RAY LARCH OFTEN marvelled at the amount of traffic accidents that were possible. Their consequences he didn't choose to think about, but such a consideration was inevitable once his mind turned in this direction. Such thoughts mostly occurred in the few hours when he wasn't driving a taxi.

If he turned too quickly on a wet road, or failed to execute an emergency stop in time when a child ran into the road, or lost concentration and plunged into oncoming headlights, or drove recklessly while too close to the vehicle in front, or fell asleep on a motorway at night, or reversed over a toddler not visible in his rear view mirrors... The opportunities appeared infinite. And as a mere speck among millions of other motorists, from the moment he turned the ignition key he knew he risked an involvement in any number of incidents, at any time, as did every other motorist. It was a lottery, and every motorist had a ticket.

He guessed the clincher about the outcome of a potential accident involving him came down to his decisions and reactions, often made in less than a second, compounded by the decisions and reactions made by other motorists, cyclists and pedestrians. Considering the outcome of the wrong choice in either respect, there wasn't much time to make a crucial choice of stop, accelerate, swerve or jump.

When he thought of the deaths, the disability, the physical torment and human misery of long term physical rehabilitation, the lifelong grief or invalidity that he could inflict through a traffic accident (in the amount of time it took a person to realise they were having an accident), he often wondered why he was even allowed to drive a car at all. Or why anyone else was allowed to drive one either.

He still had near misses. He had them all the time. He drove a private hire car seven days a week. He never slept more than five hours in any night and would haul himself, baffled and blinking, out of bed at 3am for an airport fare, or to pick up drunken girls in short skirts at the weekend when the clubs closed. The upskirt potential alone on those latter jobs could be the cause of any number of accidents, because every time he looked in the rear view mirror he wasn't checking the traffic behind his car; while he endeavoured to glimpse gusset it would be so easy to jack-knife a tipsy pedestrian over the bonnet and bring an end to their days of unassisted mobility.

The more he thought about accidents, the more he also wondered why more vehicles out there were not suddenly crashing. Or why the entire network of roads did not become a long sequence of traffic accidents. Should drivers undergo the same fallibility assessments as train drivers and airline pilots? Or did that come down to a matter of scale?

We drive because we forget, he'd decided. We forget pain, we forget fear, we forget the hot-cold paralysis of near misses, we forget consequences. We forget our vulnerability: the very fragility of our bodies, of our wobbling heads packed with brain matter, mounted on a thin spinal column, the weakest link in the entire animal kingdom. And we forget how we are dependent upon those miniscule threads of nerve tissue that – once severed – lead to legs incapable of sensation, or wheezing apparatus standing sentinel at our white-sheeted bedsides. We forget the picture of the car smashed beneath the truck on the hard shoulder, and the blackened silhouette of a figure burned into its seat in a motorway pileup. We forget the vestiges of wreckage in a newspaper picture in which four teenagers died. We look away from the dirty, wilting flowers tied to metal railings on that corner you have to slow down for, if you know the road. In time, we even forget how we felt at the funeral of a child.

Our entire existence is contingent on forgetting horror. Maybe all of our repeat infractions as a species are based on not remembering the horror of past infractions. And Ray had even begun to forget the time he clipped a cyclist on Rocky Lane two years before.

He never stopped his car and after a sudden, metallic *thunk* against one of the passenger side doors, he barely heard anything else because of the volume of his radio. At the edge of his hearing, as he passed, there was a suggestion of keys being dropped onto the tarmac somewhere behind his car.

Ray had been doing at least forty miles per hour in a thirty, and weaving around a row of cars badly parked at the curb. But he never noticed the cyclist until the back of his jacket seemed to fill the windscreen.

The kid was black, he thought, though wasn't sure. But he'd glanced into his rear view mirror and there was absolutely no cyclist in the road anymore. He'd put his foot down because he barely touched the guy, or so he told himself later. Not for a fraction of a second had he thought of stopping. Getting away had been the only conscious consideration.

When he decided against buying the next day's *Mail*, Ray realised he did not want to know anything about the night before. He avoided television too and left the radio switched off for three entire weeks. By avoiding all local news, he felt he had not been involved in what might have happened to the cyclist. By the end of his self-imposed news blackout, he was nearly certain that only the cyclist's knee had, in fact, been grazed by his car. The kid must have quickly turned his bicycle onto the pavement, which is why he had vanished from Ray's rear view of the road. Ray told himself this so many times he almost believed it was the truth.

Three weeks after the incident, and long after the paint job on his car had dried, Ray was compelled to return to Rocky Lane on his way to a fare at Alexandra Stadium. There was still a great mound of flowers at the roadside at more or less the same place he had met the cyclist so unexpectedly.

When Ray made an offhand mention of the flowers on Rocky Lane at the taxi rank on Colmore Row, as he fiddled with his phone, he learned from another driver that he had indeed killed a teenager, who had been riding a mountain bike to the Hamstead chip shop, without a helmet or lights. The other driver wasn't sure, but didn't think there were any witnesses. "Fucking cyclists," they'd both agreed, and rolled their eyes knowingly.

Ray had never again driven along Rocky Lane and still circumnavigated that entire estate if ever asked to pick-up or drop-off close to it. He'd also arrived at the conclusion that if we vividly remembered the misery of every cold, cut, and bruise, in anticipation of the next illness or misfortune, we would all go mad. Or we would all become inactive and unable to function. The ability to forget was a kind of advance braking system of the mind, and the effectiveness of his own surprised him.

So did the mad have perfect recall, or the ability to imagine the full horror of the consequences of existence? Now there is a thought, Ray thought, and turned into the street to pick up his next fare.

Ray had never made a pickup from this area of North Birmingham, and was unaware there were even houses standing in the area where Hockley became Aston and the Jewellery Quarter. The area was close to the city centre and remained a labyrinth of closed redbrick warehouses, revived industrial estates, hole-in-the-wall commercial interests attached to broader industries, interspersed with cash and carries, mostly closed retail units, developments of unsold flats, barely functioning churches and one or two old school Midlands pubs. But his satnav brought him to a small settlement of houses attached to a wall of Victorian red brick that had once been home to a local industry; the houses were opposite a patch of waste ground used for storing white commercial vans.

The residential side of the street was typical of a Midlands terraced row; permanently in shadow, slouched at the curb as unappealingly as a group of scruffy labourers stood in line for something soul destroying and poorly paid. This street had somehow escaped clearances, Luftwaffe bombs and gentrification.

The eight terraced houses also looked as though they had shuffled back from the road, as if they didn't want to meet the eye of any passing motorist. Their dark, traffic-grimed windows and peeling window frames didn't give much away about their interiors, and Ray would have guessed, at a glance, that they were unoccupied. From the rear of one of the properties, dirty black smoke rose into the sky suggesting a bonfire.

The man who came out of the terraced house numbered 129 came out with a smile that Ray found disproportionate to the prompt arrival of a taxi at his address. He wasn't wearing a coat, and his feet looked too big for the pair of brown slippers he wore, which was odd because it was raining.

The tiny front garden of 129 was a wreck; filled with sodden cardboard boxes containing bottles, rusting tins, what looked like garden waste, and a kind of bracken that sprouted so high it obscured the ground floor sash window.

The call from the controller listed this address, the name John, and a landline phone number. "Wants taking to various places" was the only instruction. Beside the last piece of information, it was an ordinary enough job.

Ray watched the grinning elderly man make his way to the driver's side window.

"Afternoon!" the man said, and then looked at a sky glooming towards a rainy dusk.

Ray nodded, and looked about the man's person as if querying the lack of a jacket. "John, is it?"

"She'll be out soon," John said.

Perhaps the tatty bastard in slippers was not the passenger. Ray hoped so; he disliked the man's half-smiling face. Unless they were attractive and female, or it was an airport fare, Ray found it hard not to greet every passenger with an attitude of weary, surly impatience. He didn't particularly like this about his customer service, but he couldn't help it. It is what working from seven until eleven did to those who provided a service to the general public.

Behind the thick spectacle's lenses John's eyes were alight with excitement. "I'll need a hand with her." He seemed surprised that Ray didn't share his enthusiasm for the task.

Not a fucking wheelchair.

"You've a very special passenger this evening. You're going all over. But she'll look after you eventually." The man winked to embellish this tantalising suggestion of a generous tip.

"Where to first, mate?" Ray climbed out of the car and wanted to hurry up the overgrown path to the house to escape the rain, which didn't bother John at all. "How many places does she want to go?"

The man stopped and in a show of exuberance spread his arms wide as if to indicate vastness. "She knows where to take us. Where to start and where to finish."

Ray took a second desultory inspection of the elderly man's grey slacks, which looked to have once belonged to a suit, and were now held above his navel by a white plastic belt. A diamond patterned pullover was tucked into the waistband of the trousers. An oddball with an elderly relative, and the fare would probably be paid out of a mobility allowance. But he would have preferred clarification on both the destinations of the journey and an assurance that this man had enough money to pay for it. He adopted a quizzical facial expression as he waited for the man in the slippers to catch up with him on the front path.

"Yes, yes, she's in there, waiting." The man said, misreading Ray's yearning for reassurance, while jabbing a stubby forefinger, yellowed with nicotine, at a black doorway. The man's pullover stank of sweat. The front of his trousers were greasy.

Even now, Ray still came across pockets of the world that hadn't changed and that reminded him of old films. This was one of them. And for good or ill, he knew houses were like people. Just as you never really know what goes on behind a face, you also have no idea what a home really looks like behind the façade.

"Takes me time to get her up. Taken me an age this year," John said. "But she is raring to go now, I can tell you. And a lot of people are waiting for us."

Ray didn't ask any more questions, because he wasn't interested and had already decided to keep conversation to a minimum. *Just get the job done.* He wondered if his disgust at the living conditions inside the house were obvious, but then realised that he didn't care if they were.

The house was cold and smelled of old bin bags and gas. And something else, like the odour that gathers around thunderstorms, which was stronger than the underlying smells of gas and waste.

One ceiling light was on in a rear room of the house and all of the curtains were drawn. What yellowy illumination existed was sufficient to indicate that John hadn't taken the rubbish out of his dismal home in a while.

Following the shabby figure, Ray saw that a narrow track had been made in the living room, fashioned between bulging rubbish sacks and cardboard boxes packed with what looked like old clothes. Perhaps the man was in the rag trade.

Ray peered inside a box. A little girl's dress and a pair of brown sandals were placed on top of other clothes inside pink plastic bags. The evidence of juvenilia in the man's house inspired Ray to look about a bit more carefully. He peered into a second box and was relieved to see an adult man's suede coat, a pair of broken glasses and some scuffed shoes.

The second room may once have been intended as a dining room, though any indication of the room's former function had been obliterated by what looked a collection of every free paper printed in Birmingham within the old man's lifetime.

"I'll get her out the kitchen," John said.

The entrance from the dining room to the kitchen was missing a door, and through the doorway Ray glimpsed a dark silhouette, as small as a child, soundlessly turn away from a counter before slipping deeper into the unlit kitchen. John vanished into the darkness as if in pursuit, but never switched on the light.

While John messed around in the kitchen out of sight, Ray peered about the dining room. In the background, he heard the old man say, "Your carriage awaits, your Highness."

Ray thought about taking a picture of the room on his mobile phone for the other drivers at the coffee stand, but his anxiety about not being paid swamped any other inclination or thought. "Alright in there?" he asked the darkness. "Minimum fare is a fiver, mate."

"Yes. Yes. Why wouldn't it be? A lot of preparation has gone into this evening, so we don't want any snags. And you'll do a lot better than a fiver too, driver. You will be justly compensated." This was said from inside the unlit kitchen with a tinge of sarcasm that made Ray suffer a sight disorientation at the man's tone.

"Ain't me that's not ready," he fired into the darkness. There was no reply.

A series of framed pictures on the dining room wall, half concealed by a bale of newspapers, caught Ray's eye. There were two framed photographs of a middle-aged woman; the second picture featured John, though better dressed and well-groomed than he was now, sat beside the woman at what looked like a table in a restaurant. Dead wife, Ray thought without a trace of emotion. It was hard to see what the middle picture depicted, a painting that gave nothing away beside an impression of black smoke billowing up from something that burned in the section of the picture that was concealed. The smoke moved across a grey sky.

John returned from the kitchen wearing an anorak, with the hood pulled tight around his face, which made him look imbecilic. Held in his arms, the lid tucked beneath his chin, was a cane-work laundry basket painted yellow. "If you get the other side, I think we can manage." The lid was secured to the bottom with green gardener's twine.

"What is...?" Ray started to ask, but didn't know how to finish.

"It's all I've got that's big enough. And it will suffice. Now, you must drive very carefully, you understand? I hope that was explained to you."

"We going to the laundrette?"

What he'd suggested was offensive enough for the elderly man's face to darken with rage, before he said, "Just get the other side!"

Ray soon felt like he was carrying the entire weight of the heavy basket on his back, while John muttered instructions – "Be careful. Careful! That's it. Careful" – as they picked a path through the rubbish on the floor. Whatever was inside the basket was also living. Maybe some kind of animal. Ray felt it skittering around inside the cane basket; perhaps seeking a way out, or a stable surface, in the way animals do in transit. Probably a dog. Was that what he had seen in the kitchen? A dog?

"This a rare breed or something, mate?"

"You have no idea of her value."

"Ain't you got no cage?"

John ignored the question.

Outside at the car, after much fussing, the old man clipped himself and the wicker basket into respective seat belts in the rear of Ray's car, which quickly filled with the odour of the old man's sweat. Ray climbed into the driving seat and cracked a window.

"Please close that, in case she... it's cold out, you know," his passenger said.

Ray sighed and started the car. "Where to, mate?"

"I have the first address."

"Let's have it."

The first three digits of the post code, B20, indicated Handsworth Wood, a mostly affluent Sikh area. And the satnav quickly found Somerset Road, a place Ray was familiar with; a long, quiet road flanked by large Victorian houses.

"A vets, is it? Or you breeding her or what?" Ray asked, while eyeing the cheap, yellow basket in the rear view mirror. "Sure you ain't got one of them carry cases? Can't be very comfortable for the animal. Dog, is it?"

The old man sat close to the basket and rested one arm across the front as if to protect the cargo if the car should stop suddenly. He said nothing to Ray and seemed content to grin at the rear view mirror in a way that started to make Ray feel uncomfortable.

"What is it?" Ray repeated.

The man's mouth loosened into a sneer. "Maybe you had better just continue with the role you have been assigned, *driver*." The way he said *driver* was oddly formal, and old fashioned, but not without a trace of condescension either.

"Some manners never go amiss, mate."

"We don't want to be late."

Ray wound his window down further and pulled away from the curb.

AFTER RAY HAD helped John and his laundry basket up to the front door of their destination, and then returned to his car to wait a good ten minutes for another passenger that John had told him to wait for at the same address, he'd begun to smell smoke.

Peering through the passenger side window, Ray watched a thick plume of black smoke billow over the roof of the house that John had gone inside, and drift into the sky. The fire must have been burning in the rear garden. Over the sound of his radio, Ray was also sure he heard a short, sharp human cry issue from the rear of the property. But the scream was immediately followed and muffled by the laughter of a large group of people.

"Not the weather for a barbecue," he said, in an attempt at humour and as a tactic for drawing out some information from his new passenger, when she eventually shuffled down to his car. "Lot of smoke back there. What's it, bonfire? Festival, like?"

The ancient Indian woman in the rear never answered him. Once she and her Samsonite suitcase had been installed into the rear of the vehicle, she had merely passed a piece of paper between the seats. Printed in capitals was an address Ray recognised in Handsworth, near the park. He wouldn't need the satnav.

As Ray pulled away, he glanced through the passenger side window so he could see into the space between the house and the equally vast neighbouring property. The sound of laughter and applause coming from the back garden continued. The scream must have been part of some Asian festival or tradition. The people who had initially crowded about the front door to welcome John and his laundry basket were all well-heeled Sikhs, as Ray had expected them to be. Though their smiles and greetings were warmer and more excitable than he'd thought possible for the arrival of a little scruffy man and his pet inside a laundry basket.

During the journey to Handsworth Park, the elderly Asian woman never looked up from staring at her withered hands that she held together on her lap. Bonfire smoke had caught in the folds of her Sari. Ray was struck with the notion that she didn't like him.

After Ray parked outside the large semi-detached Victorian house, across the road from Handsworth Park, that the old Indian woman had requested, an expectant middle-aged white couple appeared in the doorway before Ray had applied the handbrake. They came into the street to help the thin, elderly Indian woman out of Ray's taxi.

The couple looked alternative yet fashionable. Ray recognised the type, who had begun migrating into what had been an Asian and West Indian neighbourhood because the big houses and long gardens were half the price of houses in Moseley and Kings Heath. Two older children, both boys with long hair, skipped around the Indian woman's case as if Father Christmas had arrived.

The mother held a toddler in her arms and, without looking Ray in the eye, said, "We need you to take another passenger. She'll be out shortly." She handed a twenty pound note through the window.

When Ray slipped a hand inside his jacket pocket to find fifteen pounds change, she said, "No, no, keep it."

"You sure?" Ray said. "Only a fiver's fare."

"We need you to hang on for a few minutes. You know, keep the meter running."

Ray shrugged. "No problem at all. You need a hand with that case?"

But the woman had already turned away and Ray could see her husband raising the Samsonite case over the threshold of the house with the help of his eldest son. The husband never looked at Ray either. The elderly woman was already inside; she had been in a hurry to get off the street.

More perplexed than he could remember being about his work for some time, Ray waited fifteen minutes for the next passenger to come out of the house. And while he waited, he heard another desperate wail, that he guessed was human, shoot up from the rear of the property he was parked outside. The cry was cut short by the burst of a firework, that howled and shatter-sprinkled above his car.

Ray climbed out of his car and looked at the sky. The firework had already dispersed into the cold black air. But he could smell smoke. Wood smoke and meat cooking.

The door to the house that he'd delivered the elderly Indian woman to opened and shut quickly behind another elderly woman with a tartan shopping trolley on little wheels. Her association with the family was almost as incongruous as that of the elderly Asian woman he had dropped off at the address. Maybe the new passenger was a caterer and the family wanted Ray to drop her home now that the party had started and her work was done. There was lots of laughter and applause and excitable shrieking coming from the children at the rear of the house now. Someone shouted, "I don't believe it!"

The woman who had come out of the house stood on the doorstep and pointed at the shopping trolley. "Give us a hand, please, driver."

Ray went and collected the trolley. The top of the trolley was tightly secured with the elasticated cords used to fix objects on the roof racks of cars. The trolley was heavy and Ray was certain that as he raised it, something had flopped or fallen against one side of the case, then kicked itself upright. "Party they's having, is it?" he asked his new passenger.

"Once a year you gets your chance. This year mine come round," she said, but didn't elaborate. A cloud of black smoke rose from the rear of the house, then billowed up above the red roof and dispersed into the darkness that smothered the park.

"Another pet in here?" Ray asked, nodding at the trolley as he wheeled it across the pavement to his car. "Sure it's legal to have an animal inside? Can it breathe?"

The woman said, "It's all I got and she don't mind."

He dropped the woman and her shopping trolley off at an address in Sandwell Valley, close to the large farm that was open to the public. Like the elderly Asian woman, his passenger did not speak during the journey, and had only broken into, "Here, here it is. This one, it must be," as Ray pulled up outside a large white private house with high walls. "I can't wait to see her."

"Who?"

Judging by her gleeful expression, she was too excited to answer, and the woman clambered out with a groan. He received the impression his passenger had been utterly indifferent to the person who drove the vehicle she'd travelled in; the person responsible for her safety, let alone her enigmatic schedule. *Nothing new there.*

Ray wheeled the tartan shopping trolley up to the white house. It banged against his leg and he heard the scrape of claws against the trolley's lining. The trolley stank of smoke. He left it outside the front door and returned to his car.

And so the curious nature and sequence of his afternoon and evening's work continued. He'd made forty quid and was on a roll, but his curiosity about his passengers and their respective cases was beginning to stifle his delight at the abundance of work. So he decided to be more assertive with the next passenger: an elderly black man.

Ray helped the passenger position a large holdall in the rear. A little brass lock secured the end of the bag's zipper. The interior of the car bloomed afresh with the fragrance of cold air and wood smoke. Ray climbed into the driver's seat and cracked the window wider. "Where to, mate?"

"He say he gonna be here." A piece of paper was passed between the seats.

Ray frowned. It was the very first address he had picked up John and the cane basket from, at the edge of Hockley.

In the rear view mirror, Ray looked at the man in the rear. The man met his eye without even blinking: stolid, unfriendly, obstinate, and somewhat entitled.

Ray glanced at the bag beside his passenger. It was the type of canvas sports bag that teenagers favoured. It had West Bromwich Albion's badge at one end. "Baggies fan?"

"My son," the man said, and looked out of the window.

Ray drove in silence, but struggled to keep his mind on the road. Just as well he knew them so well. "Not being funny, like, but do you mind if I ask you a question?"

As if he hadn't heard Ray, the passenger never moved his head.

"But I pick your mate up at this address that we are going to. And he gets in the car with his pet in a basket. And then we go to another house and another house, and each time it's the same thing. Someone with an animal, I think, in a bag. So I'm guessing you got one in there, too, yeah? So what's it all about, yeah? 'Cus I am clueless."

The man never spoke for at least a minute. He just stared at the buildings they passed as they neared the city centre. And Ray found it hard to read the passenger's mood from glances into the rear view mirror; though he suspected he intuited a grave sadness in the man's eyes whenever the headlights of a passing vehicle flashed through the car at the same time Ray checked his mirror.

"Life is full of repetition," the man eventually said. "Same bad things keep happening."

The statement, because that is what it was, mystified Ray. Nor was it information he felt capable of responding to. "You all right, mate?" was the best he could do. "Ain't none of my business, but I'm just wondering out loud what you're all doing. Curiosity, like."

"You realise it's not just you. There's others who been through the same thing."

"What, like? You talking about John and that Asian woman, and that woman with the shopping trolley?"

The man briefly looked up from his morbid self-absorption, but never spoke.

Ray pushed. "The others, like? With the bags I been picking up here, there and everywhere?"

"Here, there and everywhere," the man said and then sighed. "I don't know them. Only met John once." He pinched his fingers in his eye sockets as if he were stoppering tears.

As his curiosity became discomfort, Ray looked forward and drove through the dark in his own silence. He only spoke after he'd pulled up outside the first address. "Fifteen pound."

The man paid him with a hand that shook with nerves, or palsy. "Help me with my bag, please."

"Right ho."

The two men held one strap of the sports bag each and carried what could have been a long, well behaved dog, zipped inside a holdall, up to the front door of John's address. The passenger depressed the bell.

Though Ray heard nothing chime inside the house, John opened the front door within seconds. "You made good time." John said this as if the passenger had driven the car. "She's been in there long enough. Bring her through." He ignored Ray.

With the bag wedged between them, Ray and his passenger squeezed into the hovel. There were more lights on inside the house now, though the place was still dim as if the shadow upon it would never allow the brightness of the lights to grow. When they passed through the room filled with boxed clothes, the last passenger paused and said, "All these?"

Over his shoulder, John said, "And more every year. Mostly kids. Nine and ten we find. Now, to the kitchen, if you please. And I'll tell you where you can set her down."

Ray struggled into the kitchen with the holdall. Whatever was inside the bag had begun to sniff at his trouser leg through the side of the canvass.

The kitchen was remarkably tidy in contrast to the rest of the house. A small table, with a floral pattern printed on its surface, stood at one side of the room with two chairs pulled out as if in anticipation of imminent use.

"He'll come in through here, Glenroy," John said to the passenger, once they were all inside the kitchen with the holdall.

"Here? You sure?" Glenroy asked his host.

Ray's bafflement and curiosity compelled him to stay a little longer. He wanted to see what was inside the bag.

"Never fails," John said, in a softer voice that Ray hadn't thought the man capable of. "This was Wendy's favourite place. And I always use it for those of you that can't entertain at home. As long as this is your son's bag, there won't be any problem, I can assure you."

Glenroy nodded and then looked at the back door. It opened onto a cold darkness that flickered with firelight. "Through there?"

"We done? I gotta get on." Ray said to both men. Neither seemed to hear him, or they were ignoring him. "Look–"

"Just set it down on the patio," John said curtly to Ray, and stepped through the back door.

"Come on, we got to get this done," Glenroy said to Ray.

"What?" Ray asked.

"Once you have helped me outside with this, it's over," the black man said.

Ray carried the bag out of the kitchen and into a small paved yard that cringed beneath what could have been a viaduct. And his attention was seized by the size of the pyre in the yard, set against the far wall. Beside the pyre of bracken and wooden pallets was an oil drum that belched black smoke. Upon the top of the pyre was an old vinyl car seat. A small set of metal steps, the kind you see in warehouses or large libraries, had been positioned at the foot of the pyre and led to the seat.

Glenroy muttered, "Dear God."

"This part is always difficult," John said, to soothe the nerves of the elderly man.

"What is this?" Ray asked, looking from one man to the other. They ignored him.

John touched the passenger's elbow. "Glenroy, believe me, you won't even notice the fire as soon as you see your son. Just go and find yourself a seat at the table and he'll be here shortly. I suggest you sit with your back to the garden to avoid distractions in what will be a very precious time. You will probably hear a bit of fuss out here, and then your son will arrive and embrace you. There is no need for you to see this part of the proceedings, though some clients prefer to make the offering a joyous occasion."

Glenroy nodded and headed for the kitchen.

The undisclosed connection between fire and the contents of the bags, suddenly made Ray eager to get back to his car. Besides being just too weird, the sinister implication of such a backyard installation was not lost on him. He thought of the black plumes of smoke he had seen at every address that evening, of the photo on the dining room wall, and of the distant screams. Ray turned to follow his last passenger out of the yard.

"Not you, *driver*." John said into the back of Ray's head, in a tone of voice that made Ray tense. There followed the sound of a zipper being quickly undone in the cold air of the cement yard. "We're not done with you yet."

Ray had heard enough. "What's your game, eh? I've been driving–" he said as he turned to confront the man standing behind him. But then lost the ability to speak, and the strength in both of his legs seemed to drain through the soles of his shoes, at the sight of what had climbed out of the sports bag and now stood upright. Something that had travelled in his car all evening. And it wasn't a dog, or a cat, or any kind of pet.

"Now." John raised both hands into the air and made a series of rapid gestures as if he were performing sign language. "You either take your seat unassisted up there" – John nodded at the summit of the unlit pyre – "or she will be forced to *seat* you."

The back door closed and Ray heard a key turn in the lock. He turned his head and watched Glenroy take a seat at the kitchen table.

"The duration of the event is mercifully short," John said. "A bit longer than it took you to knock Glenroy's son from his bicycle on Rocky Lane."

"I... I... I..."

"Yes, yes, that's all very well. But there are consequences, and it's getting late and you're the last one this year and there's no time for any fiddle, so please take your seat."

"What..."

Within the ebb and flow of the firelight and what illumination it offered, even though the thing on the patio was as tall and hairy as a fully grown male chimpanzee, what had been inside the sports bag was not an ape. For as long as he could bear to look at it, Ray could see that it wasn't a primate, because there were trotters on the end of its short rear legs. And though the thing's face was horribly reminiscent of a pig, it wasn't a pig either, because it stood upright like a child. The little figure shivered in the night air.

When it grinned at Ray, he whimpered and stepped towards the garden fence.

John's brusque voice penetrated his shock. "You'll only feel the flames for about three seconds, driver. Nothing more is required of you, then she'll bleed you out. So I always suggest that you raise your chin, or you will burn for longer than is necessary in this particular ritual. Now, to your chair please, *driver*."

Ray turned and fell at the fence. It was old and sagged with rot. He would kick it down, run.

"Soon as I drop my hands, driver, she will be released. I can assure you that you will get no further than my yard."

"Wha...?"

"Hit and run," John said with all the pomp of a scout master. The firelight from the oil drum flickered across the lenses of his spectacles and Ray could no longer see the old man's eyes. "She followed the scent of your callousness. A challenge. Guilt, shame, and even pride are more established spores. And she's had three of you today and reunited three mothers with their children, albeit for an incredibly short time."

"What is—"

With the impatience and irritation that John had shown him that day, the scruffy old man cut him short. "She became a good friend of my wife. After Wendy was killed on a pedestrian crossing not far from here in 1994. And her killer sat in the chair far longer than you will tonight, driver. So be thankful that time has mellowed me. Time ever heals, they say. You even start to forget. This is how I remember. Now, shall we begin?"

Ray gripped the top of the wooden fence. "Fuck off!"

John dropped both of his arms. The palms of his hands slapped his hips.

RAY BEGAN TO scream even before he sat buckled into the car seat at the summit of the pyre. And when John stuck a blazing taper of rolled newspaper into the base of the bracken, that had been soaked in the petrol, whose fumes now clung to his face, Ray looked to the kitchen as if to appeal for mercy.

He saw his last passenger, Glenroy, through the glass panel in the kitchen door. And over the kitchen table the old man embraced another darker and more indistinct figure. One who had already buried a face, that Ray could not see, on its father's shoulder.

Ray screamed afresh when the heat of the flames burst upwards to crisp the hair on his exposed ankles.

He thrust his head back and exposed his throat. "Now!"

ABOUT THE AUTHORS

Jay Caselberg is an Australian author based in Europe. His work has appeared in multiple venues and several languages worldwide and includes horror, science fiction, fantasy, literary and mixes of all of them, including poetry, but generally with a dark edge. His novel *Empties*, billed as a novel of brutal psychological horror, is due soon. More can be found at his website: www.jaycaselberg.com.

Zen Cho is a Malaysian writer based in London. Her short fiction has appeared most recently in *Esquire Malaysia*, *Andromeda Spaceways Inflight Magazine*, and Prime Books anthology *Bloody Fabulous*. She is a 2013 finalist for the John W. Campbell Award for Best New Writer.

S.L. Grey is a collaboration between Sarah Lotz and Louis Greenberg. Based in Cape Town, Sarah is a novelist and screenwriter and die-hard zombie fanatic. She writes crime novels and thrillers under her own name, and as Lily Herne she and her daughter Savannah Lotz write the *Deadlands* series of zombie novels for young adults. Louis is a Johannesburg-based fiction writer and editor. He was a bookseller for several years, and has a Master's degree in vampire fiction and a doctorate on the post-religious apocalyptic fiction of Douglas Coupland. S. L.'s first novel, *The Mall*, was published by Corvus in 2011.

The Ward came out in 2012 and *The New Girl*, the last of their Downside novels, in October 2013. They have also published a handful of short stories.

Rochita Loenen-Ruiz is a Filipino writer who currently lives and writes in the Netherlands. A graduate of the Clarion West Writer's Workshop, she was the recipient of the Octavia Butler Scholarship in 2009. Rochita's fiction has been published and anthologized online and in print and she was the first Filipino writer to be shortlisted for the BSFA short fiction award. Aside from writing a regular column for *Strange Horizons*, she also writes essays, reviews, commentaries and criticism. She is working on her first novel. Follow her on twitter (@ rcloenenruiz) or visit her website at rcloenenruiz.com

Helen Marshall is an award-winning Canadian author, editor, and bibliophile. Her poetry and fiction have been published in *The Chiaroscuro*, *Abyss & Apex*, *Lady Churchill's Rosebud Wristlet* and *Tor.com* and has been reprinted in several Year's Best anthologies. Her debut collection of short stories *Hair Side, Flesh Side* (ChiZine Publications, 2012) was named one of the Top Ten books of 2012 by *January Magazine*. It has been short-listed for an Aurora Award and a British Fantasy Sydney J. Bounds Award, and has been long-listed for the Frank O'Connor International Short Story Prize.

Sophia McDougall was supposed to be an Oxford English literature academic before running away in 2002 to write fiction. She is the author of the bestselling *Romanitas* trilogy (published by Orion/Gollancz and twice shortlisted for the Sidewise Award for·Alternate History), set in a contemporary world where the Roman Empire never fell. Her first novel for children, *Mars Evacuees*, will be published by Egmont and Harper Collins US in 2014. Her short stories have been published by Jurassic London and NewCon, as well as Solaris. She also creates digital art and mentors aspiring writers.

Paul Meloy is the author of *Islington Crocodiles* and *Dogs With Their Eyes Shut*. His work has appeared in numerous anthologies and magazines. He is the recipient of the British Fantasy Award, for his short story "Black Static". He lives in Torquay.

Anil Menon's short fiction can be found in a variety of anthologies and spec-fic magazines including *Albedo One, Apex's Digest, Interzone, LCRW and Strange Horizons*. His novel *The Beast With Nine Billion Feet* (Zubaan, 2009) was short-listed for the 2010 Vodafone-Crossword award and Carl Baxter Society's Parallax Prize. Along with Vandana Singh, he co-edited *Breaking the Bow* (Zubaan, 2012), an anthology of spec-fic stories inspired by the Ramayana. He can be reached at iam@anilmenon.com.

Adam Nevill was born in Birmingham, England, in 1969 and grew up in England and New Zealand. He is the author of the supernatural horror novels *Banquet for the Damned, Apartment 16, The Ritual, Last Days*, and *House of Small Shadows*. He lives in Birmingham and can be contacted through www.adamlgnevill.com

Philip Reeve is the author of numerous books for children and young adults, including the *Mortal Engines* quartet, *Fever Crumb, Larklight, Here Lies Arthur, Goblins*, and *Oliver and the Seawigs* (with illustrator Sarah McIntyre). He lives on Dartmoor with his wife and son.

Vandana Singh is an alien currently living in the Boston area, where she writes science fiction and teaches physics at a small state university. She was born and raised in New Delhi, India, and acquired an early appreciation for science and the arts, later coming to the US for a Ph.D. in theoretical particle physics. Her stories have been published in numerous venues, including *Strange Horizons, Clarkesworld, Lightspeed*, and anthologies such as *Solaris Rising 2* and *The Other Half of the Sky*. She is a winner of the Carl Brandon Parallax Award and many of her stories have been reprinted in Year's Best anthologies.

Benjanun Sriduangkaew spends her free time on words, amateur photography, and the pursuit of unusual makeup. She has a love for cities, airports, and bees. Her fiction can be found in *GigaNotoSaurus, Beneath Ceaseless Skies, Clarkesworld* and various anthologies.

Lavie Tidhar is the World Fantasy Award-winning author of *Osama*, of *The Bookman Histories* trilogy and many other works. He won the British Fantasy Award for Best Novella for *Gorel & The Pot-Bellied God* and a BSFA Award for his non-fiction, and was nominated variously for a Campbell, Sturgeon and Sidewise awards. He grew up on a kibbutz in Israel and in South Africa, but currently resides in London. His latest novels are *Martian Sands* and *The Violent Century* and, forthcoming, his comics debut, *Adler*.

Ian Whates currently has two published novel series, the Noise books (space opera) from Solaris, and the City of 100 Rows trilogy (urban fantasy with steampunk overtones and SF underpinning) via Angry Robot. He has also seen some 50 of his short stories appear in a variety of venues, two of which have been shortlisted for BSFA awards. His work has received honourable mentions in Gardner Dozois' *Years Best* anthologies and appeared in Tor books' *Futures from Nature*, which gathers the best stories published in the science journal *Nature. Growing Pains,* his second collection, appeared via PS Publishing in March 2013. Ian served a term as Overseas Regional Director for SFWA (the Science Fiction Writers of America) and, in June 2013, stepped down as chairman of the BSFA (British Science Fiction Association) – a position he had held since 2008. When not writing, Ian works as an editor, having edited titles in the long running *The Mammoth Book of...* series for Constable and Robinson and the on-going *Solaris Rising* series for Solaris. In his spare time he runs multiple award-wining publisher NewCon Press, which he founded by accident in 2006.

Rio Youers is the British Fantasy Award–nominated author of *End Times* and *Old Man Scratch*. His short fiction has been published by, among others, St. Martin's Griffin, HarperCollins, and Cemetery Dance. His latest novel, *Westlake Soul,* was recently nominated for Canada's prestigious Sunburst Award, and has been optioned for movie by Hollywood producer, Stephen Susco. Rio lives in southwestern Ontario with his wife, Emily, and their daughter, Lily Maye.

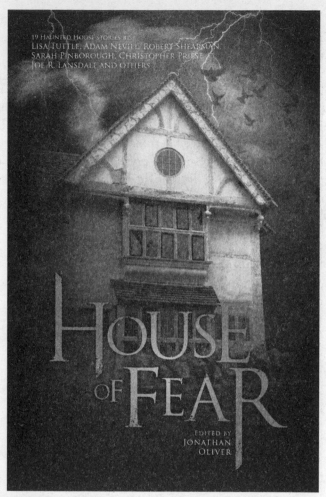

19 HAUNTED HOUSE STORIES BY
LISA TUTTLE, ADAM NEVILL, ROBERT SHEARMAN,
SARAH PINBOROUGH, CHRISTOPHER PRIEST,
JOE R. LANSDALE AND OTHERS

HOUSE
OF FEAR

EDITED BY
JONATHAN
OLIVER

UK ISBN: 978-1-907992-06-3 • US ISBN: 978-1-907992-07-0 • £7.99/$7.99 CAN $9.99

The tread on the landing outside the door when you know you are the only one in the house. The wind whistling through the eaves, carrying the voices of the dead. The figure glimpsed briefly through the cracked window of a derelict house. Critically-acclaimed editor Jonathan Oliver brings horror home with a collection of haunted house stories by Lisa Tuttle, Stephen Volk, Terry Lamsley, Adam L. G. Nevill, Weston Ochse, Rebecca Levene, Garry Kilworth, Chaz Brenchley, Robert Shearman, Nina Allan, Christopher Fowler, Sarah Pinborough, Paul Meloy, Christopher Priest, Jonathan Green, Nicholas Royle, Eric Bown, Tim Lebbon and Joe R. Lansdale.

 WWW.SOLARISBOOKS.COM

Follow us on Twitter! www.twitter.com/solarisbooks

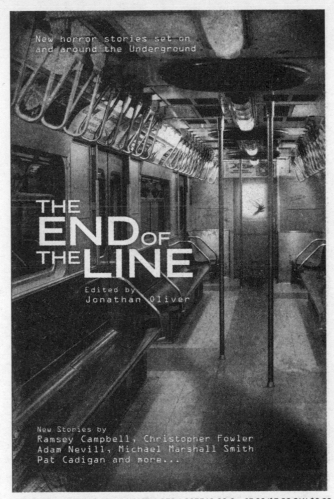

Audrey
Niffenegger
Dan
Abnett

Alison
Littlewood
Storm
Constantine
Will Hill
and others

An
anthology
of the esoteric
and arcane

Magic

UK ISBN: 978-1-78108-053-5 • US ISBN: 978-1-78108-054-2 • £7.99/$9.99 CAN $12.99

They gather in darkness, sharing ancient and arcane knowledge as they manipulate the very matter of reality itself. Spells and conjuration; legerdemain and prestidigitation – these are the mistresses and masters of the esoteric arts.

From the otherworldly visions of Conan Doyle's father in Audrey Niffenegger's 'The Wrong Fairy' to the diabolical political machinations of Dan Abnett's 'Party Tricks', here you will find a spell for every occasion.

Jonathan Oliver, critically acclaimed editor of The End of The Line and House of Fear, has brought together sixteen extraordinary writers for this collection of magical tales. Within you will find works by Audrey Niffenegger, Sarah Lotz, Will Hill, Steve Rasnic and Melanie Tem, Liz Williams, Dan Abnett, Thana Niveau, Alison Littlewood, Christopher Fowler, Storm Constantine, Lou Morgan, Sophia McDougall, Gail Z. Martin, Gemma Files and Robert Shearman.

 WWW.SOLARISBOOKS.COM

Follow us on Twitter! www.twitter.com/solarisbooks

A Dark Novel of Possession

THE Waking THAT Kills

Stephen Gregory

UK ISBN: 978-1-78108-151-8 • US ISBN: 978-1-78108-152-5 • £7.99/$8.99 CAN $10.99

When his elderly father suffers a stroke, Christopher Beal returns to England. He has no home, no other family. Adrift, he answers an advert for a live-in tutor for a teenage boy. The boy is Lawrence Lundy, who carries with him the spirit of his father, a military pilot – missing, presumed dead. Unable to accept that his father is gone, Lawrence keeps his presence alive, in the big old house, in the overgrown garden. His mother, Juliet, keeps the boy at home, away from the world; and in the suffocating heat of a long summer, she too is infected by the madness of her son. Christopher becomes entangled in the strange household, enmeshed in the oddness of the boy and his fragile mother. Only by forcing the boy to release the spirit of his father can he find any escape from the haunting.

 WWW.SOLARISBOOKS.COM

Follow us on Twitter! www.twitter.com/solarisbooks

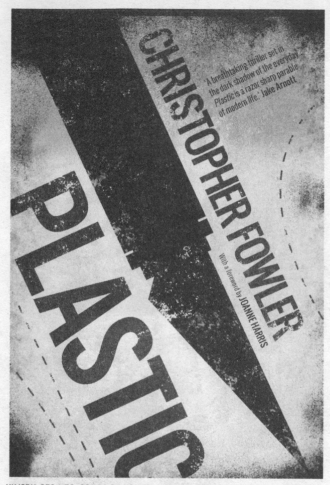

'A breathtaking thriller set in the dark shadow of the everyday, Plastic is a razor sharp parable of modern life.' Jake Arnott

CHRISTOPHER FOWLER

With a foreword by JOANNE HARRIS

PLASTIC

UK ISBN: 978-1-78108-124-2 • US ISBN: 978-1-78108-125-9 • £7.99/$7.99 CAN $9.99

June Cryer is a shopaholic suburban housewife trapped in a lousy marriage. After discovering her husband's infidelity with the flight attendant next door, she loses her home, her husband and her credit rating. But there's a solution: a friend needs a caretaker for a spectacular London high-rise apartment. It's just for the weekend, and there'll be money to spend in a city with every temptation on offer. Seizing the opportunity to escape, June moves in only to find that there's no electricity and no phone. She must flat-sit until the security system comes back on. When a terrified girl breaks into the flat and June makes the mistake of asking the neighbours for help, she finds herself embroiled in an escalating nightmare, trying to prove that a murderer exists. For the next 24 hours she must survive on the streets without friends or money and solve an impossible crime.

 WWW.SOLARISBOOKS.COM

Follow us on Twitter! www.twitter.com/solarisbooks

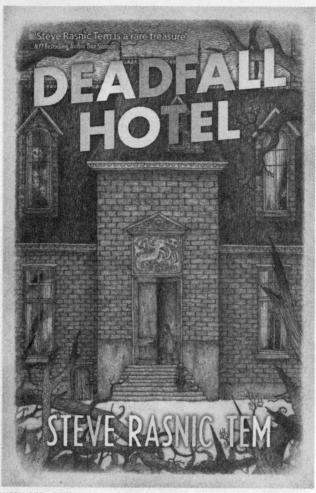

'Steve Rasnic Tem is a rare treasure'
NYT Bestselling Author Dan Simmons

DEADFALL HOTEL

STEVE RASNIC TEM

UK ISBN: 978-1-907992-82-7 • US ISBN: 978-1-907992-83-4 • £7.99/$9.99 CAN $12.99

It's where horrors come to be themselves, and the dead pause to rest between worlds. Recently widowed and unemployed, Richard Carter finds a new job, and a new life for him and his daughter Serena, as manager of the mysterious Deadfall Hotel. Jacob Ascher, the caretaker, is there to show Richard the ropes, and to tell him the many rules and traditions, but from the beginning, their new world haunts and transforms them. It's a terrible place. As the seasons pass, the supernatural and the sublime become a part of life, as routine as a morning cup of coffee, but it's not safe, by any means. Deadfall Hotel is where Richard and Serena will rebuild the life that was taken from them... if it doesn't kill them first.

 WWW.SOLARISBOOKS.COM

Follow us on Twitter! www.twitter.com/solarisbooks

'Dark, enticing and so sharp
the pages could cut you'
SARAH PINBOROUGH
ON BLOOD AND FEATHERS

BLOOD AND FEATHERS
REBELLION
LOU MORGAN

UK ISBN: 978-1-78108-122-8 • US ISBN: 978-1-78108-123-5 • £7.99/$9.99 CAN $12.99

Driven out of hell and with nothing to lose, the Fallen wage open warfare against the angels on the streets. And they're winning. As the balance tips towards the darkness, Alice — barely recovered from her own ordeal in hell and struggling to start over — once again finds herself in the eye of the storm. But with the chaos spreading and the Archangel Michael determined to destroy Lucifer whatever the cost, is the price simply too high? And what sacrifices will Alice and the angels have to make in order to pay it? The Fallen will rise. Trust will be betrayed. And all hell breaks loose...

 WWW.SOLARISBOOKS.COM

Follow us on Twitter! www.twitter.com/solarisbooks

1653: Two plots to kill Cromwell.
One to restore the King.
The other to set the Devil on the throne.

GIDEON'S ANGEL

"Splendid... Seventeenth-century Britain in all its sweaty, superstitious, blood-soaked savagery, with the bonus of added demons." – New York Times best selling author James Lovegrove

Clifford Beal

UK ISBN: 978-1-78108-083-2 • US ISBN: 978-1-78108-084-9 • £7.99/$8.99

1653. The long, bloody English Civil War is at an end. King Charles is dead and Oliver Cromwell rules the land. Richard Treadwell, Royalist, exile, and now soldier for the King of France, burns for revenge on those who deprived him of his family and fortune. He returns to England in secret to assassinate Cromwell.

But his is not the only plot in motion. A secret army run by a deluded Puritan is bent on the same quest, guided by the Devil's hand. When demonic entities are summoned, Treadwell finds his fortunes reversed: he must save Cromwell, or consign England to Hell...